Voice Of A Pretender

Book One of the Speak Your Voice
series

C.A. Wilson

ISBN 979-8-9928618-1-5 (paperback)

ISBN 979-8-9928618-0-8 (ebook)

For Journey
Thank you for being in my timeline.

Chapter One

I've been sold.

I tried not to think about it, but there wasn't much I could do to distract myself. I counted the tiny gray tiles on the bathroom floor. Traced the coffered ceiling. Reorganized my closet by color. Nothing helped.

I sighed. Rearranging my perfume bottles by height hadn't done the trick either. Why did they all smell like vanilla, anyway? Jasmine and vanilla, almond and vanilla, were there no other scents available? I hated the smell of vanilla by default.

Waiting was the worst part. I mean, I'd always known I would be sold into a marriage but it still felt like they'd thrown a ton of bricks at me, regardless.

Not like they'd ever asked for my opinion. Independent thinking and personal opinions were two qualities well beyond what was allowed for someone like me. Insipid men controlled the world. Their pathetic, feeble minds were incapable of contemplating any other purpose for a female—than to breed heirs and obey commands. And now, they'd set me up to marry one of them.

Yes, I was taking it well.

Deep breath. Slowly out. My mantra.

A foul taste spread across my tongue. I gulped down, bittering my uneasy stomach. The muted sun peaked out for a moment, reflecting the pink and purple bottles across the vanity, making their reflection appear like stained glass. I left the repetitive vanilla perfumes in disarray near the framed photo of my family at my sister's wedding. She'd been more than happy to get married, or at least happy with the attention and the expensive dress.

Maybe I can rearrange the furniture? I shook my head. *They wouldn't approve of that.*

Switching around the flora paintings on the walls seemed like an option. They all looked similar enough that their position in the room didn't matter. I'd never claimed to like flowers. They'd just presumed that I did, and these frames had appeared on my walls one day, since real flowers had ceased to exist well before I was born. The paintings only solidified my desperation for something real in life.

As the guards changed, their footsteps reverberated up the stairs. Each guard had a distinct tap to their polished shoes on the marble floors. On days the house stood silent and was locked from the outside, I could still hear the precise pattern of their steps repeated in my mind. The nauseating stench of starch lingered up the stairs as the fresh guard stood at attention at the front door.

I exhaled a heavy breath. Not slow like the mantra, but with one big *huff.* My eyes were puffy, like I'd cried all day. But I honestly had not. I just hadn't slept properly in weeks. Honestly, I can't remember the last time I slept well, maybe when I was nine or ten. It's a bit of a blur. Insomnia will do that to you.

My door opened without me hearing her. The uneven steps of the housekeeper's limp walk struck my eardrums just before she stopped beside me to set a glass of water and a pill on the vanity.

The swelling of her split lip had calmed since yesterday, but if she'd smiled, it likely would have cracked open again. But I'd never seen her smile before. She left without either of us uttering a word to one another. That was just the way things were.

The door creaked, stopping midway. She knew I found it annoying when the guard patrolling the hallway would peek in and watch me. Apparently, the creeps had nothing better to do.

The housekeeper's uneven steps faded up the stairs to her tiny room above mine. I rolled the tan pill between my fingers. They insisted it was to protect me. What if, just this once, I didn't take it?

I shrugged. Maybe, I would die a terrible death. Maybe not. Still, I tossed the pill into my mouth and gulped down the crisp, clear water. It was not the proper day to die.

A delicious scent of sage and thyme roasted chicken wafted up the stairs. My stomach rumbled. I wasn't ready to eat yet. How had the day passed by so quickly when I hadn't even left my room?

A loud bang from the front door told me Father was back from work at the Suit's headquarters. I felt a sickening drop in my stomach, and nausea rose in my throat. I cradled my stomach, trying my best to ignore the familiar feeling. My father's presence had a suffocating effect, like he'd encased the house in a tight, plastic wrap, sucking the air out.

I brushed my brown hair back away from my face. Heat rose up my neck drenching my lilac top in sweat. I clutched my chest, unable to breathe. I rushed to the window, cranking it open. The arid breeze rushed over me, drying the beads of sweat on my forehead.

The blue 'on' light of the air filter blinked to life. The house hated fresh air, or perhaps it was that the layer of smog hovering over the land was never actually fresh. Still, today's smog was light, allowing me to see the outline of the city. The Suit Corporation Mountain's factories must have had a slow day.

I shut my eyes. *Deep breath, slowly out.*

A faint chant echoed on the wind from the city of Iargulta. Muffled drum beats rose above the smog, barely loud enough to cut through the wind. Beyond the miles of barren desert, the skyline glowed with flickers of fire. The wild Indigents were stirring up trouble again.

I wanted to run in the streets with them, scream with them, feel the warmth of the sun against my skin with them. I wanted to experience life with them. If only I could feel their freedom and happiness for one moment, I could hold on to it for the rest of my life, knowing that I'd felt something real, even just once.

"Keep your eyes peeled." The guard below the window spoke into his walkie. "They're starting up again tonight." He tugged on his gun strap where it was, slung over one shoulder.

I imagined yelling down to him, *"Let me out! Climb up, and free me!" Perhaps, I should grow my hair long enough to climb down from the window.* But who was I kidding? They would have chopped off my hair before it could grow long enough.

There was no hair past the waist allowed.

There was no running allowed.

There was no screaming allowed.

There was no leaving allowed.

Where would I run to, anyway? Only the merciless desert lay between my family's house and the city. Father preferred it that way.

The final glimpse of daylight sunk behind a haze of copper clouds, spilling darkness across my room. The darkness felt familiar, not safe, but at least familiar.

I turned on the bedside light while reaching under my mattress. I focused on the door. My fingers ran along the smooth binding of the diary before I snatched it out. The scent of smoke and dirt from the brown leather cover filled my senses.

I unwrapped the twine, slipped out the pen from the binding, and opened it to the first page, still blank. Sitting on the floor, I held the diary in my lap. My hands trembled, gripping the pen.

It was illegal for me to have such a possession. It was illegal for me to have such thoughts, to stray from the norm. It was illegal for me to resist. It was against all their laws for women.

There was no freedom of thought allowed.

There was no personal writing allowed.

If they ever found the diary, it would be the end of individual thought and twisted ideas of freedom. They would beat me for having the guts to form my own opinions. The end approached, regardless of the protests within my mind.

The pen fumbled from my fingers, clattering to the floor. I snatched it up on the verge of snapping it in two. Every nerve-ending froze. I waited to hear the echo of footsteps ascending the stairs. My throat ran dry.

Deep breath, slowly out.

Nothing, just silence.

My pulse raced, pressing the pen down to the paper. A pleasurable tingle spread across my skin. But I only found enough courage to defy society with the slight mark of a pen, one letter, *I*.

A knock reverberated up the stairs. The hollow sound rattled my fragile bones. It was the carrier with my marriage contract. I bit down on my lip to keep myself from screaming.

Life stopped for a moment.

I couldn't imagine a world where I felt safe to breathe.

I frantically wrapped the twine around the diary and slipped it deep between my mattress and box spring, then smoothed out the bedding with it falling precisely, even on each side.

It must appear undisturbed—each purple piece perfectly placed upon one another. I scrambled to straighten out the perfume bottles. Nothing in the room could be out of place. I memorized the room because they knew. If something was out of place, they would suspect something was wrong. If something was wrong, it was my fault.

The man's voice came into focus over the ringing in my ears. "Hello."

I snuck into the hallway without opening my door any further. Cool air crept up my sleeves cooling my sweat. Each step closer shook me until my anxiety smacked me in the gut. I clasped my hand over my mouth as warm stomach acid crawled up my throat. The floor released a loud creak near the stairs. I inhaled deeply, stiffening my body.

"Your security outside checked my credentials, but would you like me to slide them again for you, Cardinal Freeman?"

I inhaled just enough to keep myself from fainting, then released it immediately.

"Swipe one more time inside."

Father adjusted his tie clip to prominently display his Suit insignia, Cardinal of Iargulta. He was one of five Cardinal leaders. One must never forget who they were talking to, after all.

Perhaps that's why no one ever told him slicking back his dark hair didn't hide the signs of balding. The thick, combed-back layer looked off-putting and made his forehead appear larger. It emphasized the severity of his dark narrow eyes which washed out his pasty skin even more. But I wasn't going to be the one to tell him.

The dagger-shaped metal sconces flickered, plunging the foyer into darkness for mere moments. Father scrolled down, then nodded. "Everything is in order, let us proceed."

The courier itched his chubby, sunburnt cheeks while adjusting the two stuffed envelopes wedged under his arm. The marriage contract was addressed to my father. The other envelope, kindly addressed to me, offered a slanted view of my husband-to-be's life story.

The courier adjusted his collar. "Looks like congratulations are in order."

What a pompous ass.

"Cardinal, it's a pleasure to meet you, sir." He wiped his hand on his black pants, before extending his hand to my father.

Father extended his hand robotically. "It's a special day in this house."

More like doomsday.

The courier shook his hand with a wide smile, as though it were a privilege to witness this demeaning transition.

Father retracted his hand, placing it at his side. "Let's keep this moving, I've been waiting far too long for those envelopes."

The courier nodded, holding up the scanner for him to sign.

"Thank you, sir." The courier handed over the two envelopes in one swift trade.

The sour, yet bitter taste of stomach acid boiled at my lips. I wanted to rush down and shred the envelopes to pieces. I didn't. My fingernails dug into the carved leaf and flower of the wooden banister.

Father's soulless eyes darted up to me. "Smile. You look prettier when you smile, Arabella."

My lips curled up automatically. A sharp, cold prick jabbed into my skin, stinging my cheeks with displeasure. I hated myself for smiling. I hated how compliant I was to follow my father's demand. I bit down on my cheek to stop myself from screaming.

Father tore open the envelopes and pulled out the signature page. He bent over the wooden entrance table and—he signed me away. The sound of the pen's loops and curves carved into my temples.

It began.

Tick, tock. Tick, tock.

My chest tightened. I imagined my heart stopping right where I stood, the air sucked right out of my lungs. My arms fell to my side, trembling. I was on the verge. On the verge of exploding or imploding. Either way, I would just become fragments of myself shattered across the floor. Would anyone bother picking me up? Or would they leave me to become embedded in the floorboards, to be trapped forever within the house? I knew the answer, no one would bother picking me up. No one ever bothered.

Run, I told myself. The word repeated over in my mind, elapsing the muffled voice of my father. *Run.* My knees rattled against each other.

Deep breath, slowly out.

Deep breath, slowly out.

Sweat slithered down my spine, turning icy cold.

His words came back into focus as the door shut behind the courier with a loud thud. "Get back to your posts. The Indigents are wild tonight."

"Yes, sir."

I rushed into my room, searching for a moment to escape.

His polished shoes pounded against the stairs, the sound beating against my eardrum.

Heel, toe. Heel, toe.

I spun around to face the door as he walked in. Keeping my head bowed, I stared at my fist clutching the pleats of my plum skirt. His body towered over me. I stiffened my back, holding my breath, bracing for a hefty whack against my head.

"I expect you to read this."

His feet shifted, creaking the floorboards. I gritted my teeth, my smile frozen in place as I stared at my warped reflection in his polished black shoes.

He placed the envelope in my hand. "Have full knowledge of him before both of our families meet in two days."

My mother's chipper beige heels tapped into the room after he left. "I'm so proud this day has come for you. You'll make such a pretty bride for your husband."

I sighed, rolling my eyes, hoping she didn't notice.

What was there to be proud of? That I could smile and look pretty? She placed a delicately wrapped pink perfume box on my bed. *Oh, great. Another vanilla perfume.*

"Something special for you. I can't wait until you meet him."

Once she walked downstairs, I raised my head and let out a breath. My knees wobbled, and I grabbed the bedpost to steady myself. My eyes stung with the need to cry, but I wouldn't allow it.

My parents expected a show of a false version of me they could present to society. That version I would have learned to resent.

Deep breath, slowly out.

I melted to the floor, tossing the envelope aside. The torn flap revealed a stack of white pages, each neatly labeled— *Achievements, Dislikes, Preferences,* and *History.* The files existed so I could know everything about his polished life and entertain him on command. I traced the rough, torn edge.

He'd received an envelope with my information too. *What could mine possibly say? Achievements—surviving as a prisoner in her father's house for twenty-two years. Dislikes—you and everything about you. Preferences—escaping. History—frequent thoughts of resentment and melancholy. Physical traits—brown hair, green eyes, short, less curvy, more angular, and bones break easily.*

I smirked, considering they probably sugarcoated my personality a bit to ensnare him.

Perhaps, I was being a bit harsh. Maybe, my husband would be different—someone who could save me. Or maybe I'd wake up, married to a monster, locked away, and forced to love him with a bunch of kids that boss me around as much as he does. Perhaps, he would purchase expensive stuff for me to love him like he bought me.

Yes, I am an optimist.

I rubbed my neck, still hesitating to grab the envelope. A picture might reveal what kind of man he was.

Yes, I have dabbled in moments of denial.

A picture only told what the person wanted it to say. I couldn't trust any of it.

This was how society dealt with women. My family—or rather, the men in my family—had governed the district of Iargulta for as long as the stories they drilled into us went back. But history texts never mentioned a time before the Suit Corporation's power. Oh sorry. They prefer to be called a society now. Much more palatable. The once CEOs knew how to market themselves as rulers.

My future husband would be just another Suit drone—slicked-back hair, rigid stance, and signature black suit so crisply pressed you could see the creases from a mile away. His stern jaw and direct eyes would swallow my soul and spit me out once he was done with me.

I can't do this.

I bit my lip, swallowing what little hope I had left. My eyelids weighed heavy.

Father's voice raced around my head, dizzying me. I winced and shoved the envelope under my bed, where the monster could hide until he became real.

Tick, tock. Tick, tock.

Father would only approve of a man of high ranking. Power was a strategy game, after all. The Suits grew in power as the rest were born to serve us. The ones below us, the masses, were referred to as Indigents. They owned nothing, yet some we owned. Some of those owned were the housekeepers, who were Indigents plucked off the streets to serve the Suits' needs.

Smoke from the protests in Iargulta lingered in through the open window. The Indigents were rallying, at least I imagined they were. A sting of queasy guilt resonated in my gut. I pitied myself when they had so much less, yet they lived freer than I ever would.

I breathed in deep, filling my lungs with the faint rally of smoke, then let it out slowly.

We deserved the protests against us. The Indigents deserved more.

Tick, tock.

Chapter Two

The smell of smoke faded overnight, replaced by the usual, stale scent of the house. Whatever rally for freedom had erupted during the night was extinguished by sunrise. I waited until I heard Father leave for work before going downstairs.

The house stood still in the early morning. The large, tinted windows perpetually made the interior appear as though it were approaching dusk. Bits of vapid sunlight slanted through the glass, reflecting off cascading chandeliers that hung from the cathedral ceiling in the foyer.

The oversized painting adjacent to the front door clashed with the cool, dark, gray walls. It depicted shadowed Suit soldiers saluting atop a dune, overlooking the vast desert. The screaming orange and yellow hues of sunrise bled into the flames of towns burning—towns that had once surrounded Iargulta.

It was called *The Triumph of the Great War*. Society had burned long ago for daring to overthrow the Suits. Now, there was only barren desert stretching for miles around Iargulta. Small towns were scarce, and the five remaining cities were governed by the Cardinals.

The guard at the front door watched me. I tightened my ponytail, pretending not to notice his beady eyes lingering on me as I walked into the kitchen. He looked at my body like he was inspecting it—first, my legs, then onto my ass and the slight curve of my hips. After, his beady eyes remained staring at my chest. Never once did he focus on my face—least of all my eyes.

If I'd worn a bag over my head, he wouldn't have noticed. I crossed my arms over my chest and slumped my shoulders. This guard always seemed to be working, though I was confused about his schedule. It was impossible to avoid him.

The housekeeper didn't look up as she scrubbed the dark marble countertop, already spotless. Without lifting her head, she placed a plate on the counter for me.

"Thank you," I said.

She stiffened, her pale eyelashes fluttering, but she didn't respond. Her eyes never lingered on me long enough for me to discern their color. Her cheeks were blotchy pink, as they always were in the mornings.

The housekeeper's rough skin hung loose around her square jawline, weathered far earlier than most. The damage caused by the environment infested her skin. Sunspots and crusty dry sores spread along her neck and hairline, where her dull ash-blonde hair grew in sparse patches.

I sat at the oblong island and stabbed at the dull yellow yolk of my egg. It slid across my plate, soaking into the toast. I forked a bite into my mouth.

The beady-eyed guard's shoes squeaked against the white-and-black checkered floor as he shifted his feet. The housekeeper turned on the faucet, rinsing out her cloth. Heel, toe. Heel, toe. The suffocating smell of his musky aftershave and starched uniform filled the room.

"Hey," the guard said as he entered the kitchen.

My fork clanged against my plate. I clenched my jaw.

The housekeeper remained hunched over the sink, unmoving. The guard's beady little eyes drilled into me, scanning my body, up and down, once again—as if my measurements have changed. He smirked, pressing his lips together. I shivered.

"You," he snapped, his jaw tensed until his lips thinned into a line. "You missed a spot on the table out here. When you're finally done in here, you need to clean the entire entryway again."

He paused, letting my heart take a beat.

"Useless bitch. I can see my shoe prints on this floor."

I gripped my fork, squeezing the handle until the metal edge dug into my palm. His eyes remained on me, but—I didn't look up. He spat on the floor and stepped in it, leaving a wet shoeprint behind.

Water splashed against the maroon subway tile backsplash as the housekeeper's body tensed. She didn't relax until his footsteps stopped at his post by the front door. Only then, did she exhale, her trembling hands hovering over the sink.

I froze as she turned off the faucet and rolled up her wet sleeves, revealing dark bruises encircling her wrists like cuffs.

She wrung out the towel and rolled her shoulders back. The weight in the room rose and fell with the heaviness of her calculated breaths. In and out. Slowly. In and out. A small, fresh bruise peeked out from beneath her tan shirt collar.

I whispered, "Are you okay?"

She nodded without a sound. The harsh lighting over the sink yellowed her skin making the bruises appear greenish.

"Can I help?"

She shook her head.

Sometimes, I wondered if they burned out her tongue so she couldn't speak. I often caught myself staring at her mouth, curious to see if there was anything left but a stub. She never spoke. She hadn't been set to defy. They set her to defeated long before she entered this house.

I wanted to set her free. I wanted her to feel free enough to say at least one word.

That word being *no*.

I scraped my food into the trash. I couldn't stomach eating. They broke a new part of me every day.

"I'm sorry," I whispered

A single tear slid down her cheek. She wiped it away before anyone else could see. Her shoulders lifted as she inhaled deeply, then she returned to scrubbing my dish.

I wanted life to be different for her.

The foyer was empty. I scanned the area, searching for the beady-eyed guard lurking around a corner. Swallowing the aftertaste of eggs, I strained my ears, listening for the sound of his shoes. Nothing.

A voice in my head whispered, *Run*. I shuffled to the door. *Run*, it urged louder. My heart pounded with every step. I bit down on my bottom lip, digging my nails into the cold metal of the doorknob.

Sunlight exploded into the room as I turned the knob. I squinted, shielding my eyes with my hand. A rush swept over me—a tingling sensation coursing through my body.

Run.

The air instantly dried my lips.

Run.

Miles of rust-colored sand stretched between me, vast and empty.

Run.

Beams of sunlight broke through the hazy burnt yellow and gray clouds, reaching down like extensions of hope.

Run.

I stepped forward.

A shadow loomed across the light.

Run.

The guard's voice cut through the air, harsh and cold. "What are you doing?"

The quick flash of freedom vanished.

I bit down on my lip, shrugging. "Just checking the weather."

"It's always the same. Get the fuck inside."

He gripped my shoulder and shoved me back towards the door.

The beady-eyed guard approached with a wide-eyed glare.

"What the fuck happened?"

"Where the fuck were you? You were supposed to be watching the door." The other guard spat back.

I stayed silent, my feet shuffling forward, following the first guard's push. The door slammed behind me, triggering the air purifier to whir on sucking the outside air out of the room.

The pressure on my shoulder tightened, his fingers digging in. I wanted to slap his hand away. *Run*, I wanted to tell myself. Instead, the voice in my head whispered, *Hide.*

"I just stepped away for a piss," the guard mumbled.

The voice hissed now—*Hide.*

"What was she doing out there, anyway?"

"She doesn't know." He chuckled, tightening his grip on my shoulder. "You know women. It's their prerogative to know nothing."

My hand clenched into a fist. "That's why wanderers get their feet cut off. They're damaged."

Pain shot through my palm as my nails dug into the skin.

Hide.

The blond guard released his grip, shoving me forward. I stumbled, catching myself on the entrance table. Their laughter echoed through the room, raking over my skin. Each laugh was another pin inserted into me. My nails scraped along the side of the smooth wood of the table.

I had won the birth lottery with my family, only to fail once they declared me female, therefore, incompetent.

The light shifted as the sun faded behind opaque clouds. Their shadows loomed over mine. I focused on the wood grain beneath my hands, tracing its every curve and line.

The crawling sensation under my skin didn't stop until their steps faded back to their posts. Straightening, I marched past the stairs. Each step drilled into my head, sparks of anger firing off with every footfall.

I didn't raise my head until I reached the pool room. Once inside, I shut the heavy door and turned the lock. My breath hissed out in a low growl.

My body sank to the floor. Down, down, down, until I felt buried beneath them all. I should have let myself cry—crying was normal, acceptable—for women. But that was what they wanted. To pound the tears out of me. I wouldn't give them the satisfaction.

I sprawled across the tile floor, letting every muscle relax until the pressure eased. The pressure—fear. Fear that ached in my body and trembled in my hands at the mere look in their eyes. I had to remind myself to breathe. In and out. To keep moving.

I sulked to the closet, grabbed a black swimsuit, and changed under a towel, even though I was alone. Part of me knew they had a key to unlock the door.

The pool room had been customized into a panic room, stocked with emergency clothes for every member of the family in case of an attack from the Indigents. But the very thought of being trapped in this room with my family made my skin crawl.

I sat on one of the eight bright cobalt-blue loungers lining the pool. The coarse fabric wasn't worn in. Hardly anyone used this room anymore, except me. Which was one of the reasons I liked it.

The soft blue light of the pool barely illuminated the cave-like walls, making the space feel smaller. But the door locked from the inside. That was what I liked most.

When I was little, my older sister, Vienna, had tried to drown me in the pool. She'd dragged me to the bottom, held me down, and then sprung up off of me. I remember her laughing as I reached the surface, gasping for air. She'd said she was "conditioning" me. After that, I avoided the pool until she moved out.

Now, the pool was my sanctuary. I floated on my back, arms and legs spread out like a star, the tension in my shoulders melting away.

Above me, the ceiling mimicked the sky outside—a bright blue expansive sky with fluffy white clouds drifting ever so slightly, mirroring my movements.

Hours passed as I watched the clouds. I imagined what it would be like to lay in the desert, staring at the real sky. When the colors shifted to orange and pink with the setting sun, I realized how much time had gone by. My fingertips were pruned, and my stomach growled.

I wrapped a plush navy towel around myself as the last rays of the sunset hit my face. I pretended the fake sun's warmth could energize me the same way the real one might.

Dinnertime approached.

Tick, tock.

I couldn't be late.

Tick, tock.

Tick, tock.

Family dinners were never a joy. I would go out on a limb to say I was the only pretender among them. The others were full-fledged supporters of this lifestyle. Some of the women even seemed to fancy it.

I froze at the sound of voices outside the pool room door. The two guards.

Their heavy laughter rolled through the air.

The beady-eyed guard had a hiss to his voice. It sprung up and lingered at the edge of words. "I came up behind her, bent her over the front table, and plowed into her."

The second guard's voice was much deeper, "Did she struggle?"

"Pffsh, a little," He chuckled. "I had to hold her down. She was feistier today. She's an okay fuck. Her tits are too small and saggy. Couldn't find the other one today—she must've been upstairs." He laughed. "Best part? Made her clean up after."

"Classic." he snickered. "But man, I know what you mean, the place I worked before, they bought Indigents with big plump tits. They jiggled every time they scrubbed the floor. I heard those types cost more. The Cardinal likes to keep his money, so we are left staring at pathetic ecuses for tits."

I sank. The floor swallowed me whole. I inspected my breasts, not knowing if I would be considered good enough.

Why do I care?

The guard continued, "You always get the action. I'm just stuck outside in the frickin' sand and heat."

"Nah, you got the daughter today." He snickered.

My heart stopped. I held my breath.

"Yeah, I should have taken her. Not as hot as her sister but I could get off at least. Chic looks like a troll. She could at least put some effort in"

The guards kept talking their vile words. I pressed my hands against my ears, trying to block it out, but their voices seeped through.

You're inadequate.

This wouldn't be the last time I would hear a conversation like this. I could imagine overhearing my husband talking about some housekeeper's breasts that were better than mine. Or maybe, it would be my sister that would be the object of his desire.

Why does it matter?

I clutched the towel to my slim curves that appeared nonexistent under the plush fabric. I pouted, staring at my short legs. I guess I could have made my face more delicate, prettier if I wore more make-up like the other women. I could have emphasized the features men liked.

If I could have been just like the other women and followed in line, I would have maybe qualified just above the approval line. The framework was there—all I had to do was build myself up to be defeated.

I wish I didn't care.

I tiptoed back and slipped my clothes back on, waiting for them to depart while watching the stars light up in the fake sky. One bright twinkle after another popped up.

Anger and sadness churned inside, clinging to my ribs, festering into my bones. I buried it deep, keeping it where it couldn't be seen or heard. Waiting.

After some time, I crept out. The hallway was dark and empty. Faint chatter from the dining room reached my ears as my family gathered for the evening meal.

Tick, tock.

A trail of wet footprints marked my path, Shadows crawled along the walls, infecting the corners. They seemed alive, reaching to snatch me with ghostly hands. The very walls of this house breathed with evil intentions.

Chapter Three

Father's laughter shook the walls as he rifled through the stack of mail on the entrance table— the rape table.

He tore open an envelope. "Looks like you just missed the haboob blowing in."

My brother, Starin, leaned against one of the polished black pillars, his brown eyes narrowed at me as he took a sip from his glass.

"Yeah," he said, his jaw tightening. "Looked pretty nasty."

Starin's light brown hair and delicate facial features edged toward looking feminine. He always seemed to grind his teeth in anger—perhaps thinking it made him look more masculine. His boorish behavior made up for whatever softness lingered in his face.

Father's expression soured as his eyes landed on me. "Girl, what do you think you're doing? You're a mess. You should be dressed for dinner."

I stared at the small puddle of water forming around my feet.

My voice cracked. "Sorry, sir. I'm going right now."

Clutching the towel around my neck, I turned to leave.

"And do your hair," he snapped. "You're not some Indigent. Wear it down like a proper lady." He pounded the table. "I don't want to see it pulled back again."

Appease the men. Fall in line. The mantra drilled into me since childhood ran through my head.

What would they do if I actually spoke my mind? If I remembered correctly, the punishment for that was having your tongue burned out. I pressed my tongue against my teeth and kept my lips sealed.

In truth, my silence equaled my crime. Every unspoken thought was a violation of rights—rights I didn't have.

"Yes, sir. Sorry, sir." I kept my head lowered.

Looking a man in the eyes was forbidden. A proper woman must always look slightly away, her head tilted downward.

His voice sharpened, "Your husband won't put up with this inadequate appearance, either. Dress appropriate, not because it suits your mood."

"Yes, sir," I murmured, focusing on his polished dress shoes.

"Don't just stand there. Go get ready, girl."

I trudged toward the steps.

"That girl is such an idiot," Father muttered. "I can't wait until she finally goes to good use."

A sharp tug at my hair snapped my head back.

Starin grinned over the rim of his glass, the ice clinking as he took another sip. A practiced, casual motion—like he hadn't just yanked my hair moments before. My throat tightened, my scalp stinging where fingers had been.

"She will always be no more than a little fool," Starin scoffed behind my back as I hurried away.

A sickening warmth suffocated me as I entered my room. Someone had shut the window and turned up the heat—standard procedure for entertaining guests.

I picked out a soft periwinkle dress layered with chiffon and a pearled edge. A birthday gift last year, though it hadn't been on my wish list.

My closet was full of the most expensive, pretty clothing. That was their way of assuring me that everything was okay. My sadness, they said, was just disappointment over not having the latest trends. That must have been why I had so many things.

When I grew tired of pretending, I wore my sadness like a badge, written across my forehead—*Help me. I'm not okay with this.*

No one bothered acknowledging it, anyway.

I gasped when I exited the bathroom, spotting a faded pink wind-up toy perched on the edge of my vanity, its little feet about to step off. My hair stood on end. I snatched it before it fell and frantically searched the room for him.

I was alone.

The toy had once been a little girl in a pink dress. The paint had worn off in patches, leaving only her wide eyes intact.

Starin had bought it for me at a fair I wasn't allowed to attend. Back then, he had been sweet, enjoying the sight of his little sister smiling. But something inside him rotted after he went away for high school.

The toy became a tool for his games. Wind it up, and when it hit the ground, the chase began. *Run.*

He loved his version of hide-and-seek.

The door creaked open. I jumped back.

The housekeeper limped in, unalarmed. Her flushed face had calmed, but her split lip remained puffy. She placed a pill and a glass of water on the vanity.

I tossed the toy into the trash can. "Could you take out the trash, please?"

She nodded, taking the bin.

"Thank you," I said, louder than I should have.

He rejoiced in his games. That was what made them terrifying.

I stood still.

Tick, tock. Tick, tock.

My body tingled until it went numb. My fingers crawled along the smooth edge of the vanity to the pill. Popping it into my mouth, I drowned it with a glass of water.

Before I knew it, my legs were walking down the stairs, my heart lodged in my throat. My hair and makeup were perfectly arranged. A smile stretched across my face, betraying nothing of the fear roiling inside.

My lifeless body, drained of energy, fell into line. I was in full pretender mode.

Pretending had once felt like a sickness that started in my gut, eating me from the inside. But after a while, I stopped fighting it. I let myself sink. Down, down it went until it plummeted me into the deep abyss. I was lifeless, absent of light, alone, unable to stand on my own. There I stayed where nothing hurt, nothing mattered. The darkness became home.

The women of the family waited in the small sitting room adjoined to the kitchen. The oversized floral wallpaper was of purples, pinks, and maroon flowers tangled up with green vines, looping endlessly around the roses stripped of their thorns. In the dim light, the pattern receded, but when the overhead lights were on, it screamed against the walls.

Their overpowering vanilla perfumes assaulted my nose. Each woman's hair was styled in a perfect Suit Society haircut. There were ten government-approved options for women. Choosing between them was our "privilege."

Where could I get an unapproved haircut?

The housekeepers worked silently at the stove and counter, finishing the dinner preparations. The guards, thankfully, remained outside, securing the perimeter. That seemed to put the housekeepers at ease. It certainly put me at ease.

The housekeeper with the limp checked the roast in the oven, then shoved it back in for more time before returning to chop nuts on the counter. The other housekeeper, a newer addition, seemed to have picked up the rhythms of the household quickly. Her coarse, dark hair was pulled back so tightly into a bun it looked painful. She stirred the sauce on the stove, occasionally glancing at the senior housekeeper for approval.

Liddy, my sister-in-law, glanced up at me with her giant doe-eyed dark blue eyes. She swept her blonde hair away from her face and shifted her body, a faint smile tugging at her lips. Her button nose scrunched as though she'd smelled something unpleasant.

Liddy always seemed uncomfortable, but then again, she was always pregnant. When she wasn't carrying another of Starin's children, she was on a crash diet and workout regimen to "get her body back" for him. She existed in an endless loop, constantly working to appease him.

Currently, she was on the tail end of a diet, her figure slim but her breasts still swollen with milk.

I took a seat in one of the white wingback chairs closest to her. The fabric on the armrests had started to fray at the seams from where I'd clutched them too tightly over the years.

Vienna, my older sister, bobbed her toned, exposed leg as she spoke. "He bought me this dress. It's an original—there isn't another like it."

She traced the dark maroon fabric with her hands without acknowledging my presence.

"It's lovely, Vienna. Looks perfect on you." Mother said, pressing her lips into a smile that deepened the wrinkles around her green eyes. "Don't you think so, Arabella?" She glanced over at me.

Vienna leaned forward, exposing her cleavage in the deep V neckline. She grinned like she got me into trouble.

"Yes, it's lovely. No one else could pull it off like you," I said, digging my nails into the armrest. More of the fabric threads snapped under the pressure.

"Well, no one can. It's an original," Vienna snapped, pointing her finger at me.

"I can tell," I nodded.

Vienna leaned back, satisfied with herself. Her long, pin-straight brown hair with fake blonde highlights was slicked back away from her face exposing her giant diamond earrings. Nothing was out of place on Vienna. I'm sure she worked hard on that. No one woke up as perfect as she looked. She rested her elbow on the chair and placed two fingertips on her pronounced cheekbones.

"Jealous your husband won't buy you the best in everything like mine?"

"There are plenty of other dresses in the world."

"You think this is an ordinary dress." She jumped up. "This was made for me. Just for me."

Mother scowled, "That was rude, Arabella."

Really, rude? There were so many other thoughts that popped into my head that I filtered out.

I scoffed, "I didn't mean it that way," I did mean it that way. "I'm sorry. I hope one day I'll have something that even comes close to that dress." *I don't care about the damn dress,* I thought bitterly.

"Okay, everyone, calm down," Mother said, standing. "We don't want the men thinking we're ill-mannered now. Let's settle down."

Vienna flopped down in her chair with a sour pout.

I might have liked my sister if she was remotely likable. To men, she appeared meek and charming. To women, she was conniving and ruthless. She selfishly believed no woman could ever be better than her—and, sadly, she was often right.

Liddy adjusted herself awkwardly, "Starin bought me a new ring for our new little one. He named him Jax. I like the name he chose." She extended her hands, displaying six gaudy, elaborate rings that twinkled under the light. One for each child. "A treasure for his prize, he always says."

The word *prize* made my skin crawl.

"He's so nice." Liddy smiled looking down at her rings.

Let me clarify, that it does not make him nice or sweet.

"Lovely," Mother said, eyeing the rings with a mix of jealousy and pride. "Soon you'll have one on every finger."

"If that's what he wants. I know I can give him as many children as he needs." Liddy smiled, adjusting herself.

Needs? Is he building an army with his children?

I dug my fingernails into my palms, forcing a smile, "So pretty."

"Arabella, you'll know soon enough what's expected of you," Mother said, sitting back. "You're only a day away from meeting him."

"I can't wait," I said flatly.

I hated the tedious conversations that were required for me to participate in as part of society.

The housekeeper removed the last roast from the oven, slamming the oven shut.

"Oh, life is just beginning for you, Arabella." Liddy's smile seemed almost on the verge of sympathetic.

I hesitated, returning her smile half-heartedly.

I wasn't angry at the women for enjoying being wives and mothers. I was angry that they never questioned that they had no choice in the matter. Libby always seemed too sheltered to contemplate there was more to life than her current situation.

Libby giggled, "The sooner you get pregnant, the better. That's what they say, right? A wife's first duty is to give her husband an heir." Her chipper, high-pitched voice made me want to throw up. "I've heard he is quite a looker. Has these eyes that just sink right into you."

Sink so deep, I'll drown.

"I bet you're so excited."

Sweat trickled down my temple.

I forced a breath out, "I'm so excited it's hard to keep it in."

The housekeepers loaded their arms with three roasts and half a dozen side dishes, leaving the room without a sound.

"Dinner is ready," Mother chimed in.

Swallowing the last of my pride, I took my place behind Liddy. Another family dinner awaited me. I could hardly wait.

Chapter Four

I followed the other women in a silent line into the dining room, my head lowered. The men, engrossed in conversation, didn't acknowledge us. Father tipped his glass of saps to his mouth between hearty laughs.

Women weren't allowed to drink saps or any other type of liquor. Women were deemed too emotionally unstable for alcohol.

I wonder who makes us too emotionally unstable?

The housekeepers cleared the predinner treats from the table and set down two new bottles of saps. Father scooped up a bottle without missing a beat. I tucked my chair in without making a sound.

An oversized arrangement of fake deep purple and white flowers in the center of the table obscured my view of Starin, seated across from me. Three glass chandeliers hung over the long table. All three the same, all three hanging on the edge between powerful and fragile.

Starin stood, pouring his wife a glass of water and then himself a drink of saps, "So, how much damage did the Indigents do in the city last night?"

Father pounded his glass on the table, jolting me. "Nothing. Hardly anything. Those damn fools are throwing pebbles at a tower that will never collapse."

I squeezed my hands together, resting them in my lap.

"What do those idiots think they're going to accomplish?" Starin sneered, placing a hand on his lapel over his insignia pin—his mark as next in line to govern. It gave him power without responsibility. "We control them. It's not like they're in a place to make changes."

The housekeepers arranged the food near the men at the table. Father eyed the dishes indecisively.

"We dealt with rebellions during the Great War when I was young, son. They never defeated us, and they never will. They should know from history—the more they try to fight us, the more we will take away."

I dug my nail into a chip in my pink nail polish. The tiny pink flakes fell onto my dress, creating a diamond pattern. I hated waiting for their choices, but eating before the men wasn't allowed.

My stomach growled.

We had to wait for them to begin before we could take our first bite. For years, women weren't even allowed to eat at the same table as men. Somehow, they considered this progress.

I supposed it was a step up from the gray dress sector of Suit Society. Women there ate leftovers in a separate room without speaking once the men had finished. They wore gray dresses that covered them from their necks to their plain, dark gray shoes, with gray bonnets hiding their pinned-back hair.

The men always handed out flyers to join their sector in the city as their multiple wives stood behind them with their silencer collars on and heads bowed. It was a reassurance that—*yes, it could be worse*.

A sharp kick to my shin jolted me. Starin leaned back eyeing me through the cream petals of the centerpiece.

He smiled. "I mean, what more could they want from us? We feed and bathe them, after all. And still, they're so dirty. How hard is it to clean up after yourself?"

Father lifted his fork, poking at the dishes. "People like that don't know what they want. They're all talk, no action."

Wasn't their constant protesting in fact action?

Starin snickered, rolling his eyes.

Father's voice rose, as if delivering an inspirational speech to troops. "We have a huge defense force against them. They have no chance. We're just better than them. If we need to, we'll remove the instigators. But there's no reason to worry right now. Remember, men, to own society, you must break society. Their spirits will break soon enough. The protests will stop, and our rule will continue, as it has for years."

"Damn right," Marcus, Vienna's husband, howled. "Indigents are nothing. They're lazy. They've got no power, no right to complain. We can make them do whatever we want. Dangle something in front of them, and they'll jump for it. They can't even read. They're not smart like us—they don't know the difference."

Marcus raised his fist in the air. He looked as if someone brought a mannequin to life who had soulless, dull eyes that lacked any capability of emotions. Then they programmed him to make ignorant, life-changing decisions for people he had no prior knowledge about in his life.

"They're dumb. Born dumb. Every last one of them is dumb." Saps sprayed from Father's mouth as he laughed.

Father always bragged about his vast vocabulary to belittle the uneducated. Yet, he hardly ever used words longer than four letters.

The Indigents' enmity was for their inability to better themselves—an inability imposed by people like Father.

The Indigents didn't have schools like we did. Suit males were well schooled, while Suit females were educated only until the age of ten. After that, we were taught obedience. Maybe they feared educated women. Maybe they feared that if we had access to education, we'd discover they weren't as smart as they claimed to be.

Vienna sipped her water and giggled at her husband's remarks. We were allowed to giggle at their jokes. Imagine that—a single permitted indulgence.

Women weren't allowed to speak at the table—we just were supposed to smile and laugh.

Starin shouted, "Stupid fools."

I laughed along with them.

I squeezed my hands together tighter and laughing louder.

Starin reached over the table, tipping my glass of water. I grabbed it swiftly before much spilled onto the table, though some drops soaked into the cream runner. He continued laughing.

My heart raced as I watched the water spots spread. He glanced at me, smirking. I set the glass back down over the wet patches, hoping no one would notice.

"Dinner looks good tonight," Father said, pointing out his selections to the housekeepers. "I have good taste in picking food."

The housekeepers filled Father's plate and then moved around the table, serving the men first.

I stared at my warped reflection in the polished knife beside my plate. Unclenching my hands, I traced the knife's sharp edge with my fingertip. I wanted it. Not for violence—just for security, in case I ever needed a way out.

Over the years, I'd considered many ways out, most of which left drifting away like whispers in the wind. But some options lingered, cemented in my mind forever. Those were the scariest of all.

The problem was how accustomed I'd grown to this feeling—a raw, gnawing emotion masked until I no longer could feel anything. It was an emotion I had witnessed in another, but it still unnerved me. At that moment in time, I could not fully understand it. Numbness.

It had been Jemma who triggered something in me, a free-fall I hadn't been able to stop ever since. I remembered her core reaction set behind her eyes. It had become so dark she couldn't find a light at the end to get out. Anguish radiated off of her. I would develop an understanding of her pain over time. Her eyes never smiled, although her lips told another story. It was the only way she could control what was happening to her. It was her only way out.

When I was six-years-old my brother, Starin, had been matched to marry. It was Father's dream match, his son marrying another Cardinal's daughter. Her name was Jemma. They were still sixteen years old, younger than a traditional marriage, but they rushed to close the contract anyway.

We traveled all the way to Turini to meet the Wallaces by train. The train had a dining cart and everything. I didn't get to see it though, since females could only sit at the back of the train. It still was exciting and the farthest away from home I had ever been before.

Cardinal Wallace's house reminded me of a fairytale that I once heard but then was told it must be forgotten. Fake green trees surrounded me, wrapped with lights and shimmers. Paper dragonflies and butterflies hung from the ceiling in purples and pinks. It was like I was standing in the middle of another world to meet my soon-to-be sister-in-law.

Father was almost on the verge of excitement standing beside her father, Cardinal Wallace, staring up at the stairs. Cardinal Wallace had an oddly disproportionate face. He had a short forehead but an angular tense jaw that came out into a point like a downward-facing mountain and his eyes were set too wide apart. Father was shorter than him, although he would have never admitted it.

Jemma had delayed much longer than I thought I could anticipate. I waited at the end of the stairs for her. Wide-eyed with nerves, I fidgeted with my fingers and dress: hoping I looked perfect. Her door finally opened, and the light taps of her heels echoed down the stairs. I straightened out the tulle ruffles on the bottom of my pink dress. It was my favorite dress. I couldn't have imagined a more perfect dress—until I saw Jemma's dress.

Her pale pink, spaghetti strap dress shimmered when it caught the glimmer off the lights on the trees. She had chosen makeup with sparkles and shimmers, so her skin glowed in the dim light. An extravagant series of pink and white diamond necklaces cascaded from her long slender neck.

The only trait she got from her father was his height and dark brown hair, thankfully. She had a cute button nose and perfectly set hazel eyes. I imagined she was a princess in the fairytale. Something was off, though. When she smiled, her throat tensed up. I directed my eyes to my fingers bunching up the fabric of my dress. She made me feel uneasy, like she knew a secret I didn't.

"Jemma, it's about damn time." Cardinal Wallace's gruff voice reminded me to lower my head as she walked by. "You've made your husband-to-be wait far too long."

My brother licked his lips as though he was looking at a sweet treat. His eyes made me nervous. He inspected every curve of her body over and over. He couldn't keep his eyes off her.

His youthful face had a pinkish tone which would later fade. Back then he had still looked rather young for his age and hadn't hit his final growth spurt yet. It made him bitter that he didn't look as mature as the other boys in his class. He ran his hands along the side of his head, making sure his hair was still slicked back just right.

Jemma's hair fell across her eyes. "Sorry, I'm late, sir." Her voice trailed off as she fidgeted with her fingers. "I wanted to look perfect for you, sir."

"You'll have to figure out how to be perfect and prompt, girl. Your husband has no time to spare on you." He pointed over to Starin, grinning.

"That's right." Starin added, nodding.

"Yes, sir." Her voice fell to a whisper. "I'm sorry, sir."

I smiled, trying to get her attention, but she didn't notice. I tucked my chin down low but continued smiling though, just in case she noticed.

"Proceed to the dining room. By now, it's time to eat." Her father said, directing the men in that direction.

Our families passed by her like she was a neglected statue as she stared down at her cream satin shoes. I stayed behind, waiting for the others to leave, and tugged on her dress to get her attention.

"Hello, I'm Arabella." I smiled as wide as I could. "We're going to be sisters."

Her bloodshot eyes glanced over, startling me. "Yes." She took a quivering breath. "Yes, we are."

"Why are you sad? Aren't you happy to be getting married? You are going to have a big wedding. It's going to be so grand." I clutched my hands to my heart.

"No, I'm not happy but there's no way out, is there?" Her voice became monotone. "It's not like I have a choice."

"Why would you want anything else? You have the prettiest clothes, the nicest house, and the coolest stuff. I wish I had your stuff. What else could you want?"

"The freedom to think. The freedom to choose my path, my own love. Keep your eyes open, Arabella, and you'll see when your time comes."

I giggled, "I don't know what you're talking about."

"Has your dad ever hit you?" She tried to whisper, but her voice cracked.

My eyes widened. "Only when I do something wrong," I whispered, glancing around for someone who might hear.

"Wrong according to them. Was it really wrong, or were you just doing as you had seen men do before?"

"But we may not do as the men do. We are not made like them. That's what my father says." I uttered, scared of what she might say next.

"Is that so? Come, let's go. The end is waiting for me." She extended her hand to me.

I was glad she stopped speaking such forbidden thoughts. I had been frightened someone may have heard her and thought it was me. I grabbed her hand and held it tight, swinging it while we walked.

Father was pouring Starin his first glass of saps when I entered the room. "It's time you start drinking like a man now that you're becoming a man."

Starin smiled, staring at Jemma while he took his first tiny sip. "Soon, I will."

She released my hand to place herself at the table. I tiptoed over to my place beside Vienna. I wanted to run, but I kept calm, staring at my shiny pink shoes. Vienna towered over me with her long plum dress.

She had argued with our mother about the dress because she'd wanted to buy a dress with lace at the top. My mother had told her she was too young for such lace. Vienna had won in the end. Now she grinned, running her fingers along the lace around her collarbone. Although her head was lowered, she stood proud and confident in her new dress.

Two candelabras dimly illuminated just enough to see the table. The tan walls seemed plain until I brushed past it. The coarse textured wallpaper was abrasive against my skin like sandpaper leaving behind a blotchy pink scrape.

The Cardinals sat at the heads of the table, prompting when the women could sit. Each man raised their right hand in the air, ordering us to pull out our chairs. When the hand lowered, we sat ourselves. This command typically only happened during these types of dinners, otherwise, women waited in the wings until it was time to be seated.

I was lucky enough to have Jemma seated across from me; although, she didn't seem to notice. All she could do was stare down at her silverware and plate.

"Cardinal Wallace and I have discussed it. In three months, you will be wed. That will give the women plenty of time for fittings and approval of the dresses." Father said, not taking notice of the housekeeper filling the men's plates first.

Jemma released a heavy breath, not taking her eyes off the knife and spoon. I couldn't even imagine how beautiful she would look in a wedding gown. I wondered if mine would match her dress or if I could help pick out my dress. Even Vienna smiled at the thought of a new dress.

"We've arranged for the wedding to take place at the Suit Hall at sunset." Cardinal Wallace paused for applause. My mother's face lit up.

He continued, "We will, of course, make arrangements with the other Cardinal families to attend. It will be the grandest event this generation has ever seen." Cardinal Wallace took a sip of saps before continuing. "We must stand out above everyone else for this. This union is an unimaginable match and will cement our families to reign over society."

"Damn right. It's time for us to step forward and take rule." Father lifted his glass in salute.

My brother followed with his head held high. My mother, almost giddy, raised her water glass. I remembered she had wanted her wedding at the Suit Hall, but they were renovating it at the time, so she had to have her marriage to Father elsewhere. Every time she told the story, she acted like it was the most devastating thing that ever happened in her life.

A housekeeper placed the delicious-looking food before Jemma, but she didn't move. I stared at mine, hardly finding the strength to resist the urge to start eating before the men. But Jemma didn't blink.

The only part of her that moved was her chest breathing in and out slowly. I wanted to whisper at her to make her look up, but I knew I better not do such improper behavior. I didn't want to get slapped in front of everyone. It would have been too embarrassing. Plus, I didn't want my new sister to think I was ill-mannered.

"Starin, how many children do you foresee yourself having?" [OBJ]

"As many as I can get out of her, sir." Starin chuckled, "The more children we produce, the more power we can spread over the land, right father?"

"That's my boy." Father beamed at the end of the table.

"Start early, start strong, is what I say." Cardinal Wallace nodded, "and always hope for a boy."

The housekeepers returned to their places in the shadowed corners of the room. Jemma placed her trembling hands on the table, still staring down. The men's laughter ricocheted off the walls.

A tear rolled off Jemma's chin onto the knife. Her bloodshot eyes glared up at me. I clutched my dress. I could not help but stare. Her eyes reflected a rising darkness, simmering beneath the surface.

My heart started pounding, getting lodged in my throat as her trembling fingers wrapped around the knife. She jumped to her feet, still keeping her eyes on me.

"Jemma, sit down, girl." Her father pounded his fist on the table.

Jemma raised the knife. "Open your eyes, Arabella," she whispered—calm, certain, like she had already left this world before the knife touched her skin. She dragged the knife along her long pale—throat, carving open her flesh. Blood gushed out, splattering across her jeweled neckline. Her eyes remained on me as her body collapsed to the ground.

I jumped up, screaming. Tears filled my eyes.

The men raced over, yelling, "No."

Her mother ripped the tablecloth off, throwing dishes and glasses into the air. They crashed to the floor with startling cracks and bangs, shattering shards of glass everywhere. Her mother pressed the tablecloth to her neck, absorbing the blood. Jemma's eyes stared up at the dark coffered ceiling, a mesmerizing peacefulness in her final expression.

"Do something. Fix her," Starin cried out.

A gut-wrenching scream escaped my lips, getting louder and louder until it was deafening. I thought my heart was going to pound out of my chest.

"Shut that damn girl up." Cardinal Wallace yelled, pointing to me.

Father shouted, "You tried to cheat me by selling this daughter of yours to me, knowing she's defective."

"Why would she do that?" Starin screeched, standing over her body.

"She was defective, son." Father repeated.

Their faces twisted with the perplexity of what had just happened before their eyes. They would never fathom the complexity of her mind. Her reasonings were lost in the fibers of the green and taupe rug saturated in her blood. It was a stain the family would never be able to remove.

A tear rolled down her mother's inflamed cheeks as blood soaked into her dark green gown. Her bloody hands trembled, staring down at her lifeless daughter's body.

Vienna snapped her head to me with a look of anger in her eyes. She lifted her hand, slapping me across the face. I leapt back, cradling my face—sobbing and stunned.

"Shut up, shut up." She kept repeating.

"Wallace—the deal is off." Father roared.

Her father stomped off, leaving bloody footprints down the hall.

"What a waste." Starin scoffed, kicking Jemma's leg.

The housekeeper tiptoed over, covering her body with a blanket.

I crouched in the corner, weeping. Vienna's heavy hand slapped me across my face. "Shut up, shut up, shut up." Her voice drilled into my head.

My brother had been forced to wait four more years before they vetted another suitable match. Liddy was a niece to a Cardinal, and that was good enough. She was not Cardinal Wallace's niece. He and Father were still not on good terms. When Father searched for a new match, he demanded for a stable minded woman who was quiet and obedient.

Liddy delicately smiled as they spoke with just the right amount of nodding. They had trained her well. Sometimes she reminded me of a woman with a silencer collar around her dainty neck.

Jemma's legacy, however, lingered in the shadows. Her warning—*Open your eyes*—haunted me.

***

I ran my fingers along the edge of the knife at dinner, hoping for courage, but a housekeeper's light touch stopped me. She removed the knife silently, leaving me to stare at my warped reflection in the polished silver spoon. I was never sure if she was helping me or hindering me with my escape plans.

The housekeeper limped away with the knife still on her tray after she had placed some food on my plate. Only, of course, the food permitted for women—some food they considered dangerous for women to consume. I couldn't explain society's reasoning behind this rule.

Father spoke while chewing. "Soon, we will have someone from this family placed in each branch of Suit Society. Arabella's new husband has just been promoted to a top-ranking detective position in the intelligence branch. We will have complete dominance."

The word *dominance* rang in my ears like a drumbeat. Power craved power, endlessly consuming everyone and everything.

I forked the food into my mouth. The burst of flavors elapsed my taste buds and comforted my anxiety. The housekeepers created fantastic dishes. They trained them vigorously as soon as they entered the estate. They knew the best spices and combinations to make my taste buds tingle.

"It's about time we show everyone how powerful this family is." Starin blurted out.

I grinned, nodding along. My stomach churned.

"Damn right." Marcus tipped his glass to his upturned lips.

"Ladies, count yourselves lucky," Father declared. "The Indigents outside are dangerous. They take women and do what they want with them. Just bend you over in the middle of the street and have their way."

I gasped with my hand over my mouth.

Unlike Suits, who catch you off guard and rape you over the entrance table.

He took a sip of saps and continued, "I tell you, you're safer inside with us. It's too dangerous out there. You need us to protect you from those uncivilized Indigents. They're monsters."

His words blurred as my thoughts drifted. I stared at the family portrait on the wall—my younger self frozen in time, eyes wide with fear, smile strained. A silent cry for help.—*Save Me*. A fake plastered smile stretched across my pale face. Shame and defeat weighed on me for disappointing that girl.

I let the scene unfold in slow-motion around me—the garish table with mounds of food piled along the center. The men dressed in their signature Suit look—pressed black pinstriped suit, white shirt, and a pinned down black tie. The iron creases still so crisp from the morning, they could slit my throat. The women in uncomfortable form-fitting dresses to please the men—laughing to please the men. The housekeepers, standing quietly in opposite dark corners blending into the dark gray walls, head lowered, hands clasped.

Laughter engrossed the table. I laughed along, drowning out the reasons we were laughing. Starin's dark brown eyes cut into me. Heat rose in my chest. The chase was on although there was no point in running.

Too soon, the housekeeper removed my plate. The men were done eating, which meant we were done. There was no eating before the men nor after the men.

"I'm retiring to my office to read *The Triumph of the Suits* for the night," Father announced.

Starin and Marcus nodded their heads, "Good book, good book."

I've read it. Of course, while no one was looking. I'd slipped into Father's office and snatched the book years ago. I couldn't believe he was still reading it. It had only taken me three days to read that slanted piece of crap book. It read like a preteen superhero story of the great war, where the heroes were actually the villains. It wasn't like I was going to find the alternative version of the book somewhere. The Suits had burned those books decades ago.

"You guys do as you please." Father rose up from his chair. He directed it to the men, in reality, the women had no choice; they must entertain the men.

I remained transfixed by the family portrait long after the others left the table. Their voices trailed off into other rooms, but I continued staring. I forced myself up when I noticed the housekeepers scrubbing the table.

I wished I could have saved the girl in the portrait from what was to come.

Chapter Five

Marcus' vexing voice chattered in the living room, fading as I walked down the hallway. I didn't realize where I was going until I was a few steps from the door to Father's office. I turned the doorknob without thinking. I had an urge to speak with him, something I had never found the courage to do before.

Maybe there was a way to delay the marriage? Maybe I could tell him about my treatment from the guards?

The door bounced off the wall. No one was inside—just an over-organized sleek black desk with the dim green desk lamp turned on. Papers were stacked in two even piles on one side of the desk while the opposite side had a computer monitor illuminating the bookshelves in a dim blue hue. *The Triumph of the Suits* sat on the bookshelf covered in dust. A few books beside it had fresh fingerprints smeared across the dusty, old bindings. Perhaps, he changed his mind.

I took a breath and wiped sweat from my forehead. "What was I thinking?" I slipped back into the hallway and closed the door. "He would have killed me for talking."

The sconce lights flickered like candles against the hunter green walls. A herd of retired family portraits haunted the hallway.

The realization of the world must have started around eight. In the portrait, I looked like I had been caught stealing something. My eyes widened and shocked, my smile on the verge of pouting. I remembered the emotion of the time more than why my brother was squeezing my shoulder.

Not a single portrait frame ever had a smidge of dust on them. The hallway looked like a well-kept museum maintained by an anal curator. But in reality, the housekeepers kept the house spotless.

Father once told me they were fortunate to be housekeepers. "They were off the streets, after all." He would say to me. "They should be thankful."

I believed him once when I was younger, naïve—years before that portrait. He made it seem like we were doing them a favor.

Fortunate really meant their work paid for their room and board with nothing left over to save up and prosper in life. In another place and time, they would have called them slaves, but they were called fortunate in my house.

They stirred before the sun rose to prepare breakfast and finally laid down to sleep long after I went to bed. There were two in a room that should have only housed one. Only a dull, coarse gray blanket covered each of their thin bare mattresses. The roof peaked in the middle of the room where they hung faded, fake flowers with cooking twine. Unlike the elaborate family portraits on our walls, their off-white walls remained blank.

One time, I asked why they had no family photos, and the young housekeeper simply replied, "We had no camera to take them with."

"That's silly," I giggled.

I thought they were lying and just didn't want me to bother them with such annoying questions.

The two housekeepers each had a chest to hold their personal belongings. I used to try to peek in between the rusted, warped lids. I wasn't supposed to be in their room, yet that's all I wanted to do.

One day, I asked the younger of the two housekeepers, "What's your name?"

She was an odd-looking woman with a pinched nose and large round brown eyes. She answered back, "I am not allowed to have a name within the walls of this house." She paused then smiled, whispering, "but it rhymes with feather."

I never got the chance to call her by her name before she died. She collapsed upon her bedroom floor that night. The thud woke me up. There wasn't a funeral, and no one came by to collect her remains. Her body was just removed immediately from the premises. A new housekeeper appeared the next day without a name. In her thin arms, she held a damaged chest that flaked off paint when she limped up the stairs.

I found the former housekeeper's chest in the trash that night, covered with leftover food. I held my breath when I opened it but all that was inside were ripped, dirty clothes that smelled horrible. There was a pair of shoes with holes worn in the bottoms and a dirty cup. I shifted the items aside. She must of had more to her life. I strained, reaching to the bottom, unearthing a brown leather-bound book covered by old rags. I unwrapped the leather twine and opened it, hoping to see but a glimpse into her life.

The pages were blank, one after another, blank. Maybe, she was going to teach herself how to write? Perhaps, she secretly knew how to read and write? Maybe, but she never had the chance to do either.

I had hidden the diary under my mattress that night, where it remained, digging into my side while I slept.

Every year my family did a portrait, and every year the previous year's portrait would be retired to the hallway: as a reminder. A reminder of who we were, in case, someone wasn't paying attention. Everyone knew damn well who we were.

Reminder: If you are not angry by now, you haven't been paying attention.

"Why are you down here all alone?" Starin's voice startled me.

His warm breath hovered over my shoulders. How long had he been watching me? *Run.* I clenched my hands, digging my fingernails into old wounds. My blood ran cold.

His cold fingertips grazed the back of my neck. A wave of sharp spikes shivered across my skin as he delicately twisted the ends of my hair between his fingers, over and over. His heavy breath released against the back of my neck.

I focused on the portrait, forcibly swallowing back my thick silva. "Just looking at how time has passed."

"Don't fill your pretty head with thoughts, little sister." His fingers continued looping my hair between his fingers. "Go where you belong with the other women." He gritted his teeth as saps spewed out of his foul mouth.

I wanted to say many words, but only one I uttered under my breath unintentionally, "No."

His fingers tightened, yanking my head back. "Who said you could talk?"

I clenched my jaw.

RUN.

Chapter Six

The wall trembled behind me. My skull throbbed. The sharp ringing in my ears drowned out everything—except his voice.

"Tough doesn't look good on you."

His fingers found my throat again, squeezing tighter.

Run.

Fear stiffened every muscle in my body, encasing me like ice.

His fingers dug deeper into my neck.

I couldn't stop trembling, my body withering away.

Run.

Starin's hand constricted my throat, the force wrenching my body backwards.

Run.

The vein in his temple throbbed as his crazy eyes bore into mine. He spat in my face, the warm saliva sliding down my inflamed cheek.

My head pounded against the wall, sending a sharp jolt of pain through my skull. I clenched my jaw, refusing to give him the satisfaction of seeing me cry.

My nails bit into his wrists desperate to break his grip, but he only squeezed tighter.

Oxygen was growing scarce, the ache spreading like fire through my body. His eyes stared through me, empty of anything resembling kindness. Whatever had once been there was long gone.

I couldn't hold his gaze anymore. My eyes flickered to the ground, unable to bear the growing rage in his face.

"I could break your neck, you know that? Just one snap, and you're gone, bitch."

Sweat trickled into my eyes, stinging. I couldn't fight back—not against him, not alone. I didn't know how to fight.

The faint sound of heels approached. Vienna stood in the hallway, her eyes wide. I wanted to yell for her to help, to tell her—*there are more of us than them, that together we could overpower them, that we could defeat them.*

But nothing came out of my lips.

I wanted her to see that her life mattered, to choose to stand with me.

Starin sneered, "She's not going to help you."

Vienna's eyes flickered to the floor, and then the sound of her heels faded as she walked away. Crushed, I slumped my head forward. I would crumble dead to the floor before anyone offered help.

Starin's grip tightened further. I gasped for air, each shallow breath burning like acid in my chest. He wanted me to feel powerless, and—I did.

I couldn't take it anymore. My arms went limp as the edges of my vision blurred. My breathing slowed.

A door slammed shut, striking my nerves.

"Let her go, Starin, or you'll cost me a lot of money."

Starin's hands released me, and my body smacked against the floor.

"I can't hand her over damaged. They've already paid a good chunk of money for her." Father's voice echoed as he exited his office, laughing. "Deal with the pathetic girl after the sale is complete."

I clutched my throat, coughing violently as I slumped against the wall.

Starin kicked my leg as he walked away. "What a waste."

Icy daggers stabbed across my skin. I couldn't move. Hatred seared through me, so raw it felt unbearable.

No one bothered to check if I was okay—I wasn't.

A faint buzz from the sconces grew louder as my vision came back into focus. Each breath felt like fire, filling my lungs with slow, steady air. I waited, until I was solid once again.

The guards outside spoke over their walkie-talkies. "No disturbance on this side. Over." The static crackled, followed by the base's reply, "All clear here, too."

I pushed off the wall and staggered to my feet. I hesitantly took two steps, then paused. My legs wobbled.

I wanted to run. I wanted to scream.

Running wasn't allowed. Screaming wasn't allowed.

I took a deep breath and rushed down the hallway. First, I jogged, then I broke into a full sprint, tearing across the entranceway and past the staircase. My vision narrowed to a tunnel until I burst into the pool room.

I slammed the door shut and leaned against it, my chest heaving. My heart pounded like a drum against my ribs. I reached back and twisted the lock closed.

Clenching my hands into fists, I forced myself to spread my fingers wide, then clenched them again. I repeated the motion, trying to release the trembling anger coursing through me. The energy surged and fell, but I couldn't stop shaking.

The faint blue glow of the pool illuminated the room. Steam rose in the dim light, curling towards the artificial starry ceiling. The water was calm, unbothered by the storm raging inside me.

I inhaled deeply, filling my lungs entirely, and then I leapt in. The water slapped against me, enveloping my body. I let myself go.

Down, down, down.

I forced my eyes open and released the rage. Every part of my body screamed as I spread my arms wide, letting the energy seep out of my limbs.

I screamed until there was nothing left.

Breaking the surface, I sucked in a sharp breath. Water splashed against the pool's edge as I pulled myself to the side, resting my arms on the tiles.

Only a day left.

I couldn't live like this forever.

One day.

Tick, tock.

If I let myself fall asleep in the pool—maybe I'd turn into the foam that collected on the water's surface after a few days.

Floating on my back, I stared at the stars on the ceiling. The water encased me like a security blanket. Every muscle in my body ached.

I hummed along to a song in my head that I didn't know the words. I used to hear one of the housekeeper's hum the song every day until she was reprimanded. Singing was not allowed. The sound bounced off the walls, filling the empty space.

A lone shooting star streaked across the artificial sky. I closed my eyes and made a wish.

I wished someone would save me.

I kept my eyes closed, listening to the pings of water dripping into the pool and the soft waves splashing against the side walls.

Eventually, I crawled out and curled up on a lounger with a few plush navy towels. I stared at the door for what felt like hours before sleep finally claimed me.

One day left.

Tick, tock.

Chapter Seven

I woke up gasping for air and flailing my arms around me until I realized I was alone. No one bothered to beat down the door during the night.

Behind the pool room door, there was a hum in the house. Dozens of people were scrambling around the hallways. Overnight, decorations had sprouted up and took form. Workers on ladders hung delicate gold and white flowers from the ceiling. Sheer white fabric cascaded down from the second floor. A stout man tied the ends like window drapes around each pillar.

An elaborate gold etched table replaced the wooden rape table in the entryway. A sculpted glass replica of the Suit's headquarters stood proudly at its center. The glistening skyscraper slicing through the city like the terror it was always meant to be.

I hated they were all so happy despite my lack of enthusiasm.

Four life-size marble statues of well-groomed Suit men rolled in. A decorator placed a statue into each corner of the entryway: measured precisely even. Each statue looked almost the same—same stern face, same pressed suit, and same muscular build—the only difference were their poses. One stood at attention with his arms behind his back. Another held a baton in one hand and a shield in the other. A briefcase and book filled the other statue's hands. The last statue saluted, staring up into the sky.

I tiptoed past the housekeeper working feverishly, wiping down every surface, and snagged a handful of granola bars out of the cabinet. No one noticed me rushing up the stairs as they continued decorating either. I wove in and out of the way until I reached my room at the end of the hallway.

I slammed the door shut behind me. The housekeeper jumped back from her work, one hand covering her split lip.

"Oh sorry." I said with a hoarse voice.

I ripped open a granola bar and shoved it into my mouth.

"No problem, miss." She fixed the hem of the gown spread on the bed.

I widened my eyes. *She speaks?*

I swallowed the granola bar down, releasing raw pain as my bruised throat expanded. I sighed, "There it is."

She stepped back, keeping her head bowed. "It's pretty, miss."

The gown stared at me. Sheer blush pink fabric crisscrossed the bodice before flowing into a long silk skirt.

"Yeah, pretty is relative." I shrugged before setting the stack of granola bars on my dresser.

"I'm not sure they believe in relative, miss."

"True." I shrugged, "It looks so fragile it might break."

"I think it is harder to break than you think."

My fingers glided over the smooth, delicate fabric. "It doesn't feel that way."

"It may be sewn with many fragile pieces but together each piece makes it stronger." She paused, "It's indestructible."

I rubbed my swollen neck that ached with reddish, purple bruises. "I might tear it apart."

"Then you can put it back together the way you like." She raised her head to meet my gaze. The moment was long enough for me to notice the crystal-clear blue of her eyes but just as quickly her eyes flickered to the floor as she turned away. "I will see you later, miss."

I pressed the dress up against me. Yes, it was pretty. So many things they gave me were pretty. A knot in the back of my throat cut into a shrieking pain. I tossed the gown back on the bed and sighed.

The decorators left the house in an eerie stillness. The rooms were fresher—like finally taking a breath after years of being dead. Delicate white drapes, adorned with miniature white roses, softened the stark black pillars with a feminine allure. A city of roses suspended from the ceiling with clear threads, appearing like a fairytale. I touched one to see if they were real. The meticulously crafted roses were made of a delicate fabric of gold and white. I let it go to sway in the air, free to dance with the muted sunrays.

In the kitchen, Mother hovered over the stove. On rare occasions, she cooked. I guess, the sale of her daughter was one of them. She did well enough, but I much preferred the housekeepers' cooking.

My father's broad shoulders loomed over her slender frame. His hand travelled up her back, stopping at her shoulders, where he looped the ends of her hair through his fingers.

The wall sconces barely lit the dim kitchen. Mother liked to keep the harsh overhead lighting off. She always told me too much lighting showed too many wrinkles.

The scent of spiced meats overpowered the smell of the fresh furnishings. The guard's heavy boots crunched against the crusty dry sand outside the front door. He shifted his weight, then continued pacing.

Father's voice ripped through the quiet, "Did you turn on this burner? It's not boiling yet." His fingers twisted tighter in her hair.

I snapped back, sliding behind the statue of the saluting Suit. I gripped his leg, peering into the kitchen. I was torn between fleeing back up the stairs and finding out what would conspire.

Mother politely responded, "It's warming up, dear."

Father's heavy breath swept her hair across her pale face. She stirred the pot as his fingers looped and twirled, tightening her hair to her scalp.

He yanked her hair back like a leash and slung his hand back, smacking the pot off of the burner. The water exploded across the room. I jumped.

Mother's eyes widened as he tugged her hair back tighter. Her lips quivered.

His breath heaved in and out.

I dug my fingers into the cold marble of the statue.

He snapped back, slapping her head forward. Mother kept her head hung low, her shoulders slouched. He seized her trembling hand, spreading each of her fingers out slowly.

I dug my fingers deeper, breaking a nail.

He forced her hand down on the burner. "Does that feel warmed up to you?"

My teeth chattered.

Mother shook her head, no. My stomach churned. Her eyes swelled up but did not break. She was unbreakable because she had been shattered into pieces long before.

Sweat drenched my shirt. Her jaw tightened. *Run*. I was motionless.

Father latched on to her hand. Her cheeks flushed. The flash of fright grew deep in her eyes. Her entire body trembled.

I held my breath.

He removed the boiling pot from the other burner. Mother curled up her fingers into a fist. He forcefully spread out each finger—one by one. His other hand yanked her hair, twisting it tighter and tighter until she couldn't move her head.

Run.

He constrained her hand, pressing it down upon the red-hot coil. I cringed. His lips turned up in pleasure, watching my mother's face twisted in agony. A moan of pain escaped her. She bit down on her thin, quivering lips.

Father's red face had a disturbing mixture of joy and anger. He clenched his jaw. His lips curled up in a grin.

"That is what warming up feels like." His voice rumbled just below the point of yelling.

I squeezed my eyes shut. I wanted to disappear. The scent of burnt skin elapsed the aroma of spices. I bit down on my cheek and sunk to the floor, trying to control my breathing. I hugged my knees against my chest and buried my face.

He tossed her forward. She tripped, stumbling on her heels.

"Dinner better be ready in time." He stomped out of the kitchen towards his office.

I remained hidden in the shadow of the Suit until he slammed his office door shut.

Tears trickled down Mother's blotchy face, yet she remained quiet. I tiptoed in, scooping the empty pot off the floor. She just stood there and took it as her mother had taught her. Her back appeared broken, hunched over the sink. She flinched in pain as the water rushed over her burnt hand.

"Do you need help taking care of that?"

She glanced over her shoulder at the pot in my hand, then at me.

"No, I can take care of this. You go on and get ready. It's your big day, you're going to meet Jasper tonight. I placed my body make-up on your vanity to cover those marks on your neck, by the way."

*Mark*s, she called them marks. I would have referred to them as bruises by a douchebag. It clearly needed some rebranding. The light touch of my fingertips on them brought the painful reminder back.

She tried to muster up a smile as she pushed back her dark brown hair stuck to her wet, wilted face. Her pale lips, still with imprints of her teeth, trembled. I couldn't help but feel overwhelming sadness for her.

She flung open a drawer and rifled through the suppressive pills and perfumed lotions until she pulled out a tube of numbing medical ointment—a necessity in the house.

"Let me help you," I said, untwisting the red cap to the ointment.

"Really, I'm fine. It was an accident." What a LIE. "Go get ready for Jasper."

I shifted my eyes to the wet floor. "I don't want to marry who Father has chosen for me."

My eyes welled up as I bit down on the side of my cheek.

She stopped rubbing the ointment into her palm and screeched, "What?"

The self-pity in her eyes flashed away. I took a step back. If anyone understood, it would have been her, "I don't even know this man. He might be the same as Father."

In a flash, her face scrunched up in disgust like she smelled a whiff of her burnt skin. The trembling in her lips halted. "You will do as you are told and marry who you are told. It's just the way things are, Arabella. You will learn to love him." She wrapped a cloth around her hand: ignoring her pain and forgetting her tears. "And if you don't, it doesn't matter."

My voice cracked, "You can't actually tell me that you love Father?"

She rolled her shoulders back and lifted her head. "Yes."

My shoulders slumped.

The damage that he inflicted on her mind was irreversible. There was only a warped shell of a person left. I studied her bruised, rough skin, none of it enough proof to her of the truth—there was no love in that man she called her husband.

I was disappointed—defeated. My soul curled in on itself. Mothers were supposed to protect their children.

Heat rose in my body. The pain in my shoulders sharpened.

Words boiled out of my lips, "There is a great difference between love and tolerance. Both you are in denial about, however, one you wanted to find and the other you needed to find."

Her heels echoed against the floor. Her voice was cold. "You are the daughter of a Suit, and you will marry the Suit which your father has found appropriate for you. You will do it, Arabella, and keep your mouth shut, and be the wife your husband wants. No matter how kind or hurtful your husband, might be, he is your husband. It is the way of the Suit's wife as you were born to become. Stop being selfish. This isn't about you or what you want. This marriage affects all of us. It's a strategic move for this family." Her faded green eyes were sharp. "Now, forget what you saw here, go upstairs, and get ready for Jasper."

Tick, tock.

Teetering on the verge of nonexistence, I steadied myself with one hand on the counter. The housekeepers stood still, staring at me. Embarrassment rushed to my cheeks.

Mother went back to cooking as though the pain in her hand never existed. She turned on the burner and refilled the pot.

"I said now, Arabella." She glared up at the housekeepers. "Don't just stand there, clean this water up—it's a mess."

Tick, tock.

I backed out of the kitchen. Mother ignored my presence and stirred the pot, as if nothing had happened.

My body felt hollow. I pressed a hand against my stomach. I wanted to scream at her, shake her, demand that she sees what she had become—but I knew better. My voice would only echo back in silence.

I turned away, each step dragging like I was wading through mud. My hands trembled. I clenched them into a fist. Then, I felt it. A presence behind me. Watching. Close. Too close.

A yearning, warm breath crawled over my body. His hand grazed my hip then crept down the side of my body, stopping below my butt. He cupped my butt cheek, releasing a breath of approval in my ear. The overwhelming scent of his musk aftershave suffocated me.

He smacked his wet lips together. Every nerve ending in my body was frozen yet enraged with fire at the same time. I bit down on my lip to pinch away my urge to cry. The beady-eyed guard snickered when he let go.

It wasn't the first time, and it wouldn't be the last—yet I still was disgusted—with him, with myself, with my body.

I wanted to shed my flesh and remove what was left—down to the bone.

Every hair on the back of my neck stood on end. I stared at his shadow along the floor. I was ashamed that I had let him make me feel like less than human—like just an object. The beady-eyed guard whistled as he strolled back to his post. His gaze seared into my spine.

I wished my reaction had been different. I wanted to scream, to smack his hand away. I wanted to accuse him of his grotesque act. But I knew what would happen if I did. Shame, would be placed upon me, not him.

Shame for speaking up. Shame for calling attention to myself. Shame for implicating a man who would proclaim himself innocent.

After all, it was just your butt that was touched. Why are women so sensitive? they'd say.

They would shame me for the violation itself. Shame on me for having a butt he could grab.

I stiffened my legs and marched up the stairs, but the shame still stuck to me like tar. Each step, the shame burrowed deeper into my skin.

Shame was how they kept us. How they controlled us.

It was the endless list of shames they placed upon us from birth.

Shame for wanting more. SHAME.

Shame for wanting equality. SHAME.

Shame for speaking up. SHAME.

Shame for not speaking up. SHAME.

Shame for not laughing right. SHAME

Shame for my hair not being perfect. SHAME.

Shame for my face not being perfect. SHAME.

Shame for my body not being perfect. SHAME.

Shame for my breasts not being perfect. SHAME.

Shame for not dressing right. SHAME.

Shame for not always being happy. SHAME.

Shame for not always smiling. SHAME.

Shame for having emotions. SHAME.

Shame for having a menstruation cycle. SHAME.

Shame for not having children. SHAME.

Shame for challenging a man. SHAME.

Shame for being smarter than a man. SHAME.

Shame for being funnier than a man. SHAME.

Shame for looking a man in the eyes. SHAME.

Shame for disagreeing. SHAME.

Shame for having thoughts of my own. SHAME.

Shame for disobeying the norm. SHAME.

Shame for saying no. SHAME.

Shame for being female. SHAME.

The shame of losing the 50/50 shot at the birth lottery I hadn't even known I was participating in. One outcome gave you unlimited power. The other left you powerless. That was all it added up to—a 50/50 chance at life. A life impervious to shame.

He had no clue about the shame I lived with every day.

His beady eyes remained on me, seeping into my skin like poison. His thoughts, his desires, carving into me.

I understood his thoughts. He would never understand mine.

Chapter Eight

My fingers lingered under the doorknob, tracing the smooth surface, where the lock used to be. *Hide.* I twisted the doorknob tighter and tighter, as though it could force the door to lock. All I wanted to do was lock everyone out.

I'd like to say I'd felt whole before, but that would be a lie. The Suit men had been stealing pieces of me for as long as I could remember. I imagined them collecting the pieces, placing them in jars. They stored the jars away, out of sight, until they wanted to pass them around and brag. If I found all the jars, maybe I could put myself back together. Maybe, for once, I could know what it felt like to be a whole person.

They were the collectors, and I was the pretender. Every day, I pretended this life was normal and fair while they ripped me apart little by little, until nothing was left.

The metallic taste of disgust encased my tongue. I needed to remove his touch from my body. I stripped off my clothes, throwing them across the bathroom floor. My reflection watched me as I gasped for breath, my chest heaving.

Each goosebump had goosebumps. Every bruise and scar screamed out, exposed. Damaged. I was just flesh and bones.

The only scar I couldn't remember the cause of was a small one across my hip. The tiny scars on my back were from plates shattering against me. Another scar along my stomach was from the broken edge of a dining chair. They'd told me that I was clumsy, even though Starin had chased me down and hurled me across the room into said chair.

I could still hear his voice whisper, *Run*.

Most of the reset bones left no scars. I wasn't sure which I preferred—the scar or the cast.

I dialed the water to hot, letting the steaming water scorch my skin. I cringed, but stayed.

I scrubbed my skin frantically—dragging the coarse sponge harder and harder along my thighs, trying to remove the shame with every stroke. The touch of his hands still crawled across my blotchy red skin. I scrubbed until I nearly bled.

The sting of pain pulsed through me. I wanted to bury it where I couldn't find it again, but instead, it bit through my stomach. I bent over, dry heaving.

I wrote *SAVE ME* across the shower's glass door. The letters covered the previous words I'd written, day after day. Water droplets wept between the letters. Some words faded, others—sharpened in the rising steam.

Words they called me. Words I wanted to call them.

Hundreds of words scrawled across every inch of the glass. Every word became a small part of me. Every brave thought, every lewd remark—they were etched into me. Alone in my room, I was made up only of words. Whether I liked the words or not, it didn't matter.

I exhaled, letting the water drip between my parted lips.

No one listened—no one cared.

Before exiting, I straightened my shoulders. I wasn't going to give them the pleasure of seeing me upset. I snatched my bathrobe, twisting it tightly around until I finally exhaled.

They had left my bedroom door closed. The make-up on the vanity arranged evenly apart, chosen for me, light pinks and apricots, nothing too brash.

And there, last in the row, stood the faded pink wind-up toy.

I shuddered.

My heart raced as I scanned the room. No one was lurking in the dark corners or under the bed. I swung the door open. Nothing.

Dread crawled up from the pit of my stomach. Dragging the vanity chair across the floor, I let it scrape loudly against the wood. Slamming the door shut I jammed the chair beneath the doorknob.

I took a ragged breath.

Under the toy lay a note. My hands trembled as I unfolded it.

A gift for your husband. You're his toy now.

The room grew dark, suffocating me. I clutched my chest gritting my teeth to hold back tears. It would never end.

I crumpled the note in my hand, digging my fingernails into my palm.

I pressed my hand over my mouth to stifle the cry building inside.

Deep breath, slowly out.

Snatching the toy off of the vanity, I hurled it out of the window. He couldn't do this to me and neither could my husband.

I wasn't a toy to wind up.

He would not get a rise out of me.

I grabbed the hairdryer, letting the warm air blow back my hair. For a moment, I pretended I was outside, free to run, the sun warming my skin and sand drifting in the breeze.

I needed to look the part of a prized doll. I twisted my wavy, brown hair into billowing curls, imagining my soon-to-be husband twisting them until he ripped the hair from my scalp. My face twitched with displeasure. I laid my hands flat on the vanity to steady myself.

A man's boots echoed on the tile downstairs. It was the blond man, who rarely worked inside. He pivoted, then stepped onto the stairs. The creak of wooden floorboards made my nails dig into the brush. I stiffened my back until the footsteps faded, heading in the opposite direction down the hallway.

The words *SAVE ME* seared into my back. The deeper the words carved into me, the more make-up I applied.

Who was going to save me?

I plucked up the lipstick and twisted up the pale pink color. The lipstick was cold and smooth as it glided across my pale lips. The indentations from my teeth were still prominent—just like Mother's lips. Shaking violently, my hands fell limp into my lap. The lipstick bounced onto the floor and rolled under the bed, leaving little pink smears dotting the floor.

Time ticked forward with every strike of the clock punching me in the stomach.

The end was approaching.

Tick, tock.

I focused on the brush sweeping across my cheekbone.

Tick, tock.

The time passed with every calculated breath.

Tick, tock.

I braced my wrist with my opposite hand to steady my grip.

Tick, tock.

The faded words screamed out from the glass behind me. I didn't hear a knock, only the sound of footsteps entering the house and the door clicking shut.

"Welcome to my estate." Father's voice rose to a cheerful tone. "Come in, come in."

Tick, tock.

My heart ached.

"Thank you, Cardinal," said a young, almost giddy voice.

Tick, tock.

I stopped breathing.

That was him. That was the man I was to marry.

The clock stopped.

Time's up.

Father yelled out, "Arabella, they are here." He lowered his voice. "She is still getting ready. She is very excited to meet you, Jasper."

"As am I, sir. It's a pleasure to meet you and your family." His formality made me nauseous. He sounded like a moron.

"Let's have drinks in the den. Housekeeper, inform Arabella our guests are here."

Her uneven steps had their own beat going up the stairs. I unwrapped the new perfume Mother had gifted me—clove and vanilla. It was a little better than the jasmine and vanilla one.

I sprayed it along my collarbone where a cascading pink and gold necklace rubbed against my bruised neck. It had deepened to a purplish blue throughout the day. I untwisted the cap to the half-used body make-up.

The doorknob turned abruptly, jamming up against the chair. A faint knock tapped against the door. It was the housekeeper.

I unjammed the chair and opened the door for her. She stepped into the room, bowing her head to the floor. She did not make a remark about the chair. "He is here, miss."

She placed the glass of water and the pill on the vanity, then turned towards the door without a word. "Is Starin here?"

"He was here earlier, miss, but is now gone. I believe he will be back for dinner."

"Thank you." My heart crawled into my throat. "What's your name?"

Her body stiffened, "I have no name within these walls."

"You still have a name," I exhaled a heavy breath. "Why don't you run?"

She closed the door quietly.

"You know what happens to runners. They cut off your feet." She peered over her shoulder at the door. "I'm past my time for running. I'll die here." She paused, staring out the window. "Why don't you run?"

My voice cracked, "Maybe he'll be different."

"Do you truly believe that?" She backed up, opening the door a sliver.

I shrugged.

She reached into her apron and pulled out a kitchen knife, then set it on the dresser. She stared at me, "Open your eyes."

She retreated into the hallway, leaving the door open. I averted my eyes to the envelope under the bed, although the knife called out to me.

I shut the door softly then strained to reach under my mattress and slipped the diary out.

The words *Save Me* bled into my back.

So, here it was, the moment I couldn't imagine living past. I've heard seventy percent of women wish for the world to end for everything to stop. A way out of the terror and the mundane; so, they don't have to make a choice.

It wasn't my choice after all—as she said, *It is not about you, Arabella.*

"Everything you say is about them," I whispered to myself. "When I should have a say in my life."

The choice.

I glanced down at the vitamin and water—the vitamin vital to my survival. I had never been sick. People were dying in the streets, and I had a pill in front of me to ensure a long, healthy life.

On the other side of this moment were two lives—worlds apart. I just needed to wait for the moment to pass and my life to begin.

Time was up.

Chapter Nine

I gulped down the water without taking a breath, then slammed the glass onto the vanity beside the pill. It had begun--the flip side of the moment. My husband could have been different. He—could have saved me. Or—I could save myself.

I gripped the pen without a twitch in my wrist. Excitement rushed through my veins. I wrote one word beside the I. The word screamed out.

Defy.

I flicked the pill off of the vanity.

I would no longer submit to their demands.

Run.

The open diary stared back at me, the written words exposed and raw. *Run.* I ripped the necklace from my neck. Jewels clattered across the floor. Tears streamed down my cheeks, smearing my perfectly crafted face. *Run.*

I tore at the dress, ripping, clawing away at the fragile pieces. The wind howled through the window, rattling the door. I ripped and ripped until my fingers ached. The pale dress lining pulled back as I yanked, refusing to break the reinforced stitching and boning.

I shivered, clinging to the icy goosebumps spreading across my bare skin. I inhaled deeply, letting the world stop for one long moment.

Nothing existed before or after this moment. The story had just begun, and the future was yet to be seen.

I exhaled until my lungs were emptied completely.

There was only one option. *Run.*

Run—away.

I scrubbed the make-up from my face until my skin turned an angry, maroon red. Every part of the life they had created for me, I wanted gone. I tore through my closet, throwing random clothes onto the bed. I scooped them up along with the diary and a stash of granola bars, shoving everything into a backpack.

I tied my hair back, pulled on pants, layered two shirts, and threw on a hooded sweatshirt—everything they despised.

Voices murmured downstairs, discussing money as their glasses clanged against each other. The final negotiation of marriage. Money—always won over love.

The truth was, I'd never had a choice—not since the moment I watched Jemma put that knife to her neck. Her empty eyes haunted me, refusing to let me forget. Life had never been the same after she'd opened my eyes. The only choice I ever had was if I'd get out dead or alive.

I grabbed the knife from the vanity, gripping its handle tightly, then stabbed it into the top of the dresser. The words in the diary weren't loud enough. I wanted my words to be carved into them like they had done to me. I left the knife standing in the wood, punctuating the carved words.

I defy.

I peered out the door. She stood in the shadows—the housekeeper. Startled, she stepped back. Her blue eyes held mine for a moment before she nodded and gestured for me to follow.

My heart hammered against my ribs in rhythm with her careful steps.

I gripped the backpack's straps tighter, shadowing her movements. My breath quickened with every step, expecting someone to reach out and stop me.

A burst of laughter exploded from the den. The housekeeper glanced over her shoulder. I froze, heart pounding. The voices, below the stairs moved away.

She tilted her head, urging me forward. I followed her to the bottom of the staircase, where another housekeeper stood with her hands clasped behind her back. Her sepia skin paled at the sight of me, but she nodded and turned towards the kitchen.

The guards, thankfully, were outside for the night. Classical music echoed softly, masking our footsteps.

I crept behind her as she held onto the banister.

Jasper stood beside Father facing the crackling fireplace. He was taller yet more slender than Father. His dark hair was slicked back in that calculated Suit manner.

He swirled a glass of saps in one hand as he gestured with the other. "I have plans for the place," the husband-to-be said, cocky and self-assured. "There's plenty of room for improvement."

Father clanged his glass against Jasper's drink. "I'd be interested in hearing about your plans for the intelligence division."

The housekeeper paused at the end of the stairs as the other housekeeper returned from the kitchen with a tray of hors d'oeuvres. The brown hue returned to her skin as she set herself in front of the fireplace to distract them.

"These look fantastic, Mrs. Freeman." Jasper was such a suck-up.

"Thank you, Jasper," Mother replied, her voice glittering with joy.

Father smacked Jasper on the back. "Don't compliment her too much. You know how women get. It'll go straight to her head."

I moved quickly, cutting across the entryway in full sight of them, hoping no one turned. Her limp exaggerated as she crossed the room.

Laughter roared as Mother giggled, a puppet to their insults.

My body trembled, but I forced myself to stare only at the housekeeper's back. She halted at the dark green hallway and pointed to Father's office.

I hesitated, my throat tightening. That wasn't a way out. Sweat soaked through my layers of clothing. I unzipped my hoodie, trying to breathe.

She mouthed, "You can escape from the office."

She pressed her finger to her lips.

"I'm going to check on dinner and then bringing Arabella down to meet you," Mother said, waving a gloved hand.

"I can't wait to meet your lovely daughter, Mrs. Freeman," Jasper replied, his voice grating against my skull.

"Hello, Starin. Nice of you to join us," Father called out as the front door slammed.

My pulse spiked.

I sprinted to Father's office, the eyes of every family portrait seemed to follow me.

My sweaty hand gripped the cold doorknob.

This was it.

My heart throbbed so loud I couldn't hear my thoughts. I turned the knob then crept into the room, shutting the door slowly behind me.

Four windowless walls surrounded me—four windowless walls. The room spun. I clicked on the desk lamp. Was she insane? There was no way out.

Father had left the room the day before, though. He wasn't there one minute, and the next, he exited the room. How? Maybe, she wasn't insane. Perhaps, she knew all the secrets of the house.

Mother's stiletto heels tapped up the stairs. Their laughter roared in the den. I patted down the walls desperately, my palms trembling. Then I felt it—a whisper of air. A smile cracked on my face.

I tugged at the bookcase, but it wouldn't move. I grabbed each item from the shelf—awards, statues, a rusted plug, books—until I remembered the books with dusty fingerprints. Their wooden spines read *Eclipse* and *Nightfall*.

I yanked them.

The wall groaned, opening to a stark white underground garage. Overhead lights buzzed. The space felt endless, leading to a dark opening beyond.

I approached a small, white, off-road vehicle. My hand trembled as I gripped the cool metal of its door handle. I slid into the seat, the rush of danger exhilarating.

This is going to be the new me. The me that defies.

Run.

My mother screeched. Papers floated out of the office, littering the garage.

An alarm blared.

Run.

The engine rumbled to life as I pressed the ignition.

Run.

I grabbed a water bottle left behind by Father and gulped it down.

I slammed the pedal, I had no clue how to drive.

Women were not allowed to drive.

I peeled out into the desert night, screaming at the moonless sky.

Women were not allowed to scream, so I screamed louder. Adrenaline rushed through my veins. I banged on the steering wheel.

The vehicle dipped in and out of divots in the sand. I didn't know where I was going—only that I had to keep moving. The wheels spun on the dirt.

Headlights loomed behind me.

They were coming for me.

Chapter Ten

I punched down on the gas. The tires spun, kicking up sand—grinding deeper without moving. "No, no, no," I muttered, panic rising in my throat.

Blood rushed through my veins. They were going to catch me.

Run.

The car rocked back and forth before the wheels finally caught, ripping free of the sand and zooming forward. I twisted the wheel, steering toward the faint glow of the city. The sandy haze fogged the headlights, the vehicle jolting as it hit the rough desert floor with a heavy thud. My body bounced, rattled by every bump and divot.

A thrill surged through me, electrifying my fingertips. I let out a laugh—a sound I didn't recognize. Freedom. Was this what freedom felt like?

The headlights behind me beamed brighter. Another set of lights appeared in the distance. And another. They were multiplying.

My sweaty hands tightened their grip on the steering wheel. The shadowy outlines of crumbling buildings emerged from the haze ahead, skeletal frames teetering on the brink of collapse.

The steering wheel shook violently as the vehicle bounced over the uneven dirt road. My teeth chattered with every vibration. I swayed with the curves, spinning up clouds of sand that blurred the world around me. Ahead, the faint glow of the city lights pierced the gloom.

I was almost there.

Digging my nails into the leather of the wheel, I pushed forward, the sound of their horns blaring behind me.

Glass skyscrapers towered over the decaying apartments, casting harsh electric light over the ruins. It was as if two different worlds had collided, unequally yoked, with only a fragile wire fence littered with trash tracing the city's edge.

My headlights reflected off jagged shards of glass framing broken windows. The façade of one building slid diagonally; bricks crumbled in piles near its doorway. A flickering candlelight glowed faintly between the slats of a boarded-up window on the top floor.

I hit the paved street, the gritty texture rattling the car as I veered onto the curb. A man stood in the middle of the road, his eyes wide as he stared at me.

My chest heaved up and down in the elapsing darkness. Sand rained down, blurring what little clarity was left. Their horns echoed in the hollow air.

I slammed the car into park, exhaling shakily.

"Hey," he said, scratching at dirt-smudged skin stretched over his wiry frame. "Nice wheels."

I snatched the water bottle from the cup holder and shoved it into my backpack.

"It's yours," I said, swinging the door open. "Take it for a ride."

His face lit up, a toothless smile breaking across his face," Seriously?" He leapt in and stroked the steering wheel.

"Yes." I glanced over my shoulder, my pursuers growing closer. "Take it before I change my mind."

His eyes stared at me in disbelief.

"Go fast," I said, slamming the door.

"Oh, boy." he whispered, giddy.

The tires screeched as he peeled out, leaving a trail of smoke and spinning debris in his wake. I ducked into the shadows of an alley as a floodlight swept across the street.

I flipped my hood up. Crouching behind a warped dumpster, I clutched the straps of my backpack. The smell of sour trash curled around me, but I held my breath, unmoving.

The Suit car crept forward, wheels crunching over scattered papers and bottles.

The door clicked open.

"Arabella," Starin called out. "Arabella, where are you?"

The beam of a flashlight swept down the alley, glinting off the rusted edges of the dumpster. I pressed myself against the cold brick wall.

My nails dug in deeper. The light paused, focusing on the end of the alley. My mouth ran dry. Papers ruffled against the rusted wire fence.

"Come out, come out, wherever you are," he taunted, stepping forward. His crisp shoes clicked with deliberate precision.

My feet would be chopped off.

Run.

The light paused, shining at the alley's end. My mouth went dry, my breath frozen in my chest.

"Arabella," he called again, his voice sing-song.

Run.

Wheels squealed in the distance, followed by the roar of an engine. Another Suit vehicle shot down the street, the noise sending Starin pivoting on his heels.

"There you are!" he barked.

The car door slammed.

"Get her!" he yelled.

Their tires screamed against the pavement as the car bolted down the street.

I slumped against the wall, clutching my chest, barely able to stay upright. When all was silent again, I peered cautiously around the dumpster. Empty.

A gust of wind rushed through the alley, sweeping my hair back. I breathed in the sour, sharp scent that infested the air.

Deep breath, slowly out.

My shoulders relaxed. I was going to be okay.

I crept back into the street where trash floated along the pavement, collecting on the street corners. The faint glow of candles in the grime-streaked windows hinted at life within the crumbling walls. People scurried between buildings among the shadows.

This wasn't what I had imagined.

Eyes watched me from the shadows. People wrapped in oversized, tattered clothes huddled around barrels of fire. Their frayed tarps crinkled in the chilly wind. I stared back. *What did I do?* I started something I wasn't sure I could finish.

Where were the rallies? Where were the protestors?

Moving towards an alley, a lifeless building creaked over my head swaying in the breeze. A faint smell of smoke laced with body odor hung low in the clouds. I found a spot near a chain-linked fence. The alley was mostly empty besides a family who slept close together near the street, and a lone person sleeping on the opposite side. The wind tugged at a fraying propaganda poster plastered to the fence. I tore it free, its message glaring in bold—*OBEY.*

I slumped against the cold stone wall, pulling out my diary. By the flicker of a nearby street lamp, I scribbled.

This is the day it all begins. For better or worse, this is my new life.

Closing the cover, I stared out at the end of the alley. I had waited so long to write something, yet I found myself at a loss for words. The diary was too important to write something frivolous. The words had to be perfect—they should have meant something.

It was my story now.

I promised myself I wouldn't fall asleep. I couldn't.

They could still find me. He could still find me.

My eyelids grew heavy, but I forced them open, inhaling deeply.

Deep breath, slowly out.

Chapter Eleven

"Hey, whatcha doing here?" A foot nudged my leg.

I cupped my hand over my eyes. A tall woman loomed over me, with her dark coily hair blocking the weak sun. Her hands rested on her hips, her foot tapping out her impatience.

She looked as tall as a building but as thin as a pole. I squinted and rubbed my face. Dull gray smog hung low, muting the hues around me. A faint layer of gray coated her deep brown skin, making her appear almost ghostly.

"Did ya hear me? You think you own this corner? This part is mine," she said, pointing to the opposite corner.

A torn tarp hung over a pile of frayed blankets near two stacked splintered crates, their surfaces coated in layers of melted wax. "Ya gonna steal my stuff?"

She was going to kill me. I cowered deeper into the corner, hugging my knees.

"Um." I cleared my throat. My voice shaky, "No, I don't want your stuff." I shook my head. "I don't need any belongings." Sand fell out of my hair as I spoke. "I'm new. I didn't know."

"New?"

I extended my trembling hand toward her. "I—I just got here last night."

She kept her hands on her hips, making no move to shake mine. I wasn't sure if she didn't understand the gesture or if formality just wasn't her thing. Awkwardly, I got to my feet, keeping one hand on the wall and the other shoved into my pocket.

Her face scrunched up. "Ya new? We don't get new peeps. That's not a thin'."

Run.

I zipped up my backpack and swung it over my shoulder. "Well, I'm new. That's all I can tell you."

She wiggled her big toe, which poked through a hole in her dirty tennis shoe. "Where'd ya come from then?"

"Umm...Gohan," I mumbled.

The lie came easily, the first city that popped into my head. I had never been there, had no idea what it looked like or smelled like. All I knew was they supplied our food and had a large trader's market.

She shrugged. "Hmm, that's kinda far from here, isn't it?"

I nodded.

"How'd ya get here?"

Damn it. Was Gohan really that far?

I stared at the pebbles between her torn-up shoes. "I snuck on a vehicle that delivered here last night."

Her voice lightened. "Oh, on one of those supply trucks? They're makin' night deliveries now?" Her hands dropped from her hips to a loud clap, startling me. "I thought I heard one roll by last night." She smiled, revealing stained, crooked teeth.

"Yep." I squeezed my backpack strap tighter.

"Wow, that's kinda brave of ya."

"I guess?" I shrugged.

"I mean, what if they woulda found ya?"

"My feet would have been cut off." Her brown eyes widened. "I mean probably. Just a guess." I sputtered.

Her expression shifted into something flat and unamused. Clearly, I wasn't making the best first impression. My career as a liar was spent. I would have to go back to the drawing board for career choices.

"It was a joke," I mumbled. "Obviously."

She burst out laughing, tossing her head back, "You're a funny one." She slapped her thigh. "I wouldn't put it past those guys, though." She licked her dry, crusty lips. "Well, come on, I'll show ya around."

"Um...thanks."

She slapped my back and instantly, my shoulders stiffened. "I heard Gohan is nicer. Why would ya come here?"

Shit. Why did she need to know so much about me? Was she writing my biography? I hadn't asked her a single thing. Was I supposed to? I was clearly terrible at meeting new people.

I smacked my hands together, creating a small cloud of dust. My skin appeared desaturated from the lack of light. "Just running from a guy," I said finally. "A few, actually. Violent, controlling." I elided the fact it was my father, brother, and husband-to-be.

She nodded. "Yep, I know that type. Think they own ya, right?"

"Exactly." I dragged my feet, trying to scuff up my shoes.

"Is that where ya got those bruises on your neck?"

I placed my hand over the marks. A flash of pain reminded me of their presence. "Um, yeah."

"My bad, I didn't mean to bring up bad memories." She said, furrowing. "Well, he's not gonna find ya out here."

"Really, you think?" I asked, slipping my hood over my head.

"Yeah, there's a ton of places to hide here. Come on, let me show ya." She skipped ahead, turning back to add, "I'm Delilah, by the way. What's your name?"

"Um." I hadn't thought of a name. I stared at her blankly. "I—"

Her voice dropped to a whisper, "Oh yeah, right, you're hidin' from someone. No need to tell me. I'll call ya no name if ya want?"

As she got closer, her sour body odor overwhelmed me. I gagged quietly, burrowing my nose into my hoodie.

She smiled a lot but of her own accord. "Just sayin'," she added.

"Maybe, I'll think about it."

I fell a few steps behind her out of habit, watching her rhythm as she walked and trying to mimic it. My impression needed work. I reminded myself to keep my head up and not to focus on her shoes.

We wove between the trash littering the street, me tripping around the heaps. Litter lined the roads like weeds, clustering into piles at the corners. Bits of paper floated above the streets like insects, pollinating the sour scent of decay.

The place was anything but a fairytale.

Delilah kicked a crushed can down the road, humming to herself. Indigents strolled past—dodging makeshift camps and hollowed-out vehicles.

The siding of the buildings peeled off like tree bark, ready to take its last breath. People lived stacked on top of each other, from the street level up. The looming, dirt-streaked apartments blocked what little sunlight seeped through the smog.

"Why's ya nails have colors on em'?" Delilah asked, pointing to my chipped polish.

I stuffed my hands into my pockets. "Um, I got bored on the truck and colored them."

"Oh cool, cool. Ya got the colors still?"

"Not anymore, sorry," I said quickly, shaking my head. My gaze drifted upward to the tattered clothes flapping on lines stretched between shattered windows.

"No, worries, we can find lots of cool stuff around here."

It felt like I'd stepped into another world. A void reigned over the city where color vacated the land one somber evening and never returned.

Delilah skipped ahead, unaffected by the echoes of crying children and the groans of the elderly. Layers of splintered wood and plastic were nailed haphazardly over the lower windows. A tarp snapped in the wind and I ducked into an alley, my heart racing. But it was just noise. Nothing more. I slipped behind Delilah again without her noticing my absence.

It was hard not to stare at the Indigents. Layers of grime distorted their faces, blurring their features until they all looked the same. They hovered somewhere—between life and death, though death seemed to be winning at the moment.

"Hey, stay with me." Delilah motioned for me to catch up. A thread from her frayed black gloves floated to the ground, landing on a propaganda poster embedded into the pavement. The word, *OBEY,* screamed back at me.

"So, this is the main street," she said, gesturing ahead. "If ya follow it, you'll hit Suit headquarters. I don't hang out there much. It's kinda boring. All of em' look the same, right?"

"Right?" I said, choking on my words.

The stench of rotting trash burned my nostrils. I tried breathing through my mouth, but it didn't help.

"Anyway, ya found a good corner. Besides the fact it's near me, it's close to everythin'," Delilah pointed to the unmarked, dilapidated buildings like they meant something to me. "Pretty awesome, right? I mean, where else will ya find a location like this."

"So, I can stay there?" I interrupted before she could keep rambling.

"Yeah, ya seem cool enough." She shrugged and continued, "The water center's just down there." She pointed to a circular concrete building. "Water day's every third day of the week. Gotta get there early before they cap it off. Looks like ya didn't bring your jugs with ya, so we'll find ya somethin' in the dumpsters."

Dumpsters? I was not going into a dumpster.

"Um, what do you mean water day?"

"Ya gonna tell me ya didn't have water day in Gohan? Ya got water every day?" She threw her arms up.

I stayed calm.

There was only water once a week? How did they survive? No wonder everyone smelled so bad. This was an outrage. I wanted to speak to a representative. And when I say speak, I mean glare at them from a safe distance. How could they deprive me of water?

"Well, yeah. Twice a week," I said carefully. "So, we called them water days."

Her jaw dropped, "Twice a week? I don't even know what I would do with all that water. Damn. How does Gohan get away with that? Ain't there a drought? I heard even the Suits only get water a few days a week."

"What drought?"

"You know, the drought. We don't have water. Duh."

I bit my tongue, the Suits weren't conserving water. I usually spent half of my day in the pool.

I smirked, "Yeah, I'm not sure how they get away with it."

"Damn, maybe I need to move to Gohan, so that I can bathe twice a week." She stared into the sky. "Well, make sure ya load up next water day, so it lasts the week." I nodded. "Food is served twice a day in the food center, sunrise and sunset. Is that the same, or ya gonna tell me ya got three or five meals a day?"

Yes, I did get three meals a day, as any normal person should. I nodded, "That sounds the same."

What was there to do between sunrise and sunset, anyway?

"Good, if ya woulda said they got three, I woulda lost it. Plus, I heard we ain't got food to waste." She cupped her hand like she was telling me a secret.

Lies again: I have a few trash cans back at my father's house that would have begged to differ. She needed a better news source, clearly. Maybe, one that wasn't produced by the people in charge.

"Who lives in the apartments?" Not that the barely standing buildings seemed much better, but it was a form of a shelter.

"The apartments? Those guys work their asses off. They work for the Suits: moving rocks, cleaning the streets near the capital, ya know none of the jobs the Suits wanna do. Usually, a few families move into a room for em' to afford to pay the landlord. Crammed in there, I dunno how they do it. I would rather be out here where there is space to move." She spread her arms out and spun around. "If ya wanna live in one of em' ya gonna have to find a labor job that will kill ya in a few years and another half a dozen people to share the rent with."

Tons of work for just a room that wouldn't even be my own. Me, crammed in a bed between a snorer and a mouth breather, who kicked a lot during the night. I would stick to the alley for now.

"No, I'm good out here," I mumbled.

How were people ever supposed to climb out of poverty? Perhaps, I made a mistake. This life didn't seem like freedom at all. The Indigents were all still under the Suits' control; they just hadn't realized it yet.

Where were the protests and the fighting against the Suits? Where were the rally cries? The only cries were of destitution.

"Let's get some grub before the food center closes."

She bobbed along towards the cement building with a faded red sign reading, *Food Center*. Why did they label the buildings if Indigents couldn't read?

Trash overflowed from bins, staining the pavement with oily residue. The splatters on the cement walls dripped from the top, cumulating into blotches of black at the bottom. Faded red and orange food trays and crumbled paper bowls littered the floor. I covered my mouth. Nausea crawled up to my lips from the overwhelming repulsive scent.

Delilah pushed open the doors. "Chow time!" she called cheerfully.

Inside, the food center was starkly bright, probably to make sure people couldn't sleep inside. I tiptoed over the food-stained cement floor behind Delilah towards the metal food counter. The circular room was mostly empty, with a few late arrivals sitting down alone at different long tables. They slumped over their food with their eyes glazed over. They didn't notice time started to stand still for them.

The food smacked wetly into my bowl. Steam curled off the brownish mush that jiggled as I walked to a small table with Delilah. The cool touch of the metal chair struck my back, shocking me as the uneven legs sloped to one side. I sat there unsteadily, waiting for Delilah to start eating her food.

"Damn it; I never find a non-wobbly one in this whole place." She ripped down a propaganda poster from the wall, folded it then wedged it under one of the legs. She sighed, "Now, that's better."

I clasped my hands in my lap, waiting. Delilah didn't hesitate for a moment and shoveled the brown slop into her mouth. The slop made a wet sound as she chewed. I paused, stopping just before the food entered my mouth. I couldn't imagine the mush touching my tongue. The smell was horrible.

"Oh, Gohan has better food too?" She rolled her eyes.

I frowned, "It's just the smell."

She sniffed the food. "The smell? I don't smell anythin'. I think I'm used to it or can't smell or somethin'. Actually, I don't smell much anymore. It's weird." She shrugged and continued eating.

"Huh, that's weird."

"Just try not smelling it." She chewed as she spoke.

That would have been impossible.

I nodded, giving her the thumbs up, "Good call."

I held my breath and took a bite. The bitter, tangy flavor made me gag, but I forced it down. Maybe each day had a different flavor? Tomorrow might have been better. I doubted it, though.

The door swung open. Expensive shoes tapped against the cement. The heavy scent of cedar wood cologne followed. A debilitating prick encased my body like someone had paralyzed me, inhibiting me to move.

Hide.

I lowered my face into the stench of the food. The heat rose into my nostrils. I squeezed the plastic spoon.

The Suit's footsteps stopped behind Delilah. He ripped a faded poster from the overrun bulletin board, letting it float to the floor, landing beside his polished shoes.

He unrolled another poster and pinned it with a tack on each corner. "You will be rewarded if you find her."

The spoon handle snapped. The Suit turned away, revealing the poster of me with my scared green eyes darting out into the far reaches of the cafeteria. I shivered, flipping up my hood and keeping my head lowered.

His footsteps faded out the door. The door slammed shut. I couldn't breathe. *Run.*

Delilah spun around to the poster. "Huh, some pretty rich girl, of course. Probably ran off with some guy."

Just the opposite, actually.

She shrugged. "Ya ain't gonna find that type of girl out here." She tilted her head to me. "Couldn't hack it here like us, am I right?"

I snickered. "Right."

I was sitting right in front of her. How could she not notice it was me? I swallowed the slop down, one spoon full after another. Maybe Delilah was losing her eyesight too.

I scraped the bottom of the bowl just as she finished. "See, told ya not smelling would work."

"Yes, you were right on that one." I couldn't stop staring at myself. "Hey, can we get out of here?"

She licked the remainder of the food off the rim of the bowl. "Yeah, they're gonna be locking up soon, anyway. Plus, I got some more to show ya."

"Where do I put my bowl?" I asked while searching for an empty trashcan.

"Oh, right over there." She pointed to a pile of crumpled up bowls in a heap of garbage in the corner.

I tossed it on the top: one bowl wasn't going to make a difference. The same people still sat hovering over their bowl without moving an inch. Maybe, they died that way, and no one bothered noticing. It was bothersome.

I opened the door to see every corner, every lamp pole, every window had a poster of my face plastered on it. I stepped back, hitting the door. The window rattled. I peered over my shoulder to a wanted poster then to my reflection. During the night, the wind covered my face with sand and dirt. The light sand made my face appear ghost-like. The dirt smudged around my nose made it appear larger. Sand even embedded into my hair, making it appear lighter. The poster taped on the window didn't look like me; I didn't look like me.

"What's wrong?" asked Delilah.

I smiled with a hint of tang remaining in my teeth. "Nothing, I just tripped on my own feet."

"Ya gotta watch yourself. These streets ain't the cleanest." Like I hadn't noticed. "Come on, let me show ya all the fancy buildings. Watch your step, though." She chuckled.

The posters increased the farther we walked into the center of the city. Some posters took up entire sides of buildings, others were layered on top of each other, covering half of my face. Some posters were labeled *Wanted*, while others were labeled *Missing*. They all stared out back at me, watching me walk by them.

The old crumbling stone buildings gradually morphed into sleek metal and glass structures. Trash dissipated with every step. Soon, the only crunch under my feet was from a stray paper blowing in from behind us. The Suit Headquarters stood erect in the distance, looming over the city. The structure's glass windows shined against the dull sky.

Cameras hung on the corners of the buildings, scanning and refocusing. They were always watching, even in the streets. I kept my hood up and my face down. I lagged just behind the camera's scan.

The air smelled cleaner, fresher, but the faint smell of rot remained. Shattered, bordered up windows changed to spotless, shiny storefronts.

Hanging on one of the doors was a sign reading, *Indigents Not Allowed*. Another read, *Indigents Need Not Apply*. Beyond the signs were expensive gifts and electronics. Another store's window read,

Indigents Keep Out: behind the sign was a display of women's dresses made with the most luxurious fabrics.

Why did they bother putting up signs if no one could read them?

Through the window of the television store, the screens showed distractions—fashion, drama, and a wealthy life. Blinding colors swept across the screens, flashing a news alert. My face popped up under the scrolling title, *Missing*. I dug my nails into my palms. Every screen in the window displayed a reflection of my face. On the opposite side of the street, the words flashed across a monitor, *Alert: Missing*. Then another screen on the adjacent building read the same. Another screen above my head broke through with a news alert.

The street continued opening to the Capitol Center, where the screens rose as tall as buildings. The monitors layered upon each other, all plastered with my face. Each wall contained rows of posters upon posters—all with my face.

I was surrounded.

Hide.

I was trapped.

Run.

Everywhere I looked, my eyes stared back at me. The buildings spun. I braced my knees. Delilah squeezed my shoulder. I tripped backward, gripping her arm.

"Hey, ya okay?" Delilah's brown eyes came into focus.

She held onto my shoulders, steadying me. Her sour breath was warm on my sweaty face. My eyes welled with tears. I held my breath not to cry. *Deep breath, slowly out.*

I swallowed, catching my breath, "Yeah." I paused, steadying my feet. "This place is just overwhelming."

"Yeah, let's head back." She looked around. "They don't like us around here, anyway."

The bronze statue in front of the Capitol caught my eye, a Suit man saluting, his bland face eerily familiar. His eyes followed me as I exited the intersection.

I followed her, keeping my head down as Suits passed, oblivious. They didn't even acknowledge our existence. They all looked the same. Pinstripes today, basic black tomorrow.

Chapter Twelve

It became easier to breathe as the trash visibly accumulated on the sidewalks, the potent smell of rot replacing the sterile stench of Capitol Center. The overwhelming Wanted signs thinned out to sparsely placed between buildings, then to lampposts interspersed with propaganda posters.

One propaganda poster depicted a Suit handing out food at sunrise and sunset. Another featured a care package filled with water instead of meals. The images were meant to inspire hope, but all they did was make my stomach churn.

Delilah's eyes grew anxious. "Feeling better?"

I blushed, wiping the sweat off my forehead, "Yes."

She let out a sigh, "Phew, scared me for a minute when you were wigging out."

I kicked a pebble across the street. "It was just a lot to take in."

She shrugged, "We'll check it out another time."

I nodded, "Sure."

I never wanted to go back.

"Hey," she said brightly, "let's go find you some water jugs and stuff for your camp." She spun around, pointing back toward the city. "The good stuff is closer to the city. We don't gotta go all the way to Capitol Center, though. The dumpsters are in the back alleys. Ya good with that?"

Back closer to the Suits? My heart thudded at the thought.

"Yeah, as long as we stay low key and don't get caught." I nodded, although my pulse quickened.

She flung her arms in the air. "Please, they never notice us. We blend into the trash, anyway."

I instantly became overcome by guilt.

"Oh, I can't wait to see what we find today," she said, with a grin.

"Alright."

So, this was what life was going to be like—existing somewhere on the scale between human and trash.

"This is gonna be the best part of my day." she said, squeezing her hands together.

What's the worst part then?

The heat intensified as the day stretched on, trapping the smell of rot under the city's ever-present smog. I thought I might pass out with each passing breath. Delilah led us behind a row of buildings, slipping into a narrow alleyway. Overhead, the Suit headquarters loomed ominously, its reflective surfaces watching like a thousand eyes.

They were always watching.

The back alley felt like a grim convention no one wanted to attend. People hovered in clusters, pulling trash from overflowing dumpsters. Some gossiped in circles, their voices low and conspiratorial. Others lingered in the shadows; their gazes predatory.

I tightened my grip on my backpack straps, scanning the alley. I half-expected someone to lurch out at me. Society's inability to grow had caused it to rot until it died out. The rot wasn't just in the garbage—it was in the walls, the streets, the air, and, I feared, in us. We had all begun to rot.

Delilah motioned for me to follow as she wove through the crowd. The further we went, the fewer people we encountered.

"Hey, stay close," she whispered. "We don't wanna lose each other."

I tiptoed; my voice low. "Why are you whispering if this is safe?"

"Because trash doesn't talk," she said, deadpan.

She stopped near a faded blue dumpster. "We're behind all those shops, near the center."

I licked my dry lips, the thick saliva sticking to my tongue. I was beyond thirsty.

The stench of the garbage churned my stomach. I placed my sleeve over my nose and inhaled the faint scent of vanilla and clove. Delilah climbed onto the warped edge of the dumpster, then dropped inside with a dull thud.

"Come on in," she called. "It's not that bad."

Yuck.

I stepped onto a bar running across the bottom and hoisted myself over the edge, landing awkwardly on a pile of cardboard. My feet slipped, and I stumbled deeper into the heap. Heat rushed to my cheeks as I scrambled for balance.

Delilah laughed, extending a hand, "Need help?"

I took her hand, cringing as she pulled me up.

"Have ya never dumpster-dived before?"

I peeled a slimy wrapper off of my leg, flinging it away. I whined—I needed a shower—maybe multiple showers. Every surface of my body was grimy, sweaty, and dirty. "I was never good at it."

The next time she said it would be the best part of her day, I needed to reassess her opinion.

"That's obvious." She dug through the trash with glee. "Score!" She held up a crushed plastic jug. "First dumpster and already winning."

Her expectations for winning were low.

"But it's all crushed up."

"We can fix that." She tossed it to me. "Damn, you're lucky—that's a good one."

I stared at the jug. Its sides were crushed and contorted, barely resembling its original shape. The cap was missing, and a crack was forming at the top.

What does a bad one look like?

Delilah continued rummaging, pulling out a ripped gray blanket. She stretched it open, revealing a gaping hole in the center.

"Still nice. Can't believe they threw it out," she said, tossing it to me.

I gagged as the musty, trash-laden fibers hit my hands. The brown stain in the middle reeked of decay.

"Do you ever find food in these?" I said pushing the trash around my feet, trying my best not to touch anything.

"Why would they throw away food?" She said, alarmed.

I shrugged, "Maybe by accident?"

"No." She unearthed another jug, this one with an alarming green residue inside. "Here," she said, tossing the jug to me.

Maybe it'll kill me.

She held up a large sheet of plastic, tilting her head. "This could work."

"For what?"

"To cover your corner," she said, cheerfully. "There ain't any tarps in here, but this'll do."

The girl lacked any sort of intelligence but at least she had an imagination.

I nodded. "Yeah, I can see it."

"Let's get going before someone notices us."

I thought no one would *notice* us.

"Is this all I need?" I looked down at the few items I was supposed to use to survive the rest of my life.

Delilah looked down at the items. "What else could ya need?"

Maybe a house.

"Oh, nothing. Just making sure." I attempted to smile.

Delilah leapt out of the dumpster easily. "Toss me ya stuff."

I threw the items over the edge, letting them land wherever. Left alone in the dumpster, I suddenly felt the oppressive weight of its dark, stinking contents. I tried climbing out but slipped, my foot hitting the metal with a loud *thud*.

"Ugh," I was going to be in there forever. I might as well just set myself up to live inside the container. My residence would be one dumpster lane.

I finally tossed my leg over the edge. I toppled out, landing hard on the ground with a smack.

"Ouch." I muttered, rubbing the back of my head.

Delilah doubled over laughing. "You're so bad at this."

I was well aware, thank you.

"I never said I was good."

The back door of a nearby shop creaked open. My breath hitched. A Suit stepped out; his slicked-back brown hair immaculate. His cold, calculating eyes locked onto mine.

"Get out of the trash, you Indigents." He barked.

He saw me.

Run.

Chapter Thirteen

I clutched the blanket tightly against my chest, the coarse fabric rough under my trembling hands. *Did he recognize me?* I didn't look back to check. The plastic tarp whipped behind me like a cape as I darted through the alley, weaving around trash and people.

My foot came down hard on someone else's. A sharp cry erupted, but I didn't stop. The Suit had seen my face. They were coming for me. Footsteps pounded behind me, echoing my racing heart. My lungs burned, but I couldn't stop.

Run.

I pushed myself harder—every step slamming against the pavement, every breath scraping through my chest. Suffocating heat rushed over me as panic blurred my vision. I bit down on my lip, the sting grounding me. They'd have to catch me first.

Their breath was on my neck.

"Man, you can run," Delilah panted, her voice strained but amused. She juggled the crushed jugs in her hands, her footsteps pounding just behind mine.

I glanced over my shoulder and saw nothing but an empty alley. It had been Delilah the entire time. My chest sank as reality settled in, heavier than my exhaustion. My pace slowed. I wanted to scream at myself for being such a fool.

Bending over, I braced my hands on my knees, heaving for air. "I thought they were coming for us."

"Nah," Delilah said, between deep breaths, "they don't care that much about the trash."

Was she talking about the discarded items—or us?

I stretched my arms above my head, trying to ease the ache in my back. Around us, people moved with a mechanical apathy, their lives an endless cycle of empty, trudging monotony. My breakdown had gone unnoticed. The weight of my paranoia crushed me.

I was the only person clearly losing their mind.

How am I going to live like this?

I scuffed my shoe against the pavement, a small protest against the universe's indifference. This wasn't the life I had expected. The world I had imagined—one of resistance and rebellion—was so far from the truth, it might as well have been a different planet.

The world I expected was so far from the truth: there was no resemblance. People passed me, not bothering to notice me. They moved without purpose: without power. Their expressions chilled my bones. How did these people live like this, day in and day out?

The family at the entrance of the alley waved at us. Their gray, decayed teeth sent shivers down my spine. I ran my tongue over my smooth teeth, counting each one in quiet gratitude. The mother's skin peeled in angry, inflamed patches. I wondered if she could still feel pain.

Delilah crouched in front of the little boy; her energy infectious. "What's up, lil' man?"

"Nothin'," he giggled, puffing out his exposed belly as he skipped in a circle. "Wanna play?"

She grinned. "Can't right now, buddy. Gotta help her set up, okay?"

"Otey," he said, before scampering off, to join his sister.

Delilah tossed the jugs into the corner she had claimed for me. "Let's get started," she said, rubbing her hands together. "I've got some rope hidden."

She pulled up a crate, revealing two water jugs—one half-full of murky brown liquid—and an assortment of other treasures — a ball of twine, a dull knife, a half-melted candle, a dented cup, and a small flashlight.

"Hmmm." She unrolled the twine, stretching it across the corner with care. "I want this to be perfect. Can't waste this stuff—it's too valuable."

Her tone was serious, reverent, as if the twine were worth its weight in gold. I nodded, though I didn't fully understand. She gazed at the twine for a moment with such pride. The small ball of twine meant so much to her, yet she was willing to use it to help me, a stranger.

The boy played with rocks at the far end of the alley, his laughter ringing out.

"When does he go to school?" I blurted before realizing how absurd the question was.

"School?" She stopped, looking up with a curious look. "School? Like those fancy buildings the Suit kids go to?"

I nodded, biting my tongue.

"No, no, no schools. When would he have time for that? He's gotta look for stuff like the rest of us." Her gaze softened as she watched the boy play. "He's not good at it yet, but he'll learn. Did Gohan have schools for everyone?"

"Uh, no," I stammered, desperate to change the subject. "What can I do to help?"

She handed me the twine. "Stretch this across the corner. Let's see if we can make this work."

"Thanks for doing all of this," I said.

She smiled. "No problem. It's great to meet a new friend."

A friend? I never had a friend before. I had heard about them but never actually had one. "Yeah, a friend." I smiled, cracking my bottom lip open.

"If I had a new friend every day, I would have a bunch of friends." Her math was accurate; there was no doubting that.

She let the plastic collapse to the ground. "O'kay, that looks right, I'll take that back."

She grabbed the knife and crisscrossed her legs. She zeroed in, whittling at the twine. Each cut took her longer than my patience wanted. Her teeth would have been sharper than the knife, yet she persisted.

The little boy moved on to play with his older sister. Her hair might have been blonde if she bathed. The ends were clumped up into knots dangling out of an unsuccessful ponytail.

"What do you guys do all day?" I asked, taking a sip from Father's water bottle. The single sip was torturous—I wanted to drink the entire thing.

She shrugged. "What did you people do in Gohan all day?"

Good question, I wish I knew.

"Um, well, you know people watch and hang out. They have a market there so you can check that out."

Gohan was known for its large trader's market: mostly items, sometimes people. I had never been, but Starin often talked about how unfair it was that anyone could sell goods there.

"Oh, cool, yeah, the market, must have been cool. What was it like?" She tore apart the last piece of twine. "Can you hand me the plastic?"

"Yeah, lots of stuff, really cool stuff. Toys, fancy dresses, delicious smelling food." I tossed her the plastic.

"Whoa, yeah, we don't have anything like that here." She dug the knife in, trying to make a hole in the plastic. "The only thing we have close to that here is the Suit's Marketplace, but it's inside and closed off to us. I imagine it's just like that."

"Maybe." It wasn't the same.

The Suits' marketplace was exclusive. It had fresh foods, new inventions, and specialty items for purchase.

I stretched out my legs, rattling a piece of metal wire across the ground. "This might be better at making holes in that." I grabbed the rusted piece of metal wire.

"Oh man, that will totally work." She twisted it in until it poked through to the other side. "I spend a lot of my days searching for stuff. That's why I have such good things." She pointed to her corner of junk, "some of these guys don't know what they are missing. Usually, I start with cleaning out all the sand in the morning and doing some stretches. Gotta keep this place and me in tip-top shape ya know." She wove the twine through the holes. "Then I get some grub, and after that, I can pretty much do whatever I want. Sometimes, I hang out with some good folks. You know, I like living here, it's nice. How do you like it here so far?"

Nice wasn't the word I would have chosen. "So far, so good." I mustered up a grin.

She sprung to her feet. "Let's see how I did."

Two corners of plastic sheet were tied to the fence with the third end tied to a rusted hook protruding out of the crumbling bricks. The wind swept through, buckling it up.

"Looks like it's gonna stay." She propped her hands on her hips. "Now we just need to find ya some kinda box to hide all ya good stuff in. I'll hide your jugs with mine for right now. We'll search again tomorrow. Make sure ya sleep on ya pack, just in case."

The sun-faded, although I hadn't seen a ray of sunshine all day. The ash-gray haze deepened to charcoal as the air grew colder with each breath. The wind rattled my plastic roof.

"Time for din," Delilah announced.

"How do you know what time it is?"

She shrugged. "Ya just know."

The line at the food center stretched out the door. Hordes of people shuffled forward, their coughs and grunts creating a symphony of sickness. I was living in a petri dish. I covered my mouth with my sleeve, longing for the faint vanilla scent that had long since faded. I guess vanilla wasn't the worst scent in the world.

A man in front of me wobbled with each step dragging his feet forward in line. He leaned against the wall with his black soot blanket covering his slumped shoulders. He looked like at any moment; he could have dropped dead.

"Oh, man, I hope we can get a seat." Delilah stood on her tiptoes, peeking over the line. "We gotta rush to one before one of these guys get one."

The man's cough rattled his bones. "Maybe we should stand; I don't want to start a fight." It seemed like other people needed to sit over us.

"Hmmm, okay if you wanna." She set her hands on her hips. "But if there are seats open, we should take them."

"Deal." I nodded, stepping forward.

Grime and dirt crawled up my neck, festering in the creases of my skin. I needed a shower. I was so filthy I started getting a headache. I imagined the gentle drops cleansing every inch of my body. My mouth watered at the thought of crisp, clear water.

The man in front of me grazed the bowl underneath his bowl with his crusty finger. I picked up two bowls and gave the top one to Delilah.

Yes, I'm well aware, that was wrong.

The man behind the counter plopped the brownish food into my bowl.

"Um, do you have any bread?" He remained silent. "So, um, is that a no?" No response. "Thanks." I smiled at the grumpy man with overgrown nose hairs.

He didn't smile back. As a matter of fact, I think I irritated him more by smiling. I stopped smiling immediately.

"Yum, this looks good tonight." Delilah licked her lips.

It looked exactly the same as the food we ate that morning.

The poster of my face on the bulletin board was now doodled over in black marker since I last saw it. I had a handlebar mustache, a star eyepatch over one eye, and three teeth that had been blackened out. I was suddenly thankful for good old vandalism.

Delilah jumped up and sat down on the counter in front of the bulletin board. I followed, sitting in front of the poster. The word *Wanted* screaming out above my head like I was on display.

I dreaded the taste but spooned a lump of food into my mouth. I tilted my head back to swallow It was disgusting.

Delilah swung her legs, bouncing them off the cabinets. "What's bread?"

"What? Oh, um. You don't know what bread is? Really?"

"Nope." She scooped another spoon full in her mouth.

"You bake it?" She shook her head. "It comes as a loaf, and you cut it into slices? It's soft. You can take two slices, put food on it, then make a sandwich?" She looked at me with a blank stare. "It's delicious."

She snickered, "It's soft, and ya putting food on it. Are ya pulling my leg?"

"No, it's a thing." Was she pulling my leg?

"How would it even hold the food if it's soft?" She laughed, finding her ignorance hilarious.

I sighed, "It's not soft as in a liquid, it's solid."

She slapped her knee, laughing. "You have the silliest things in Gohan."

I rolled my eyes. "It's not silly."

Tilting my head back, I gulped down the food without it touching my tongue.

"You're so funny."

"Bread is great." I mumbled to myself. "I wish I had bread."

Delilah continued chuckling while she ate.

"You're not gonna lick that clean?" she asked, her brow furrowing.

I couldn't imagine putting my face so close to the bowl's stench—I would have suffocated. Maybe if I had bread, I could've smeared the leftovers onto a slice, but apparently, that idea was absurd here.

I shrugged, "No, I'm full."

"Aw, man, I'll take it then." She snatched the bowl, pressing her face into it and licking the rim.

I tried my best to not look repulsed. I was unsuccessful.

People around us moved in a constant flow, collecting their bowls of food and retreating to corners to eat in solitude. Feeding time here seemed less communal and more isolating.

"We should leave to make room for the others," I said, hopping down from the counter.

"One more lick." She licked the rim of the bowl then jumped down. "Alright, let's go."

As we walked back, the night revealed a darker side of the Indigents. The night sang with darkness, both within the people and the land. Barrels of fire roared at intervals, their flickering light cutting through the gloom.

Muffled coughs and the occasional grunt punctuated the air, carried on the whispering breeze that grew stronger with each passing hour. Sand whipped against my face, stinging my cheeks and eyes.

I curled up under the blanket and gripped it tightly as the wind howled around me. I was alone—somehow, that frightened me more than being miserable. The most uncomfortable thing about misery is finally getting out and not knowing what's next. The emptiness made the night feel more frigid.

The night stretched on, every sound amplifying my paranoia. Each step, each movement jolted my body awake. My eyes burned from the effort to keep them open, but I refused to let myself sleep. Even after the fires faded and the others' breathing slowed to a dream state, I stayed awake.

Footsteps scattered between buildings, the faint scraping of a shoe dragging across pavement. I froze, clutching the blanket tighter, raising it to my mouth to muffle my breathing.

A shadow loomed closer. A light flashed across the alley, piercing the darkness.

The footsteps stopped. Silence. My heart pounded so loudly, I feared it would give me away. My sweaty palms hovered inches from the ground, ready to push me up and run.

Then, a child's voice broke the tension. "Daddy."

The little boy dashed into the man's arms, his small shadow merging with the man's lanky frame. For a moment, the boy's figure made the man look broader, stronger.

A painful sting welled up in my chest, my throat tightening as I slumped back against the wall. The tension in my shoulders melted away, but my hands still shook.

I am okay. I will be okay.

Nothing made sense. I was too scared to think rational thoughts.

The little boy's laughter echoed faintly as he nestled against his father.

If I could just sleep like a normal person, I wouldn't be so paranoid. But—no—I had to stay awake, imagining every worst-case scenario.

I know, I am obviously developing a healthy mindset.

The truth was, they weren't looking for me in the middle of the night. Their priorities were too skewed, their attention too self-serving to search dark alleys for a single runaway. Besides, they'd looked me in the eye earlier and hadn't even recognized me.

Still, I couldn't stop thinking about the housekeeper. I hoped she was okay.

My eyelids grew heavier as the hours stretched on, my thoughts growing muddled. Eventually, I couldn't fight it anymore. Before I could stop myself, I drifted into an uneasy sleep.

Chapter Fourteen

The snap of fire crackled in the distance as a log broke, plummeting into the embers. Silence reigned for hours until the unison march of their footsteps stomped up clouds of dust, creating a thick haze blurring their black armor. Ballistic helmets covered their faces. The pungent smell of musk and sage choked me.

They were coming for me. Every nerve ending in my body misfired, paralyzing me. Tick, tock. Tick, tock. They were coming. I tried to scream, but nothing came out. It was over.

I lunged forward, catching myself.

The streets were dead. No one was there.

Delilah glanced up from biting her nails. "Ya good?"

It was just a dream. No one was coming for me.

I nodded, leaning back to catch my breath. The thin clouds peacefully swirled between white and light gray in the early hours of dawn. My eyes burned, but it was too beautiful not to stare endlessly.

The scent of body odor turned up in my nostrils. Unfortunately, the smell was my own. I desperately needed a shower or at least find some soap. I had started to get a dull headache throughout the night.

Rubbing my fingers against my inflamed cheeks burned like an open wound. A slow sunburn developed across my exposed skin, and my lips were perpetually parched. I couldn't even hack it for a day. A career as a survivalist was out of the question. I was a wreck after just one day of exposure.

"Ya should put some mud on that," Delilah said nonchalantly.

She apparently didn't notice I severely lacked one of the main ingredients: water. One more day until water day, and it still felt too far away. I gulped down more water than I should have, cutting myself off just before the water bottle was empty. The sour taste of yesterday's food lingered on my taste buds. I cupped my hand over my mouth to smell my breath. It smelled as bad as it tasted.

It was a new day; anything could happen. Right?

Absolutely, nothing new happened.

The day repeated itself. First food, then searching for items out of dumpsters. The mundane lifestyle of being able to do anything, just concluded to me doing nothing all day. To add to it, I was voluntarily putting myself in garbage throughout the day, which was not the least bit rewarding. The dumpsters only contained a week's worth of old rot and a depressing void. My body ached from the sunburn and only worsened by midday.

Delilah's finds for the day were: unwanted shoes with the sole peeling off one and an old smashed up wire trash can. On the other hand, I found a half-used white candle that smelled like vanilla, a cap for my jug, and a stained pashmina gray scarf. I immediately wrapped the scarf around my head several times, elapsing my mouth. Delilah's eyes lit up at the sight of each find, but let's be honest, I scored more than her.

We peeked inside each dumpster on the way back, but nothing left. The garbage truck followed us throughout the city, making a screeching sound every time it lifted a dumpster. I think they were taunting us.

The Suits watched from above like it was a performance, and we were all on stage. The sun glistened off the spotless buildings, blinding us from seeing the show that was on display inside.

The crusty patches on the scarf scratched against my raw skin, but I didn't remove it. My face was invisible with my hood up, and the scarf covering my mouth. I'd wash the scarf on water day. In the meantime, I was beginning to taste the smell.

I coughed, irritating my dry throat. I couldn't stop thinking about how little water I had left, which only made my thirst worse. I tried to swallow, causing the sour taste of breakfast to return to my lips. I yanked the scarf down and spat on the ground. My saliva was warm and thick; a sharp pain churned my stomach.

"Ya okay there, buddy?" Delilah patted me on the back.

My voice cracked, "Yeah, just a little scratchy throat."

"Yep, I can feel it right here." She rubbed her throat. "Actually, it kinda never goes away. Sometimes, I forget about it, I guess." She shrugged. "I tell ya it's kinda like this knee pain I have."

Oh great, such things to look forward to in life. She continued talking but I zoned her out for a few minutes to catch my breath. I stared at the bricks on the side of a building until they came into focus.

"Anyway, wasn't today a blast?" She smiled, showing the leftover food wedged in her teeth.

"Yes." Her definition of a blast was slightly different than mine.

A sudden shiver raced over my skin. What was happening? An overwhelming heat boiled up from my stomach in a quick flash, drenching my face with sweat. I couldn't control my body from trembling. A vigorous pain started to stab me in the gut. I clutched my stomach, staggering over to a building. The sour food from breakfast was viciously crawling up to my lips. I keeled over, spewing every last drop out of my stomach.

"Oh, man. That sucks." Delilah frowned.

Everyone and everything was decaying around me slowly. Now, I had started the process of decaying. Maybe I should have stolen some of the vitamins before leaving. I stayed huddled for a few minutes, shivering, then pulled myself back up, wiping my mouth.

"Ya good?"

I nodded. "Yeah, let's get out of here."

A group of men were huddled together on the side of the street, chatting to each other. Years of hard labor left their faces covered with dirt, so much that you could only see the whites of their eyes.

I staggered behind Delilah watching the men's interactions with one another until a shiny black truck rolled to a stop in front of the group. I pulled my scarf up over my mouth and nose. Before anyone had even stepped out of the vehicle, the men leapt towards the truck. They crowded around the tinted windows, screaming out their abilities.

"I can lay rock." One man shouted.

Another man spoke over him. "I'm good with my hands."

"I can do it all, no complaint." Said a man waving his hands in the air.

The window rolled down and a hand emerged, pointing at two of the men. A roar of disappointment spread over the group. The defeated men backed off, returning to the sidewalk. They looked on longingly to the two appointed men who jumped into the back of the truck.

"What just happened?" Delilah tossed a shoe in the air. "Oh, that's where we stand if we wanna find work. Some people stand there all day and never get anythin', then the next day, they do it all over again."

"What kind of work?"

"Odd jobs, nothing the Suits wanna do themselves. Some jobs last a few days, some last a few hours. The cave jobs last for weeks, maybe months. The factories can last their whole life, ya know. Little pay for a lot of work usually, I hear." Delilah dismissed my worried tone with her hand.

"Cave jobs?" I quickened my pace to keep up with her. "What are they doing in the caves?"

The Suits were always up to something.

"I don't know, dig?"

"Is that how they choose housekeepers too?"

Her eyebrow curved up. "Ya wanna be a housekeeper?"

I shook my head, "No, just curious."

"Didn't they choose housekeepers in Gohan?" I shook my head no. "Well, it's random and always happens the day after the water day. They line up all the females and look us over—every inch. Then ya are taken. They don't ask if ya wanna go either. I hear once ya taken, ya get traded around from house to house." She spoke with such ease like it was just a matter of fact. "It depends on how good ya are." She tossed the shoe in the air then caught it in the basket. "I've never met someone who was let go from a Suit household and returned here. It's easy to hide on the days they are choosing the housekeepers and the days they choose the women for comfort also."

"Comfort?"

"I guess life is hard for the Suits, and they need a hug sometimes."

I shook my head, "I don't think that is what they mean by comfort." My heart sank.

"Who wants to live with Suits, anyway? This place is great. Breathe in the fresh air." She widened her arms to the sky.

Fresh wasn't the exact word I would have used to describe the air. My stomach rumbled. I couldn't imagine eating food, let alone another bite of the slop from the food center, though. The flavor stuck to my taste buds long after throwing it up: like the scum lining a dumpster.

My ears rang with the slight splash of the water in my water bottle. It bounced along in my backpack as I walked, beating against my brain. I would wait until later in the day to drink the last sip. I licked my cracked lips, tasting the dry sand stuck to them.

The little boy and his sister were sleeping on a pile of frayed blankets when we returned. The filling of one of the blankets spilled out, rolling down the street. Their parents had left the fire in the barrel to die out slowly, a dull pile of warm embers remained at the bottom.

Delilah jumped up, twirling around me. "Oh, I hope they found work today. Ya didn't see em' on the corner, right?" I shook my head no. "Great. They're trying to get in one of the apartments with two other families, ya know? They've been saving up for years."

Years and they still hadn't made it yet? They needed to work years to even get a roof over their heads. A roof that didn't even have adequate coverage, and too many bodies occupying it to be considered healthy.

I had only been living on the streets for a few days, and I was exhausted. It needed to get better. There had to be a way out for these people. It was all unbelievably defeating, yet, Delilah remained optimistic about the entire scenario. Her complacency over this whole place was starting to worry me.

Delilah punched out the bottom of the basket, then twisted the metal until it broke off. She fidgeted with the basket, rounding it out.

"There." She hung it over our heads on a hook that was sticking out between the bricks. "The kids are gonna love this." She balled up a piece of paper and tossed it into the basket. "Score." She threw her arms up.

What the hell was she doing? The little boy woke up, stretching out his tiny soot-covered arms. He rubbed his thick, matted hair, looking around for his parents.

"Hey," Delilah whispered to him as he shuffled his feet towards her. "Cheer up, little man. I have a game for ya." He scrunched up his button nose. "I'll show ya how to play. First, find a poster and crush it into a ball." She crouched to the ground balling up a poster. "Then once you have it good and tight, you toss it in the basket."

The crumbled-up poster hit the building then bounced its way through the basket. Delilah flung her arms up, jumping in the air. The little boy watched the ball land near his feet. I guess her misshaped wire basket was more of a score than my two self-serving items in the end.

Delilah nudged the little boy with her elbow. "Come on, it's fun. Play with me." He kept his arms unenthusiastic by his side. "It's your turn." She picked up the crushed-up poster and handed it to the little boy.

He frowned, "It's too high. I can't do it."

"Yes, ya can. Ya can do anythin'." A smile expanded across her face warming her deep brown eyes. "Stand where I'm standing. It's a good spot." The boy shuffled in front of her. "Now, when ya ready to throw it, jump up."

His wide grayish-blue eyes looked back to her. He exhaled, staring up at the wired basket. The paper ball hit the wall below the basket. Delilah smacked her hands together. "Okay, good first try."

She glanced over at me.

"Yep, good try." I agreed in a hurry.

The boy picked up the paper ball. "Do I have to do this?"

She clapped her hands together. "It'll be fun when ya get the hang of it. Come on, let's try again."

He shuffled his feet quickly, making a cloud of dust but he persisted. His little arms tossed the paper ball as hard as they could. I held my breath. The paper ball hit the basket. I clutched my hands into fists, ready to cheer. His face lit up for one quick second until the ball bounced off the rim then to the ground.

"I almost got it." He leaped up. "Again."

"See, it's fun. Try again, then I'll try." She gingerly patted him on the back.

He shifted his feet from side to side then pushed off. After a defeating first round, he made the basket. I slapped my hands together, cheering.

His eyes lit up. His contagious smile warmed my heart. He raced around the alley with his arms wide like an airplane. I caught myself giggling. What an odd feeling that was, which was equally delightful. The pains in my stomach diminished, leaving me at peace.

I joined in, laughing and skipping along with them. His sister rumbled up from bed, watching us jump around.

"I did it. I did it." He yelled. "Let's do it again, again."

"Told ya, ya could do it." Delilah rubbed the top of his head.

He yanked his sister's arm. "Play with us. I'll teach ya." He rushed her over to the basket. "We gonna need more balls. That way, we all can play."

I ripped out the posters woven into the fence, crushed them into balls, and then tossed them by his feet. He smiled with approval then picked up two of the paper balls, giving one to his sister. "Ya win if ya make it in." He said, quite sure of the rules of the game.

Again, he made a basket, jumping into the air. His sister followed, laughing, although she didn't make it in. Delilah picked him up and lifted him to the basket. "Dunk it in."

The boy cheered when he touched the basket and dropped the ball in. Their guileless, innocent laughter filled the air. I breathed it in like it was contagious. There was a glimmer in their eyes I'd never come across before. I gathered this was the definition of fun.

The little girl rushed into the street, ripping down the vandalized posters of my face off the walls then crumpling them up. Her giggles were loud yet soft. She leaped up and bounced one off the basket's rim. She chased the paper ball down the alley and tried again, making the basket.

Delilah tossed me a balled-up paper. "Come on your turn."

The uncomfortable thought of joining in made me nauseous again. What if I was bad at it? What if I made a fool of myself? I tossed the ball, bouncing it off the basket. Heat rushed to my face.

The little boy jumped up and down, clapping his hands. "Try again, again."

The encouragement tickled me. I exhaled, letting myself smile. All three of them stared at me, waiting for me to throw the paper ball. Sweat dripped from my hairline. I really didn't like trying new things. I crumpled the unfolding edges up tighter. I tossed it up.

The paper bounced off the back of the wall then went through the basket. I jumped up, cheering. Embarrassingly, I was unbelievably proud of myself. I had achieved something, getting a ball in a basket. I counted it as a win in life. I needed all the wins I could get. The children raced around me, cheering.

The little boy looked up at me. "I knew ya could do it."

I stopped clapping. His words filled me with warmth like a hug I never knew I needed. No one had said those words to me—ever. My eyes swelled up. I bit down on my cheek to force myself not to cry. A smile grew, over-taking every inch of my face.

"Are ya okay?" Delilah looked concerned.

"Yeah, I'm actually great." I smiled back at her.

Chapter Fifteen

Teeth chattering, I burrowed my fingers under my blanket for warmth. The temperature drastically dropped, leaving a chill in the air that bit through the blanket. The wind whipped against the plastic, buckling it up.

In the distance, a low rumble rose across the starless sky. A pitch-black curtain was closing over the desert. I pressed my palm against the ground, feeling an odd vibration radiate up my arm. Something was wrong. This wasn't a dream.

The wind exploded into a roar, rushing towards us. *Run.* The dense air choked my lungs. Something was coming. *Run.* Adrenaline shot through my veins. I shook Delilah.

"Wake up." Sand rained down like mist. "Wake up," I screamed.

Her eyes sprung open. "What?"

Dust filled the air. I covered my mouth and pointed, "Look."

"Shit," she screamed. "A sandstorm."

"A haboob?" I shouted.

"Get inside."

I grabbed my pack. "Where?" My feet scrambled, not knowing which way to go.

She tugged me. "This way."

I tripped forward into the family's camp. Delilah pulled on the mother's arm. "A sandstorm is comin'."

The dust rolled in, spraying through the fence. The thunderous wind beat down. I squinted to see the wall of sand rolling in. Delilah tightened her grip on me, tugging me forward. I smacked into someone and kept running with zero visibility.

Frantic screams rose and fell with the wind. My lungs scraped against their walls like sandpaper. The roar of nature beat against me, ricocheting my body back and forth.

"In here," a voice screamed.

I stumbled up the steps into a dark hallway. Coarse sand scratched my eyes. I rubbed them, trying to wipe the sand away with my tears.

I crept along the wall until I bumped into Delilah, who was bracing her knees. The apartment building swayed with the wind. I leaned against the wall, trying to steady my breathing.

This will pass, I told myself. *It can't last forever.*

Everyone huddled together, shaken. The little boy cried near the door, clinging to his mother. Sand sprayed in through the cracks. I gasped as the door slammed shut.

The slight flicker of a candle illuminated the hallway. The young girl's hands trembled as the wax dripped off the edge of the chipped plate, falling to the floor. Her wide eyes filled with tears as she stared at the flame. Silence fell among us.

I held my breath as the brunt of the sandstorm hit, a blasting force against the structure. The walls rattled, shaking my body. I crunched down on the sand in my mouth as I gritted my teeth. Digging my fingernails into my palms, I released the fear.

The wind became deafening. Rocks pelted the bordered windows, one after another. The wind punched through the door. I shrieked.

A few men leaped up, barricading the door with their bodies. I forgot to breathe for a moment watching them strain to keep the door shut in the shadowed narrow hallway. They weren't saving themselves; they were saving us without hesitation.

Why would they do that?

The candle blew out. A communal gasp ricocheted to the door.

Sand sprinkled off my hair onto my arm. I closed my eyes, focusing on my wheezing breaths. Thunder rolled in, followed by the jolting clap of dry lightning. The quick flash of greenish blue split between the slits in the windows, illuminating frightened faces.

I repeated in my head—*This moment will pass.*

I concentrated on my breathing. In, out. In, out. *Deep breath, slowly out.* I focused on that act alone until everything else faded away.

We stayed huddled together all night. Most of the children calmed down and fell asleep. The rest of us remained alert as the wind and sand slithered into every crack in the building while the low thunder rumbled overhead.

Chapter Sixteen

I wiped away the crusty saliva stuck to my lips and cracked my neck. My backpack had proven not to be the most comfortable place to bury my face during the night, but in my current predicament, alternative options were limited.

The atmosphere was eerily calm now that the sandstorm had passed. A few people had already cleared out, leaving the door ajar. Daylight illuminated sand particles floating in the air, beyond that, the stark sun struck, bleaching the scene. Time seemed to suspend in the moment. It was strange how gently the sand settled on my palm after terrorizing every soul in the city the night before.

I pulled myself upright, doing my best not to disturb Delilah beside me. She mumbled something in her sleep and readjusted, sprawling into my spot. Carefully, I tiptoed over outstretched legs and scattered belongings until I reached the door. The blistering sun pierced through the haze. I squinted against the light to see a blanket of silt in rippling waves along the street.

Ghostly footprints tracked paths through the sand, leading to nowhere. I exhaled slowly. A gentle breeze swept along, pushing the sand against the apartment walls. My feet sank into ankle-deep drifts as I stomped through to the alley, where piles of sand had grown taller than me in some places.

Pieces of the family's camp poked out from beneath the sand, a tragic reminder of how fleeting anything stable could be here. My own camp, of course, was obliterated. Nothing was left except the crunch of the plastic tarp under my feet. I yanked it free, tossing clumps of sand into the air. Taking a deep breath, I noticed the storm had sterilized the usual stench of body odor and rot.

"Man, this happens every time I get it looking perfect." Delilah appeared behind me, surveying the damage with her hands on her hips. "Do ya know how long it took me to get it the way I liked?" She didn't wait for a response, though I imagined the construction hadn't taken more than ten minutes when she'd originally built it. "Oh well. I guess this gives me somethin' to do." She clapped her hands together.

"How often does this happen here?" I asked.

Well, there was another mild one the other day." She shrugged. "Sometimes, they come a few times a month. Sometimes, there's months in between. I lose track of time, though." She began pushing sand aside with her shoes. "I'm gonna go borrow a broom," she announced and dashed off.

A broom? She needed a plow. Where was all this sand supposed to go?

I grabbed her crate and started digging for our belongings, using the slats in the crate to sift the sand. I found the end of her twine, unspooled and buried, and followed it almost to the street until I reached the other end.

Delilah returned empty-handed. "I can't believe I forgot!" she exclaimed.

"You forgot the broom?" I asked, still rolling up the twine.

"No! Do ya know what day it is?" Her voice brimmed with excitement, as if she'd forgotten the disaster around us.

I tossed the twine into the crate. "No. What day is it, Delilah?"

"It's water day!" she yelled, jumping up and down. "We gotta find our jugs—quick."

"Water day." No, correction, it was the best day ever. "It was about damn time."

She began frantically shifting through the sand. My excitement at the prospect of water was slightly dampened by exhaustion, but I forced myself to join in. I unearthed one of her jugs, the sloshing sound of water still inside.

"Found this one!" I called to her. "It still has water. What do you—"

"Give it to me," She snatched it from my hands, gulping down the murky liquid like her life depended on it. My own mouth watered as I watched. She paused to take a breath, then shoved it back toward me. "Quick, drink it."

My eyes welled up. I tilted the jug back without hesitation, letting the water wash down my throat. It tasted faintly of mud, and I would've gagged if I hadn't been so thirsty. The water ran out before I needed to take a breath. The last gulp coated my mouth with sludge from the bottom, sending me into a coughing fit.

At the end of the alley, I found my two crushed jugs buried alongside the vanilla candle. For a fleeting moment, I considered rubbing the candle all over my body to rid myself of the stench that was quickly returning.

A blaring alarm went off, jolting me out of my thoughts. The sound echoed from speakers on every street corner, sharp and urgent.

Delilah tugged on my arm, exclaiming, "They're releasing the water. Let's go."

She scooped up her two jugs, leaving my battered ones by my feet. I grabbed them and hurried after her, stumbling over the sand. The crowd swelled as people pushed and shoved, their containers swinging wildly in their hands.

Delilah disappeared into the throng. I craned my neck, trying to spot her, but everyone looked the same—desperate, filthy, and frantic. The line led to a brick building, its missing top floor adding to the chaos. The roof beams swayed sticking out like broken bones with white curtains wrapping around them like bandages. Debris littered the ground, creating a bottleneck at the water station.

I gripped the water jugs in each hand, hoping I wouldn't screw up water day, somehow.

The murmur of the crowd quieted to a buzz, and then to silence. Everyone slowed to a stop. I got to my tiptoes, peaking between heads in the crowd, but I couldn't see anything.

My heart sank to my gut. I squinted, bracing myself for what might happen next. They raised their containers above their heads. I took a deep breath, choking out the mass stench of body odor surrounding me. Their faces tilted upward in a strange, shared ritual. I followed, raising my jugs as they did.

A mechanical beep broke the silence. The massive doors of the building creaked open, scraping against the pavement. The crowd surged forward, pressing me into the people around me. Brownish water gushed from the spouts, spraying into the air. Mist landed on my face, carving clean lines through the dirt.

I was sure the color would clear up by the time I reached the water station. My mouth salivated at the sight. I shuffled forward with the others, elbows jabbing my ribs. No one at all was following line etiquette. I fidgeted with the dents in the jugs.

This day kinda sucked.

The murky water didn't clear up as I'd hoped. The spout was just as brown as when it had started. *Where could a girl get some clean water around the city?* I wondered how the Suits rationalized that they deserved the privilege of clean water over the Indigents.

I quickly filled one jug, draining and refilling it several times to clean out the green residue inside. The green liquid drenched my shoes. The person beside me scuffled at me. For a moment, I pondered forgetting the jugs and standing under the spout myself.

The water pushed each crushed dent out, letting each container fill to its max. A firm shove from behind signaled it was time to move on. Clutching my full jugs, I pushed my way out of the crowd, heart racing but victorious.

Back at the alley, Delilah had swept most of the sand away. She handed me a broom and sighed. "I can't find the basket anywhere. He's gonna be so disappointed."

"Maybe, it will show up." I said, surprising myself with optimism.

"Maybe," she muttered, not sounding convinced.

Eventually, I pushed enough sand to the side of a building to make a clear path to the street. I was definitely not as efficient as Delilah. I plopped down on a mound of sand and snatched one of the jugs. I, regrettably, gulped down a fifth of my first jug. Somehow, the water managed to be refreshing yet dehydrating at the same time.

Delilah wiped her hands on her ripped pants. The sand festered into the dry cracks in her knees, leaving red marks. It was like the environment started to become part of her.

We made a dent at the other end of the alley by dumping the sand in her crate lined with a tarp and throwing it over the fence. It seemed like the only place for it to go.

Delilah dropped the crate on the ground and examined the cleanliness. "Ready to shower off?"

"We get showers?" I almost leaped in the air.

"Yep." She nodded.

"Yes." I almost screamed, but I reigned it back. Water day was starting to crawl back up to the best day ever again. "You mean a real shower, right? Not like the one you imagine while you pour sand over yourself?"

Her face scrunched up. "What? Why would ya do that? That would make ya dirtier."

It really seemed like a valid question at the time. "I'm just messing with you?" I laughed it off.

"Oh, good one." Her fake laugh was high and over the top. "I'll figure out ya humor. Give me a chance."

"Yeah, me too." I paused, dreaming of the shower. "So, the shower?"

"Oh, right." She nodded. "Let's put our jugs under the crate. Out of sight, out of mind for people." I handed her the jugs. "I like to bring as little as possible with me. So, I leave most of my stuff here."

She removed her holy sweater and folded it over her torn dark gray jacket on a crate. I slipped off the hoodie and placed it on my blanket that was covering my backpack.

"Leave your shoes too. That's the one thing everyone steals at the showers."

"Why?"

Wait, there were thieves among us?

"Come on, ya know how difficult it is to find a shoe, let alone a pair of shoes. Especially nice ones like yours. How'd ya find ones without any holes in em'?"

I smeared the dirt on the side of the formally white shoes. They weren't going to be without holes for long. I wished I had taken two pairs of shoes with me.

I shrugged. "Luck, I guess."

"What dumpster? I need to find some like that."

I shook my head. "Oh no, it was back in Gohan."

"Oh right, damn Gohan. They have all the great stuff." She sighed, eyeing them in disappointment. "Yep, leave those here. You'll regret it if ya don't."

I slipped them off and tucked them underneath the backpack.

The showers were in a rectangular brick building set behind the food center. Passing by the cafeteria reminded me I hadn't eaten since the day before. My stomach growled.

The majority of the people in line were completely naked, with only a layer of filth covering their skin. They stood without shame, arms by their sides mumbling to themselves. The sharp pebbles dug into the bottom of my feet as I waited patiently.

A torn wanted poster dangled on a corner of the building. Children had drawn tattoos across my face with assorted colors. A cold shock raced over my skin. Once I took a shower, I would be exposed. The line moved forward. I stood still. Maybe, I could have lived in my filth. The smell made me nauseous. My breath made me ill.

Delilah nudged me forward. I needed to take a shower. The thought of it not happening upset me more than being identified. I needed the warm water to cleanse my skin and wipe away every last drop of the Suits.

The building amplified the scent of body odor by adding moisture. Benches lined the narrow walls of the entrance with clothes bunched up on top of each other. Some tested the shoe thieves by tucking their shoes underneath the bench in plain sight. It opened up to a large room with five lines. At the end, large overhead showers sprayed water.

I stripped down layer by layer, covering my breasts with one arm and my bottom with the other. I lowered my head. I didn't want to stare or, worse, notice someone else staring back at me. I meandered to the back of the line, slouching to keep myself covered.

Mud stuck to my feet from the wet, cold floor where clusters of black spots spread out to the brick walls. The red bricks had faded into a grayish white. Sparse light shined in from the two small rectangular windows near the stained, peeling ceiling.

A shiver ran over me from the dank air circulating in the vast room. The person in front of me wasn't old—she was just past the point of living. Sand rattled in her lungs when she coughed, stepping under the shower. She rubbed her face, smearing the dirt around but not quite getting it off. The blackened water trickled to her crooked toes. The thought of the warm water dripping over every inch of me delighted me. She shook off, then smiled, exposing the decay festering in her teeth.

I stepped forward. The shock of the water jolted my body. It wasn't just cold—it was fucking cold. The icy cold water stabbed my skin with every drop. To stay any longer underneath it, my lungs would have frozen in place. My head throbbed as my face turned numb. Why was it so cold, damn it?

I frantically rubbed my face. I reached for the soap. Where was the soap? I glanced from right to left. Of course, there was no soap. I should have realized soap was too much to ask for from the look of this place.

I inspected my body before exiting. My skin was once again a pale peach with a slight undertone of sunburnt.

Exiting the shower was more of a relief than refreshing. My head pounded with every step. An uncontrollable shiver encased my body.

How did people shower with such cold water? I couldn't feel my lips. I touched them to make sure I still had lips. They were there, just shivering uncontrollably.

I was not overreacting.

I slipped my shirt over my head. The fabric stuck to me, scratching against the peeling patches of my skin. I hadn't thought about bringing a clean shirt from my pack with all the commotion. My fresh clothes would have to wait until next water day, I guessed. My old clothes smelled of sweat and filth. A grim notion washed over me. I was never going to be clean again.

Struggling to get the clothes back on took longer than it did taking them off. No one cared to help, though. Their eyes stared at their feet until they exited. Before I left, I noticed the clothes remained piled on the benches, but the shoes were no longer there. A small child ran past me, giggling with a pair pressed against his chest.

There are really shoe thieves.

My body didn't start to warm until I exited the building. My fingers burned with an ache burrowed deep within my bones. I gripped my clothing tighter for warmth.

Delilah sighed beside me. "Ah that felt great." She stretched out her arms. She was back to her positive self.

"How are you not cold?"

Her face lit up. "Oh, I ran in place for a while. You should try it." She rubbed her hands together.

That wasn't happening. My head could have exploded. Plus, my teeth wouldn't stop chattering, and my stomach was growling. Yep, I was having my best day yet.

I shivered back to my corner of the alley. The sky repressed back to its normal vapid state ceasing to contain any joy. Why did I think the day would be filled with sunshine and a sense of cleanliness? I reached into my backpack and grabbed a granola bar. I tore the wrapper while still in the bag. I didn't want to share. I did realize that it was terrible for me not to offer her any, but I didn't really care.

I crumbled off a piece and snuck it into my mouth. Delilah hummed to herself in the corner, rearranging her belongings. I wrapped my hoodie around me as I rocked myself to warm up while chewing the granola slowly. It was unbelievable: nutty and sweet. I hadn't tasted something with any flavor in days.

A stout man with a dark grizzly beard approached us slowly. *Run.* He held a stack of posters in his hand. The granola bar fell from my fingers. I flipped up my hood, keeping my head lowered, and I pressed my feet into the ground. If those posters contained my face, I needed a way out.

I calculated each step to dodge him. If I cut across his body and spun to his left, his large frame couldn't turn as quickly. At least, I hoped. It was my best option. Realistically, I wasn't as agile as I thought.

"Hey ladies, what a fine day it is." He said in a cheery voice.

"Whatcha want, Kel?" Delilah rolled her eyes.

"Ouch, no hello for me?" He placed his hands across his chest like he was offended.

"I'm not takin' up your cause." She ignored him, adjusting her tarp.

"It's not my cause, it's all of our cause." He paused. Delilah groaned. "And we are having a rally later if you wanna join."

"I'm good." Delilah said without looking at him.

"I wasn't talkin' to you. I was talkin' to her."

The man looked down at me then handed me the flyer. I glanced up at his jolly red cheeks. A pinch of excitement raced through my veins. Was this it? Was it what I had been looking for?

I scanned the flyer—and the quick flash of disappointment set in. It was all just scribbles. Was he just an insane man with time on his hands and an ample supply of markers?

The letters were next to letters that didn't go together to form any sort of words. They misspelled words far past anything remotely legible. I flipped over the flyer to see my face colored over in red and black doodles.

"Oh great," I played with a fraying seam on my sleeve while placing the flyer near his stained boots. "Thanks." I had no clue what it said or if it meant something.

"See ya there." He smiled, backing out of the alley. "Get there early to get in front."

Delilah rolled her eyes. "I keep tellin' that guy not to come back, but he just keeps comin'. Ya can toss it." She mumbled.

I flattened it out on the ground. "I can't read this. Does this say something?"

"You can't read?"

I'd like to state I can read; those weren't actual words written on the poster.

"It's something like blah, blah, blah...we are gonna change the world. Blah, blah, blah, join us at the protest."

"Really?" I turned the poster around, looking for some sort of code. "Where does it say that? When is it?"

"Oh, not you too." She stomped her foot. "Chants aren't gonna change anything'."

I traced the letters, trying to make sense of the order. "But when is it?"

"It says right there." She pointed to the bottom of the flyer.

It said nothing. "Where?"

She sighed, "It's tomorrow at sunset. Ya really need to learn how to read out here. People will take advantage of ya for that."

They had their own written language? My mind was blown. How did the Suits not realize it yet?

"Yeah, everything is just so different out here." There was nothing on the flyer that appeared as the word tomorrow or sunset. "Can we go?"

"I'm not into all that." She wiped the dirt off the tarp. "People need to be happy with what they got."

"Come on, please? It's why—" I paused. "It'll give us something to do. I really want to experience one." I neatly folded the flyer in half. "I'll go alone if you don't want to go, it's fine."

She let out a loud huff. "You'll get lost if you go alone. I'll go."

"Yes, thanks."

I couldn't believe I was about to go to my first protest.

"But if something goes down and the gunmen come, we're outta there, quick."

I nodded. "Got it."

Gunmen? Shit, maybe it was more dangerous than I expected.

I grabbed a handful of crushed up granola and popped it into my mouth. The excitement of the protest filled a void that had been growing inside of me.

Delilah laid back under her tarp. "Those flyers are such a waste of paper."

Technically, he was recycling.

"And it's a waste time for him to hand them out. I mean, everyone always knows when they are happenin'." She propped her head up, placing her arms behind her head. "Make sure ya bring somethin' to cover your face, like a rag."

"Why?"

"Pepper spray," she said casually. "The Suits aren't big fans of protests." She paused. "It's not really a big deal."

My stomach dropped. "Doesn't that hurt."

She chuckled, "That's what the rag is for."

Her nonchalant tone did little to ease my nerves. Pepper spray. Gunmen. Chants that wouldn't change anything. Was I making a mistake?

I gripped the flyer tighter, staring at the messy scrawls. No. I had to see this for myself, no matter what...but I thought she was leaving something out.

Chapter Seventeen

Their voices struck me like a hammer, pounding over and over. "Get out. Get out," they shouted.

I pinched myself. Was I dreaming? No, this was all too real. A dim light scanned the dark street, cutting through the shadows. I scrambled forward, then backward, unsure where to go. The spotlight swept across the apartment buildings, illuminating their peeling walls.

I held my breath. My muscles tightened.

A child's scream pierced the night. I tossed a pebble at Delilah.

"What are ya doin'?" she mumbled, barely awake.

I widened my eyes, pointing at the black-suited armed guards marching down the street.

"Th-they're coming for me," I stuttered.

Run.

"Nah, they're just comin' to collect the rent from the people who can't pay. Relax. It's not for ya. Go back to sleep." She rubbed her eyes and yawned. "Why would they even come for ya?"

"Um, I-I don't know," I mumbled, shrugging.

Pebbles shifted around my feet as an armored truck rumbled past the alley. Guards lined the street in formation, and in the center, a black vehicle idled. A man in a pressed suit stepped out, a stack of money bags clutched under his arm.

I slumped back into my corner, hugging my knees.

Delilah sat up, her tone suddenly serious. "This can't be good for em'."

"Why?" I whispered.

"They never bring this many guards just to collect rent. Something's wrong."

I wiped a hand along the soot-stained stone building and smeared the black residue across my face. The faint scent of starch from their uniforms lingered in the air. Tugging the strings of my hood tighter, I buried my face in my knees, toes curling as I tried to disappear.

Delilah crawled closer and whispered, "Last time this happened, there were fights in the streets all night."

"For what?" Fights? I hadn't heard about that.

She shrugged. "Somethin' about electricity being cut off without notice. They had welded all the fuse boxes shut overnight. No big deal."

My heart sank. It seemed like a pretty big deal. "Why at night?"

"Ya know, to catch em' off guard," she said, as if it were obvious. "I've never had electricity, and I've survived. They whine about the stupidest things."

"But they were paying for it."

"Well, they're fine now without it." She stretched her arms out, yawning.

Two guards dragged a man out of the front door of the apartment building. He tripped on the steps, landing face-first on the ground.

One of the guards kicked sand into his face. The man curled into a fetal position, covering his head.

"Get up," the guard yelled.

The electric zap of a taser crackled. The man convulsed on the ground; his face twisted in pain.

I shattered. Why were they hurting him?

Another guard swept the crowd with a floodlight.

"What are you looking at?" he screamed. "Get out of here!"

The crowd stumbled back.

"Get to your feet, you piece of shit," the guard spat, kicking sand at the man.

The man staggered to his feet, teetering on the verge of collapse. The Suit landlord approached with an air of indifference, thrusting a clipboard in front of him.

"Your rent has increased. Pay now, or you're out," the landlord said, pointing to the clipboard.

The man gripped his hair, shaking his head. "I can't pay that! That's triple what we're paying now!"

The landlord nodded to the guards. "Evict his family immediately."

Three guards in full tactical gear stormed into the building.

"No, no, no," the man sobbed, collapsing to his knees. "Please, sir, wait until morning!"

"Why wait? You're no good to me." The landlord looked past him, uninterested.

The man didn't get angry—he wept. His shoulders slumped in defeat.

My eyes burned as tears welled up. I wanted to help, but I couldn't even stand. What they were doing was cruel, unnecessary. It was the Suit's way.

The guards returned with a barefoot woman clutching a crying toddler. Two more young children followed, sobbing and terrified. They ran to their father, wrapping their arms around him.

This despicable process continued through the night. Family after family, unable to pay the inflated rent, were thrown into the street.

The Suits knew these people couldn't afford the increase. They didn't need the money, it cost them more to evict tenants than to keep them at the old rent.

The guards boarded up the windows with wooden planks, bolting the doors shut. Families littered the streets, some crying, others standing blankly in shock. A few fought back, kicking and screaming.

The guards didn't hesitate. The blunt crack of batons hitting flesh echoed through the streets. My stomach churned at the sound.

I wanted to scream, *Stop! Take me instead!*

But I was frozen in fear, cowering in the corner.

When the spotlight finally shut off, the street plunged into darkness. Faint cries lingered in the air. I couldn't sleep. Delilah, somehow, dozed off clutching her belongings.

Was this what breaking society looked like to the Suits?

***

I woke to a child's whimpering. Her bloodshot brown eyes stared at me, unblinking.

"Where are your parents?" I asked, my voice hoarse.

The girl jumped back and scurried out of the alley.

"It's okay. I'm sorry," I called after her, but my voice only seemed to scare her more.

I coughed, my throat dry and raw. The thick, gritty saliva in my mouth tasted of dirt. I refilled my water bottle with the murky brown water, trying not to think about what was in it.

I figured a water bottle a day would just barely last the week. I forced myself to stop drinking before I emptied it.

The streets were eerily silent. Flyers drifted aimlessly in the breeze. Families huddled together on the sidewalks, some asleep, others staring blankly into space. One family slept upon another clustered in front of the bolted doors. What little pride they'd had was stolen overnight.

Delilah stretched. "Ready to get some grub?"

I hesitated. "Shouldn't we wait a bit, so we don't disturb them?"

She waved me off. "They're used to it. Didn't this happen in Gohan?"

I shook my head.

"Well, every few months, the Suits jack up the rent and kick everyone out. Then they work themselves half to death trying to pay it back. That's why I stay in the alley—no drama in my corner."

"But why would they do that?"

It felt more like a lesson they were trying to teach them. I wasn't sure what the lesson was yet.

"To get everyone working harder?" She shrugged. She didn't know either.

Maybe it was a reminder of who held the power. Delilah didn't seem angry. The disturbing part was that she showed no anger or fear, she was indifferent.

"And still, you don't see a reason to protest this cruelty?"

"I like to stay out of this, it's not my business." She walked away from me.

It had everything to do with her. Everything they were doing was against her.

"But it affects you." I blurted out.

"Oh, not you too. Ya gonna love the protest. After this," she gestured to the cowering figures lining the streets, "it's gonna be huge."

"Really?"

"Yeah, now get food with me before I change my mind about going."

I jumped up. "Deal."

The evicted watched us as we passed. I couldn't help but stare at the trails of blood along the streets branching out into the city. The abandoned children wandered from building to building, calling for their daddy on the verge of tears. This might have been the exact time where I should have helped, but I didn't. Instead, I stood there staring.

I should have helped.

It was so unusual that by mid-morning, the people wallowing on the streets picked themselves up. The wandering children lost their dismay and started kicking cans in the street. Just like the day before, they lined up looking for jobs.

It wasn't until late afternoon, some returned to their buildings, prying boards off the windows and scaling walls to reclaim their homes. I would have just wallowed in a corner somewhere if it was me.

Items fell from the top floors crashing against the pavement. Blankets floated down gracefully, almost peacefully, followed by furniture smashing against the ground. Children raced by, scooping the items up.

It was mesmerizing to watch them for hours.

"Are ya ready?" Delilah waved her hand in front of me. "Whatcha starin' at?"

The sun finally burned through the smog giving the sky a grayish blue color. I cupped my hand over my face. "Ready for what?"

"The protest. We can skip it if ya wanna; I have no problem with that. There are plenty of other things I need to get done today."

I straightened out my hoodie. "Yep, I'm ready."

"Okay, let's go." Her eyes widened. "It's gonna be crazy after what happened last night; I mean crazy."

I nodded, nerves and excitement twisting in my gut. I had no idea what I was walking into.

Chapter Eighteen

S o, this was it—the moment I had been waiting for since I'd escaped. I wiped my sweaty palms on my pants, the sour taste of dinner still clinging to my tongue. I tried to swallow it down but I was unsuccessful.

The sun blazed in brilliant gold and orange, spreading across the sky. Drums thundered like distant claps of thunder. Every muscle in my body tightened with each beat—*boom, boom, boom*.

A tingling excitement coursed through me. I rubbed my thumb against the tips of my fingers repeatedly, anticipation mounting. People filed onto the main street, streaming towards the Capitol. My adrenaline surged. The pieces of the puzzle were falling into place.

Delilah handed me a handkerchief. "Ya forgot this. Cover your nose and mouth—there's gonna be smoke tonight." She skipped to the rhythm of the drums as we approached the imposing Suit headquarters.

Store owners stood in doorways, arms crossed, glaring in disgust. Employees scrambled to lock doors and flip their signs to "Closed."

Some shopkeepers raised guns, aiming at us from behind their windows.

A sting of anxiety caught my breath. I tied the handkerchief over my face, casting a wary eye at the overhanging cameras. The danger was electric—exhilarating and terrifying all at once. The crowd swelled, multiplying into hundreds, pouring into the square from every street, every alley.

Handwritten posters in street language waved high above people's heads. A cloud of sand and dust hovered over the street. The fiery hues of the setting sun reflected off glass skyscrapers, making them appear ablaze.

Drummers pounded in unison on metal barrels stationed at every other corner. Their rhythm reverberated off the buildings, creating a dome of sound. Fires roared in charred barrels on the opposite corners, their red-hot sparks dancing into the sky.

Above us, three enormous skeleton puppets in tattered suits swayed and danced. Black-masked figures loomed at the street corners, wrecking bars swinging in their gloved hands. These people were here for more trouble than I had anticipated.

They raised metal pipes above their heads, clanging them to the beat of the drums. I shied back, sticking close to Delilah, mesmerized by the chaotic sights and sounds.

A chant grew within the crowd. At first, only a few voices echoed the phrase—"We will rise. We will rise." Then the entire crowd took it up, their voices swelling. My heartbeat quickened with every repetition.

Delilah rolled her eyes. "Here we go."

I grinned and chanted along, making sure to shout in her ear. "We will rise. Come on, Delilah." I nudged her playfully. "We will rise."

"Nah, I'm good." She shook her head, although there was dance in her step, a freeness. "Why aren't you dancing? It's the best part of the protests."

Dancing wasn't allowed.

Her dancing became contagious. Everyone around us danced along—except me. I yanked my hoodie tighter and crossed my arms.

I shrugged, "I don't know how."

"I don't, either." She grabbed my arms, trying to move me around.

"I'm not going to dance. It's foolish."

"Foolish? This whole thin' is foolish." She nudged me.

Reluctantly, I swayed my hips a little to appease her. Heat rose to my face. I must've looked ridiculous.

She smiled, "See? It's fun."

She skipped forward, grabbing my hand to follow. I couldn't help myself. Being in the moment, I felt free for the first time in my life. A giggle escaped my lips as I skipped like a child.

I clapped along, bouncing every time I clapped. At first, it felt unnatural, but after a few minutes, I was enjoying it. I didn't notice I was smiling until my cheeks hurt.

The crowd surged around the towering Suit statue in the square's center. Its raised arm saluting to the sky. The sunset cast a shadow over the Capitol building, stretching across the steps leading to a makeshift platform.

Clenched fists pounded the air in time with the chant. "We will rise. We will rise."

A rugged, tall man emerged from behind the statue, a gun strapped across his chest. His olive skin glistened with sweat and soot in the fading sun. Intimidation radiated off him like an odor, making my heart pound harder.

It was difficult to focus on him without feeling unsteady. He stomped to the platform's edge, scanned the crowd, and gave a hand signal before retreating to the side. Four others stepped forward—two men and two women. The crowd erupted into cheers.

Who were these people? These had to be the rebels. Who was the leader? How could I join? Was there an application process?

A young man took center stage. His light blond hair glowed in the sun, and his boyish, clean-shaven face exuded an air of innocence. Goosebumps prickled my arms. It felt as though he was staring directly at me.

He stood still for a moment, soaking in the crowd's energy as their cheers grew louder. He was handsome—or, at least his presence was magnetic. He wore only a stolen Suit vest and baggy, worn-out pants, but he seemed regal in the fading light.

Beside him stood a striking woman with bright red hair that twisted like flames in the air. Her clothes clung to her curvaceous figure as if they were a second skin. She removed her bottle-cap goggles and stared boldly into the crowd without a hint of insecurity. I couldn't believe a woman stood side by side with the male leader. She fascinated me.

The rugged man scanned the building tops, ignoring the crowd. Another woman, dressed all in black, stood next to a man with his hair tied back. Their eyes fixed on the center of the stage without moving an inch.

"Who are they?" I whispered to Delilah.

"They call themselves the Rebel Underground."

"Who's that?" I pointed to the blond man.

"Blondie?" She nodded towards him. "That's Phin. He's the leader of the rebellion. Everyone thinks he's so cute. Looks like a girl to me." She pointed to the red-haired woman. "That one's some kinda computer genius—also a stuck-up bitch." She rolled her eyes. "There are others, but I don't pay attention much." She shrugged. "I have no clue about those guys, just guards, I guess."

Phin raised his fist in the air, and a surge of excitement swept through me. I shouted along with the crowd, standing strong. He was the person who was going to change the world. I strained to see him on my tiptoes. We should have arrived earlier to be closer.

The drums halted. Phin lowered his hand, and the crowd quieted.

His voice, robust and steady, cutting through the air. "We will rise. We will overcome this. They are nothing but people like us. We've feared them long enough. It is time for them to fear us." The crowd howled, in response.

"We will rise and shatter that glass tower they hide inside. They will fall lower than us. They will fall so far, they'll have no way of getting back up." He paused. The cheers grew deafening. Fists pumped. "What they did last night was horrible, and they will pay. We will not be torn down."

The words echoed out of his entire body. "We will not be silenced. We will become louder every time they try to silence us. We will become stronger every time they try to weaken us. We will rise above them."

The crowd roared. "*We will rise!*" they chanted, their voices swelling into a thunderous wave.

For a moment, it was like witnessing magic.

Phin's voice boomed again. "We will be equal as one. No longer will we starve. No longer will we work ourselves to death. No longer will your gender say what you can and can't do. No longer—"

A bang shattered his words. I gasped as a metal canister whizzed through the air, trailing red smoke. Another followed, streaking the sky. The rugged man cocked his head, raising his gun towards the rooftops. More smoke erupted, filling the air.

Delilah nudged me. "Keep your face covered. Get ready to run."

"What's happening?" I frantically scanned the rooftops but saw no one.

She met my gaze, her voice low and haunting. "The Suits are coming."

Chapter Nineteen

*H*oly shit, they're coming.

Elbows and hands flailed wildly in every direction.

Delilah screamed, "Let's go. Let's go."

The rugged man leapt in front of Phin, firing at the rooftops. I stumbled backwards, then forwards, slamming into someone. *Run*. I ricocheted from body to body, for every step forward, I was shoved back by two. Delilah grabbed my hand and yanked me forward. I gasped for air, clutching the handkerchief over my mouth.

The dense air mixed with the red smoke. My heart strangled my lungs. I froze, watching a dark shadow emerge through the smoke.

The black of their tactical uniforms grew deeper as the Suits advanced, gas masks covering their faces, batons ready to swing. The Suits infested the crowd.

A quick flash, then a bang. People hit the ground screaming. Blood splattered across the street. A Suit's baton dripped deep red as they brought it down for another strike.

I hunched over, shielding my head. The smoke engulfed the square. Gas hissed from canisters rolling at our feet. Above the chaos, the towering Suit statue stood mighty, looming over the smoke and gas.

I leapt over the shattered remains of one of the fragile Suit skeletons, now mangled on the street. Sirens blared, their red emergency lights flashing. My pulse raced. *Hide.*

Where was I supposed to go?

My eyes burned uncontrollably, tears blurring my vision. My nostrils and throat seared with the sharp scent of pepper. I coughed, pressing the handkerchief tighter against my face. I lost Delilah's grip and stumbled forward, chasing her faint outline.

I had no idea where we were heading. The relentless noise—the strikes, the screams, the sirens—numbed my senses.

A piercing screech whizzed past me. The doors of a black van swung open, and protesters were yanked inside. Their muffled screams escaped from beneath black hoods covering their heads. Their arms flailed, desperately grabbing for help. Armed guards surrounded the van, pulling in anyone they could reach.

A hand clamped onto my shoulder and yanked me back. I jerked away, flinging myself in every direction until I tripped forward. I shoved through the crowd, desperate to get away from the van.

Another hand grabbed my wrist, pulling me back. I flailed, and a second hand gripped my other wrist. I tried to scream, but only a hoarse yelp escaped.

"It's me, it's me." Delilah's voice cut through the chaos. "Follow me!"

She dug her fingers into my wrist, dragging me into an alley. I wiped my stinging eyes with the filthy handkerchief, but the pain persisted. I wanted to claw my own eyes out. Gasping, I bent over, bracing my knees. I couldn't go on.

At the end of the alley, Delilah slipped through a narrow doorway into an industrial building. I dragged my feet after her.

"Wait—wait," I coughed between shallow breaths. "I need a moment." I couldn't catch my breath.

"They'll find us," she snapped.

"I can't see," I whimpered, rubbing my swollen eyes.

"Fine, let me find somethin'." She sighed and crouched. "This might help." She tilted my head back. "Open your eyes."

"I can't," I whined.

"This is why I didn't want to come. It's all a bunch of nonsense," she scolded.

Delilah pried my eyes open and splashed dirty water into them. The pain didn't stop, but I could see her face faintly. I knelt on the ground, struggling to catch my breath. I couldn't contemplate what was happening.

My entire body felt like it was on fire.

The burn encased every nerve ending, spreading throughout me. I unzipped my hoodie, letting the stagnant air touch my sweat-drenched shirt. Slumping my shoulders, I lowered my head. She only gave me a few moments to recover.

"Better?" she asked. I nodded weakly. "Okay, this way." She pulled me towards the stairs.

We climbed one flight before she slipped through a shattered window onto a fire escape. Every step made my chest tighter and tighter.

I dug my nails into my palms and whispered my mantra. *Deep breath. Slowly out. Deep breath. Slowly out.*

It wasn't working. I couldn't breathe deeply or slow my breathing. *Just forget the pain, just keep moving. This will be over soon.*

I staggered out the window onto the fire escape. The cross-bridge wobbled beneath my feet. I gripped the railing, praying my sweaty palms wouldn't slip.

One second Delilah was ahead of me, the next she vanished through another window. I leapt in after her, landing on the second floor with a hard thud. A flash of black darted past as I hit the ground. I groaned, rolling onto my side.

Delilah grumbled beside me. "That stung." She stood, dusting herself off. "Alright, let's walk the rest of the way."

Pain radiated through my leg as I tried to put weight on it. Limping, I followed her down the cracked stone steps to the first floor. My vision blurred in and out. She paused at the bottom, waiting.

"Come on," she urged.

"No one's gonna come in here," I wheezed. "There's a huge boulder in front of the door. Let's wait until the noise stops."

"Fine." She threw her hands in the air.

I slumped against the wall and slid to the floor, watching my vision slowly return. My wheezing subsided, but the burn lingered in my chest. We sat in silence, listening as the screams and cries outside began to fade.

When my vision cleared, I realized I had no idea where we were. Dust settled on the gray and white mosaic floor of the abandoned Capitol building, its structure crumbling. Each floor was hanging on the verge of collapsing. Parts of the roof had caved in, letting red smoke drift inside.

Debris from the upper floors had fallen into a heap at the center of the room. Beside it stood an oversized desk with its drawers pulled out and scattered. Sand coated the paper scraps littering the floor. Above the door, Father's gold insignia hung, tarnished. Below it, the words *record holdings* were missing the "c" and "l."

Sirens still wailed faintly as the sun sank below the horizon. A helicopter's floodlight swept across the roof, illuminating the yellowed white paint on the walls. I scurried, pressing myself against the wall, hoping to avoid detection.

Exhaling, I traced a line in the thick dust on the cool floor. "Why did they do that?"

"Do what?" Delilah stretched her legs, exhaling.

"Attack them like that? Father never—" I hesitated. "I thought the Suits didn't care enough to bother with people chanting in the streets."

She sighed, "It wasn't the protesters on the streets they were after; it was the Rebel Underground."

"Aren't they the same?" A sourness churned in my stomach.

"No, not really. Those people on the stage want to create their own power. But all who rise will fall, they say." She shrugged. "Ya know, they plan to overthrow the government. That's why they want em' dead."

The words struck me like a punch to the gut. She was talking about a coup. My hands trembled. I knew in my gut that the city would burn before the Suits allowed that.

"Do you think they can do it?"

She shrugged. "I don't know why they'd wanna change a good thing."

"A good thing?"

"They feed us. They give us water. They take care of us. Why not be happy with what ya got? They struggle too."

They had set her to defeat too.

"They're not struggling, Delilah," I snapped. "They waste more food and water than you could imagine. They're lying to you."

"How do you know?" she spat back.

"I—I know because." I paused. "Because I just know."

"That's what I thought; ya don't know. Ya just believe all those rumors ya hear on the streets."

Why did she have such loyalty to people who didn't deserve it?

"I'm not. I've seen it with my own eyes." I persisted.

"Sure," she said dismissively. "Back in Gohan, where everything's so different."

Damn Gohan, for ruining my street cred.

"They're not taking care of you. They're controlling you." I snapped back.

She rolled her eyes, "You sound just like em'." She leaned against the wall, shaking her head.

"Maybe, I do. How do I join?"

"Join?" She snickered. "It's not somethin' ya just join." My heart sank. "No one knows where they are, and no one who does know is gonna tell ya. They don't just let anyone in, ya know."

Ouch, that stung. My burning eyes swelled with tears. I sank into silent defeat before I'd even tried. "But—"

"But what?" she added, eyeing me seriously, "Ya better keep your mouth shut. They'll come after ya. Be happy with what you've got."

Her complacency grated on me. *How could she not want more?* Delilah's satisfaction with being miserable made my skin crawl. It was like she set her face too close to the bars constricting her in society and forgot to take a step back to see she was the one in the cage.

The helicopter's light swept past the window again, and she seemed small—scared. I wanted her to dream bigger, to fight for—more. We sat in silence across from each other for hours until it was quiet outside.

"Time to move." She sprung up, cracking her back. "Back to the alley."

"Is it clear?" I asked cautiously.

"Yep. Don't hear or see anyone out there."

The dissipating red gas clung to the shadows. People cowered under torn blankets in a nearby alley, muffling sobs. The Suits' patrol car rumbled by. I kept my eyes fixed on the cracked pavement.

"Stay off the streets. Go back to your homes," the speaker blared.

What homes? No one here has a home.

We nodded and quickened our steps. A stillness blanketed the streets, paired with suffocating anxiety. The instigators were long gone, hidden away. All that remained were the helpless.

Father's words echoed in my mind—*To own society, you must break society.*

This was what breaking society looked like. And the Suits wouldn't stop until every last one of us was shattered into a million pieces.

Chapter Twenty

Anxiety kept me awake the entire night, and I wasn't aware other people had moved on until mid-morning the next day. I was still coughing out the last of the peppery burn as dumpster pickers argued over who had found a wagon first in the back alley, their squabbling punctuating the silence. Meanwhile, a group of kids played tag in the street, giggling between skips. On the other side of the road, two women hummed while sweeping out their campsites.

What a bizarre world I lived in now.

Delilah skipped along the street, her eyes scanning her next great treasure. "Isn't it a great day?"

I nodded, absently, glaring up at the speakers droning the same phrase over on repeat. "This is your Cardinal speaking. Obey, and disband. We are here to protect you. All protesters will be imprisoned." His voice crawled into my bones, embedding deep in my marrow. There was something about his voice that always felt like a dagger being driven into my ribs.

A faint, constant buzz hummed through the speakers between phrases. Something about it sounded familiar.

"Do you hear that buzzing noise over the speakers?" I asked, exhaling heavily. "What is that?"

Delilah shrugged. "I don't know. Never noticed it before."

My heart sank. I knew that noise. It was the sound of a wind-up toy. My eyes darted to every corner of the street for him. "Where is he?" I mumbled.

"What's up with ya?" Delilah asked, her tone light.

"Oh, um… nothing. Just looking around," I replied quickly.

My heart pounded against my eardrums. *He's only taunting me.* I repeated the thought over and over, trying to steady myself. *He isn't really here. It's just a noise.* I gulped down the rising fear.

No one else seemed to find the sound unusual. Everyone carried on as normal, even though streaks of dried blood stained the streets. Less than forty-eight hours had passed, and yet the Indigents had already returned to their routines. Somehow, their spirits had rebounded, their resentment seemingly erased after a single restless night.

Delilah laughed and stopped skipping. "Ya know what's great about this place?"

"What?" I bit down on my cheek to stop myself from rolling my eyes.

"Ya have all the time to do whatever ya want. Wanna play tag? Play tag. No one's gonna stop ya. Wanna build a sandcastle? Go for it. We've got loads of sand. There are endless possibilities." She paused, grinning. "As long as ya find happiness in what ya are given. It's great. It's really great."

Well, the sun wasn't shining, but with her upbeat demeanor, it might as well been the brightest day ever. I hunched my shoulders, dragging my feet alongside her. She wasn't entirely wrong. There was a strange freedom to street life that made my former one seem almost claustrophobic. I could have settled for the street life.

People looked happy—or at least good at pretending, perhaps. Maybe I could have made a life for myself here.

But just as quickly as the resignation began to grip me, a flash of gray dropped in front of me, followed by a loud splat. I jumped back instinctively. The body hit the ground so hard that the back of her skull shattered into fragments.

"What the fuck?" I screamed.

Her gray bonnet floated down to the ground beside her open, scarred hand. Her bruised legs contorted unnaturally peeking out from under her gray dress. My breath heaved in and out. My hands trembled uncontrollably, yet I couldn't look away.

She was unrecognizable, although she looked relatively young, her haunting blue eyes fixed on the sky. The remnants of a silencer collar charred the skin around her neck. Fresh, deep scratches showed where she had torn it off. She wouldn't be silenced in death.

Delilah shrugged and stepped over the broken body. "It happens."

"What's wrong with you?" I hissed.

My heart threatened to explode out of my chest. I darted my gaze to the faces around me, but no one reacted. No one even looked. Their eyes remained focused on themselves. How could they not see her?

Delilah continued walking away, throwing her hands up.

"Yeah, it happens every couple of months. Some rich girl can't handle their life. Oh, poor them, right?" She snickered. "Like it's so hard being them."

Blood seeped into the fibers of my shoes, merging into misshapen stains. The woman's face twisted in my mind into someone familiar.

"Jemma?" I whispered to myself.

An invisible weight pressed on my chest, stacking bricks upon bricks, suffocating me. My hands trembled, my vision blurred, and yet Jemma's lifeless eyes bored into mine.

"Open your eyes" I heard her whisper against my ear. I gasped for air but there was nothing. Sweat drenched my face.

"This is your Cardinal speaking. Obey, and disband. We are here to protect you. All protesters will be imprisoned." The speakers repeated the message, followed by that same winding buzz drilling into my head.

My ears rang as the world around me spun. The screech of car tires sliced through the haze. Two black cars approached, their headlights cutting through the dust. I stumbled backward; my legs unsteady. I gritted my teeth as I squeezed into a narrow passage between two skyscrapers.

The windup toy buzzed through the speakers.

Collapsing to the ground, I cradled my face in my hands. Tears seeped through my fingers as my body trembled violently.

This wasn't happiness. It was a lie everyone told themselves a million times until it became a fact.

I squeezed my eyes shut. *I'm going to die. There's no air left in the world. I'm on my own. I'll always be alone.*

The pain in my chest was unbearable. Why did it hurt so much?

I couldn't just let them kill me this easily. *This will pass.*

Deep breath. Slowly, out. Deep breath. Slowly, out. Deep breath. Slowly, out.

Time crawled as I fought to control my breathing. When I finally got back to my feet, my legs wobbled beneath me.

No one noticed as the Suits loaded the poor girl's body into a black car. No one flinched. They were too preoccupied with their own problems.

The reluctant tenants didn't even flinch at the sight of the black cars while they used a pry bar to remove the newly replaced two by fours bordering up the apartment doors. A few evicted tenants removed their belongings and stacked them in the street. The others relocated themselves back into their apartments. Life in the slums churned on, indifferent to the chaos.

Delilah crouched beside the little boy, who was grinning from ear to ear. "Why ya so happy?"

He bounced on his toes, clapping his hands. "My mum's lettin' me go ghost huntin'! It's gonna be awesome!" His eyes sparkled with excitement.

She chuckled. "Where ya going, huntin'?"

He turned, pointing to the newly abandoned apartment building. "In there! My friend said they're in there at night. I'm gonna catch one and show ya!"

"Oh man, I don't know what I'd do if I saw one. Are ya scared?"

"Nah, I'm strong." He flexed his tiny arms.

"Not scared at all?" Delilah teased.

"Nope!" He shook his head confidently. "It's gonna be so cool. I gotta go. I'll tell ya tomorrow, 'bout it, otey?"

"Awesome." Delilah gave him a high five.

His scampering feet kicked up tiny pebbles as he ran off, waving back at her.

Delilah leaned back, a dreamy smile on her face. "He's gonna have the time of his life tonight."

"Is it safe? No one's supposed to be in the apartments," I muttered.

"Yeah, why wouldn't it be safe? They're just kids foolin' around. No one's gonna bother em'. Ya gotta chill out."

I clenched my jaw and let out a slow breath. I wanted to tear the smile off of her face. Yes, *chilling out* was clearly an emotional option for me.

She shut her eyes and began humming softly, entirely detached from the world around her.

"This is your Cardinal speaking. Obey, and disband. We are here to protect you. All protesters will be imprisoned."

I pressed my hands over my ears, blocking out the voice. But it was already too late.

***

A sour feeling churned in my stomach all night. I woke up drenched in sweat. The speakers were silent, and a soft crackle split open the stillness of the night. Thick smog filled the alley.

I covered my mouth, coughing. It was strange for the alley to be this hot overnight. Wiping the sweat from my forehead, I tiptoed toward the street.

I gasped. It wasn't smog, it was smoke. The apartments—they were on fire.

A hollow snap echoed, followed by a crash that shook the ground. The crackling wood erupted with ember sparks through the slits in the boarded-up windows. The apartments glowed against the darkness, shrouded in rising smoke.

The inferno roared into the sky. I stood frozen, wide-eyed in horror. My heart sank into my acid-filled stomach.

I shook Delilah. "They're on fire." She moaned, pushing me away. "There's a fire. Wake up," I pleaded, shaking her again. "Wake up, damn it."

Rubbing her eyes, she muttered, "What? Stop being so dramatic."

I pointed to the apartments. "They're on fire."

"Shit." She sprung up. "Shit!"

Smoke billowed into the dark sky, smothering the faint stars. I raced to the street and stumbled back. I couldn't process what I was seeing.

Flames devoured the rooftops, scorching the tired wooden frames. The fire intensified, racing through the slum neighborhood.

Hide.

Before we could react to the horror that was unfolding, the fire tore through an abandoned building beside it, leaping to the next. Bright orange flames climbed the walls, jumping from structure to structure.

Run.

The blaze rose high into the sky. Bone-rattling screams echoed from inside the burning buildings. The nailed-shut doors rattled as trapped residents pounded against them.

They had been locked in before the flames were lit.

A blood-curdling scream tore from the little boy's mother. I braced myself, paralyzed. What could I do? We needed water, but there was none.

Run.

There was nowhere to run. My entire body trembled. This was the Suits' doing—a brutal reminder not to cross them.

The door splintered open with an explosion of flames. My heart stopped as the smell of burnt flesh filled the air. A body collapsed out of the doorway, encased in fire.

Run.

My eyes welled up. An excruciating scream ripped through the night as the person writhed in agony in the sand. The flames consumed them, leaving only a charred, motionless body.

The little boy's father charged toward the door, but the fire exploded outward, hurling him back. I gasped. The boy's mother dropped to her knees, wailing, her face buried in her hands. The little girl clung to her frail mother, sobbing.

The fire was too immense, too merciless to enter. Madness took hold of the onlookers as they began grabbing buckets. But instead of water, they filled them with sand. I joined the desperate line, passing bucket after bucket, tossing sand into the flames.

It was futile.

The blaze only grew stronger. My arms went numb from the effort, but adrenaline pushed me to keep going.

By daylight, there was nothing left. The Suits had made their fury deafeningly loud by the havoc they caused. The destruction left the city drenched in an endless, oppressive darkness. A madness brewed within me.

Ash floated down like snow, delicately covering the charred corpses. Flickers of fire still glowed faintly among the rubble. The buildings were reduced to piles of scorched wood, soot, and ash.

I scrubbed at the black soot caked on my skin, trying to erase the terror, the hopelessness, and the brutality of what had happened. But it stuck to my flesh like a second skin, a reminder I could never shed.

As I wandered through the wreckage, a man emerged from the smoke. In his arms was the lifeless body of a child—the little boy.

"My baby," his mother cried out, stumbling toward him.

Please, not him, I thought, clutching my hands together.

She rushed forward; her tear-streaked, soot-covered face contorted with grief. She snatched the boy's body from the man's arms.

I held my breath, frozen in place.

It couldn't be him.

Bubbling blisters marred his tiny cheeks, melting the last traces of recognition from his features. His ragged shorts were scorched into his charred skin. Smoke still rose from his body, but his mother held him tightly, sobbing as she fell to her knees. His blackened skin flaked away, mixing with the ash to be carried off by the breeze.

Tears burned down my face as I stood motionless, the remnants of his life slipping through my trembling fingers.

Delilah knelt beside the weeping woman; her voice barely audible. "No." She rubbed the woman's back, then glared at me. "This is your fault."

"Me?" My voice cracked, choked by the knot in my throat.

"See, this is what rebelling gets ya." Her words carved across my forehead. "This is what happens." Delilah's eyes boiled, filled with hate. "Are ya happy now?"

"I didn't do this. The Suits did this. They're responsible."

She jumped to her feet. "When ya rebel, people get hurt."

"They'll hurt people, either way. They don't need an excuse. Your complacency, your willingness to be controlled, gets people hurt." I wanted her to stop looking at me the way she was.

"What are ya talkin' about? Those ain't even words ya saying. Ya know nothin'. You're not one of us. Ya don't belong here. Leave."

She might as well have stabbed me through the heart. But she was right. I didn't belong here.

I couldn't make her see the Suits for what they truly were. I couldn't take her with me.

"I know," I said quietly, wiping away my last tear.

No Suit came to help. Not a single drop of their precious water was used to save the Indigents. The Indigents used what little they had, but it was never enough.

The fire consumed everything until only ash remained—ash of people, ash of lives. The flames left black scorch marks up the stone walls, like the souls of the lost.

It blanketed every corner of the street. Bloodshot eyes followed me as I passed by. Black soot coated everyone from head to toe. My skin felt raw and burnt, though the flames had never touched me. Five more days until water day, and all I had left was a half-drank water bottle and two empty melted plastic jugs.

I wandered for hours, my feet dragging through the ash and sand. The noise and chaos dulled to nothing.

Near the Suit headquarters, the streets were silent. They had taken the day off after their long night. There were no limits to what they would do to break society.

A picture of my missing poster flashed on the screens in the square. The words *Missing. Please contact authorities with any information* scrolled across the screen. Was it all my fault? Freedom didn't feel as good as I'd thought it would.

I collapsed to my knees in the middle of the street. Ash lightly fell, settling upon my hair as the screens lit up with my face staring at me, surrounding me.

I should have cried.

I should have felt something.

But I didn't.

I wasn't any better than the Suits.

I hadn't even bothered to learn the little boy's name.

Reminder—If you think the Suits are the good guys, you haven't been paying attention.

Chapter Twenty-One

Months passed without Delilah and me talking to each other beyond the occasional hello. I avoided mentioning the rebellion in her presence. I knew how hostile the topic made her.

We were still neighbors, but that was all that remained between us. The little boy's family had moved out the day after the fire—someone said they'd gone across town. I thought Delilah might have gone with them, but she stayed put.

Food rations for breakfast and dinner grew lighter in the days after the fire, and still, there was no bread. The Suits claimed the shortage was our fault, that we'd have to go without for a while. I knew it was a lie, but who would believe me?

I couldn't get my internal clock to line up with food times. I always arrived either too early or too late. My stash of granola bars lasted until the second week, then I started looking elsewhere.

Most days, I spent scrounging for food—rummaging through garbage cans behind Suits' homes under the cover of night. My pride was long gone by the time I started eating out of the trash.

It hurt that Delilah no longer wanted me to share the same air as her, but it fueled me to focus on the rebels. My brain was wired to not focus on being alone and any negative emotion. I searched for the life I wanted—a life that should exist—but I couldn't find it. The only thing keeping me going was the hope of finding the Rebel Underground. They were my last chance.

Everyone seemed to know the rebellion existed, but no one knew much beyond that. The only signs of them were the red spray-painted "R" and "U" symbols that had begun popping up on buildings and underpasses.

I made a map of the city by drawing on the back of a wanted poster, marking every block I explored. I discovered something new each day, searching every corner for a clue. Occasionally, I'd hear rumors that led me to an abandoned building. But they were always empty, the only traces of anyone were faint footprints in the dust that led to dead ends. Each time, I marked another X on my map.

Now, there were more Xs than unexplored spaces.

I'd hoped to find the rebels at a protest. The protests had become quieter—no loud chants, just murmurs and poorly spelled signs the Suits couldn't read. I'd spent hours trying to decipher their Street Language, but it was chaotic and illogical. Whoever created it clearly didn't care about sounding words out.

Although there were no riots, the protests always ended the same way. It didn't matter how peaceful the crowd was, gas cans were thrown, and shots fired into the air. People were beaten in the streets while the upper class watched safely from their luxury condos. I hope they enjoyed the show.

No one ever heard from those taken during the protests again.

For a while, I worried Father had captured the rebellion leaders, as he'd threatened. But if that were true, he would've paraded their defeat before the Indigents. That meant they were still out there—I just had to find them.

There were rumors that if you searched the crowd, you could spot the rebels marching alongside us. I scanned every face, but I never saw them.

Months later, Phin appeared out of nowhere. He climbed onto a second-story terrace overlooking the street.

His voice cut through the air with a megaphone. "People listen to me. The unjust work of the Suits will not be tolerated anymore."

He looked like a giant up there. I craned my neck, nearly tipping backward to get a better look. His blond hair glinted dully in the muted sunlight, but his presence radiated hope until the thick, sour air choked me up.

He continued, "Stand with us, and we will rise."

My heart leapt. The crowd surged with energy; the air alive with possibility. This was what we needed—a revolution. A coup was the only way forward. The rebellion was more profound than the protests. I needed to follow him and, more importantly, find a way into the Rebel Underground.

"We will rise," the words tore from my throat, joining the chorus. "We will rise."

Phin stepped back, and then he disappeared.

The crowd swarmed the building, chanting, "We will rise!"

I pushed through, searching for his blond hair among the throng. My eyes darted from face to face. Rushing forward, I pushed people aside but he was gone.

There was my chance, and it was gone. Frustrated, I stepped onto the curb and scanned the crowd. "Where did he go?"

A light tap on my shoulder startled me. I spun around to find an elderly man with yellowed eyes and wiry white hair sticking up in every direction.

"Ya looking for em'?" He asked.

"Huh? Who?"

He didn't seem like a trusted source for information. Yes, I based this on his looks alone. I am well aware that type of prejudgment was wrong.

"That blond fella who wants to save the world," He smiled, revealing one dangling tooth left in his mouth. "I know where he is."

The stench of his breath made me gag. I turned away, pretending to adjust my hood to avoid reacting.

Forcing a polite smile, I turned back, "Oh yeah? Where?"

He leaned in conspiratorially. "They live underground, ya know. That's why they call themselves the Rebel Underground," he giggled, nodding his head. "He and his friends like to come down and blend into the crowds. I followed 'em once—very quietly, so they wouldn't hear me. They are in there." He pointed to the old bank building.

The front doors were welded shut. I knew because I'd tried getting into the building a month ago, unsuccessfully.

I laughed, "Seriously, in the middle of town? That would be the worst hiding spot in the world."

His eyes widened, shaking his head as if I were stupid. "No, underground. Ya check it out. You'll see." He wagged his finger at me then stomped off into the crowd chanting the wrong words to the wrong beat.

The Suits didn't bother us during the protest that day, which concerned me. I waited, watching the crowd pass by the bank. Why would they live underground? How could they even get underground? The man's tale made no sense. I needed to get into that building to prove the crazy old man wrong. Why did I need to verify the old man was wrong? Because I knew I was right.

The protest ended midday, so all I had to do was wait for darkness. The old stone bank stood abandoned for at least a decade since the Suit's built a towering glass building that housed every document from financial to personal. Somehow, it remained standing on the cusp of the new sleek downtown area: in the shadow of the Suits' headquarters. They could view everything from where I was standing.

Once I returned to the alley, I unfolded my map. Delilah hadn't returned yet, thankfully, so I could search the map without her rolling her eyes. I found a flashlight that spontaneously flickered in someone's trash a few weeks before. It quickly became my favorite find.

I shined the flashlight on the map and X-ed out the old schoolhouse where my brother attended his first two years in school. They built a state-of-the-art school closer to the center of the city. I attended the newer school; it was okay, if you're into obedience training and propaganda speeches.

My map became an unfortunate mismatch of scribbles, Xs, and weird shaped buildings. It lost more of its identity the more I added to it. The problem now was I searched every abandoned building drawn on the map.

"Where could they be if they were living within the city?" I muttered to myself.

Delilah skipped over to her side of the alley and curled up under the tarp. "Ya missing out, ya know."

Wait—was she actually speaking to me? I quickly folded up the map and slipped it into my backpack. "What?"

She groaned, removing her coat. "Some guy's handing out stuff. I'm not sharing" She rolled up her sleeve. "They stole it from the Suits or somethin'."

This was the most extensive conversation we'd had since the fires. Delilah placed six blue vials and needles beside her on the ground. It didn't seem like something the Suits would use. I hadn't heard of a medication that made them stronger. Someone was lying about something.

My stomach rumbled. I had missed breakfast that morning because of the protests and my poor timing. At least, it was time for dinner soon. But, if I inspected the bank after dinner, I would look more suspicious. Maybe, I could make it back before dinner ended. If not, I was willing to make that sacrifice.

"Nah, I'm good. I've gotta go, anyway."

"What ya doin' that's so important?" She scoffed.

"Breaking into a bank." I muttered, still wondering if I was the crazy one, listening to the old man's theories.

"Through the tunnels?"

"You know about the tunnels?" I exclaimed.

"Yeah, I live here." she said, tightening a torn piece of fabric around her frail bicep.

"Have you known where the rebels are all along?"

"Maybe." she said smugly. "We were right there hiding after the protest. Do I have ta tell ya everything?"

My blood boiled. She had been watching me for months and said nothing. I exhaled a heavy breath. "You said you didn't know."

She snapped, lunging towards me, "I said shut your mouth and ya couldn't even do that right."

She enjoyed watching me look like a fool. I bit down on my cheek to stop the tears welling up in my eyes. She grinned sitting back tapping her arm.

"You don't know what's in there. It might kill you," I sprung to my feet.

"I guess, we will see?"

"The Suits wouldn't give you something to better you." I said sincerely, knowing she was still blind to her controllers.

The sun set quickly around us, shadowing our bodies until we were folded into darkness.

"Well, I'll be stronger than ya when ya get back from them rejecting your sorry ass." She spat out before injecting herself, "Just you see," She mumbled, tilting her head back, and letting out a heavy breath. "No more pain." Her words trailed off as her eyes closed.

I swallowed down the knot in my throat as her heavy snoring let me know she was still alive. I had been to the records building multiple times. There was no door leading to an underground tunnel. I'd have to try going through the bank's front door first.

The streets were stirring. There was something new in the air, an excited energy. Instead of people returning to their corner of the city and huddling by the fire, they mingled like they had some big news they needed to spread before daybreak. Strange.

They whispered to one another then scurried off in another direction. I squeezed through the groups huddled in the street engrossed in conversation. They didn't notice me, too enrapt as one man unveiled a blue vial.

A collective gasp sprung up, then murmurs of strength just as Delilah had mentioned. Whatever fad they were interested in I could become crazed about tomorrow. I couldn't get distracted.

The streets reeked of an unfamiliar smell, like bathed dirt. The echo of chatter followed me as groups disbanded in different directions. I couldn't help but watch them meander into alleyways with intent for once.

"Pst!" Someone hissed behind me and I whirled.

Lingering in the shadows, a man stood with a blanket draped over his head. "I've got some good stuff. You want some."

His voice made my skin crawl. There was something off about him, but I couldn't put my finger on it. I couldn't recall ever seeing him before. Although, I couldn't see much of his face covered in shadows.

"No, thanks."

"It's good—Suit stuff. It'll make you feel better—give you the vitamins you need." He slipped the ominous glowing blue vials out of his pocket.

"Vitamins?" I snapped back.

"It's free." His voice was alluring.

I'd learned long ago from Father—nothing was free in life. And in all my time among them I'd never seen anything good come from the Suits.

I took a step forward to see his face better—was he a guard or worker from Father's house? Was that how he'd stolen the supply? But the man stepped back into the shadows, returning the glowing blue vials to his jacket pocket.

"Hmm."

He let me walk away without another word.

But as I walked, there was someone on almost every corner handing out the mysterious blue vials. Their whispers called out to me as I passed by them—promises meant to lure me in. Silhouettes lingered from building to building as if they were anxious ghosts. They whispered between breaths and avoided the glow of the streetlights. Someone was up to no good. Why didn't anyone else find this strange? Why weren't they questioning this free gift when they all spent their days fighting for what little they had?

It was empty near the Capitol. No armored trucks patrolled the streets nor security officers positioned in front of open shops. The speakers were silent—not even the buzzing of a wind-up toy coming through the underlying static. The downtown area was eerily silent and dark, as businesses closed early. Dull lights at an electronic store displayed televisions in the store windows running attack ads on the Indigents.

The current ad showed how violent Indigents were towards women. It was unsafe for women to be left alone within the city because they could just be taken and never seen again. The actor playing the Indigent had dirt smeared on his face and fake teeth blacked out. It was strange to see the ad again now that I lived among them. Now I knew the actor was too well-fed to ever pass for an Indigent.

That's what was strange about the men in shadows, their teeth were fake. The next attack ad flashed up spreading lies about diseases. I glanced back at the crowds of Indigents, in the distance, dispersing. Maybe, I was wrong.

I moved on, but it was strange walking freely downtown without having to obey the normal street etiquette of not being seen. Even the little red lights on the surveillance cameras were off.

I might have assumed there was a blackout if the blinding lights from the television screens weren't still playing around me. Father only turned off the cameras when he did something he didn't want recorded. What were they up to? At least no one would see me attempting to break into a bank.

The building's gray stone façade had started to chip around the corners. Someone had covered the windows to the bank with paper so thick that no light would be able to breach. The building was solid, though. Tearing down the old bones of the building would have been difficult, which I imagined was the only reason it was still standing.

Standing there, I felt naked, unable to hide between the shadows. I watched and listened one last time, but there wasn't a sound. I held my breath and knocked. My heart sank when there was no answer. I knocked louder—still, nothing.

I scanned for a doorbell, but there was none. I pushed on the heavy metal doors then attempted to pull them open. They didn't budge. What was I thinking? I already knew the doors were welded shut—I knew I was right

"Crazy old man," I muttered, kicking the door.

In the distance, I caught a glimpse of the records building's odd shape poking out from behind the rows of sleek Suit buildings. Maybe all those times I'd followed dusty footprints to dead-ends had something more to them? My curiosity was quickly getting the best of me. Or maybe my desperation.

"Hmm, I wonder what stories you have to tell?" I leaped down the stairs. "Well, I believed a delusional homeless man today, why not believe a girl who just injected herself with an unknown substance?" I paused. "Why am I talking to myself out loud, walking down an empty dark street? Who's the delusional one now?"

As I neared the dusty brown building, the streets grew more desolate with only the buzzing of a flickering streetlight over my footsteps. It was unnerving to be entirely alone. I stopped in front of the building where the sharp edge jutted out with a sign infested with sand read, *Records Holding*. The streetlight flickered again, illuminating the street behind me. No one. *Where is everyone tonight?*

The city had set a boulder to cover the building's entrances so that no squatters could get inside. Over time, the corner of the rock started to crumble, leaving divots that perhaps could be used for climbing. I had entered the building through a cross-bridge by first entering two other buildings the previous two times. The thought of meandering my way through some other strange structures in the middle of the night gave me goosebumps. Before, when Delilah and I had been trying to escape, we'd slid down the boulder, meaning there was an opening somewhere. It sounded easy enough.

I found it to be a more difficult feat than I thought initially.

I bit down on the filthy flashlight while I gripped the cracks in the crumbling boulder—one hand then the other. My fingers slipped. I grunted, scrambling to find my hold. My body slid, smacking my butt against the ground. Grunting, I wiped my sweaty palms on my pants.

I repeated, grabbing a piece of the boulder sticking out. The rock crumbled in my hands, then bounced off my face. This was harder than getting out of a dumpster. I sighed.

After a few tries, I was covered with rock dust and cuts across my arms. I spit out the flashlight. This was ridiculous. I was glad no one was around to witness me looking like a fool.

"It's just a piece of rock. I can conquer this," I told myself.

Deep breath, slowly out.

I searched the hunk of rock with less than a subpar flashlight, scanning each crevice. A metal curved rod jutted out midway up. I jumped, but it was too far above my head. I backed up, stumbling over a wooden box. Even with the box, it was over my head. I sat on the box, defeated, pondering my next move. If all my decisions up to that moment were wrong, at least the box would have been a good find.

But there was no turning back now. I had come too far. I moved the box a foot from the boulder, then stepped back until I hit the other building.

I placed the flashlight in my bag and told myself, "You can do this."

I held my breath, sprinting to the box, and pushed off of it. The wood splintered. I stretched out my arms.

My fingers barely gripped the cold rod. I scraped up against the coarse rock as pain streaked up my side. I grunted, straining to hold on. It wasn't time to give up yet. I gritted my teeth, swinging my body around, tightening my grip. My foot wedged into a crack that started to crumble. I scrambled for another, finding a sturdier ledge.

I heaved myself up onto the bar, then lifted myself to a smoother edge of the boulder. My feet faltered, skidding. I reached up to the top and steadied myself. I was almost there.

I collapsed into the building, out of breath.

"Ouch." I groaned.

Scrapes covered my hands and knees, but I would live. The building was quiet, with only the faint breeze swaying the collapsed roof. Moonlight lingeredin along the bordered-up windows as specks of dust settled on the floor. Shadows created what looked like monsters reaching out. I shuddered, clenching the flashlight.

It was hopelessly dim inside, and the flashlight sparsely lit my footsteps. The shoeprints were hardly visible as I inspected them. They were much larger than mine, probably a man's shoe. I could tell they were the same ones I'd noticed in different locations before, but this time, another set of newer impressions continued in the same direction. I followed them as they led to a windowless hallway.

The wind swept past me, making me feel hollow. My heart pounded into my throat. I shuffled my feet, hoping not to step on anything or anyone. What if the old man was trying to trap me? My hands shook the flashlight and it blinked out. I stepped forward, smacking into a wall. Why did I think this time would be different?

"No, no. Not after all this work." I spat.

Was I just an idiot, after all? The flashlight flickered back to life. I hurried to examine the impressions on the floor. The footprints were going in a distinct direction until they disappeared.

I scratched my head. One imprint straddled between the hallway and beyond the wall. I traced each corner of the wall.

I knocked on the wall. "Hello?"

No one answered.

I knocked on the wall beside it. "Hello?"

The wall sounded different, hollower.

I knocked again on the first wall.

I stepped back, inspecting the end of the hallway. "Is this a door?"

My fingertips scanned the cream-colored wall dividing at the center by molding. There was no doorknob nor handle, nor magic bookcase I could rifle through like my father's office.

The wind whipped through, blowing my hair into my face. I breathed it in, smelling the bitter scent of the day. It calmed my anxiety. I focused on the sounds in the building, shutting my eyes.

There was a soft whistle sound coming from where the wind seeped between the walls. It had to be a door. I patted the sides of the walls, then slid my hands over the molding until the breeze slipped over my fingers.

Deep breath, slowly out.

I tapped on the molding, then pushed it in and over. It was a pocket door. A rush of excitement shot through my veins. The full footprint laid exposed before me, leading to a dark stone stairwell.

I slipped in and slid the door back in place. "I hope I didn't just lock myself down here." I exhaled. "Well, here's to thinking things out first."

I crept down the steps, hoping no one who would hurt me was down there.

"Hello?" My voice echoed back to me. "Hello?"

No one answered. I crouched down to enter the small tunnel. It stank of sewer and trash, which was surprisingly worse than my own odor. I covered my nose and attempted to breathe through my mouth. The tunnel opened to a center, where three more tunnels expanded out in different directions. Great. I was already lost.

I threw up my arms. "What, no signage? How do you people live?"

I spun around, looking back and forth between the tunnels. "Well, this is anticlimactic. What tunnel did I even come from?" I paused, "Wait, I have a map."

I unzipped my backpack and laid out my homemade map. The flashlight flickered. "Oh, come on, don't die on me now." I traced the route—finding the Record Holding building, then walked my fingers over to the old bank. I shined the light back down the tunnels. "I came from there, so they are going to be this way." I shined the light over to my left. "I think?"

The flashlight flickered in and out. I smacked it. "What is wrong with you?"

If anyone was down there, they would have thought I was insane. And rightfully so.

A different smell laced this new tunnel. The further I went down, the more it smelled of wax. Now there was an accumulation of melted red and white wax randomly splattered alongside footprints.

The flashlight flickered, then went out. The darkness devoured my sight. I smacked the flashlight again. This time, nothing. My luck had finally run out.

"No."

I was in a strange tunnel without any way to see where I was going, which didn't really matter because I didn't know where I was going in the first place. I hurled the flashlight across the tunnel and grunted.

I closed my eyes. *Deep breath, slowly out.* I needed to relax. I was determined to find my way out or be lost down there forever. The latter seemed more likely at the moment.

"Okay, it's probably not that far. You can do this." I reached out, patting down the rough, uneven layered stones of the tunnel walls. A pebble bounced off my toes, startling me. My heart pounded, deafening my ears.

Deep breath, slowly out.

Deep breath, slowly out.

I tiptoed forward, one step after another. It was an agonizing walk, with the constant possibility I might walk off the edge of the tunnel and drop further underground.

"Ouch." I stubbed my toe. I bent down to feel a step, then the next one and the next one. After pressing my foot down to make sure it was firm, a giddiness rose in my chest. I climbed each step until I bumped into a wall.

I sighed. This would be the deciding moment. It was either complete defeat or success. I slid my hand along the edge of the wall until I hit a cool metal ring. My fingers gripped around the ring, and I pulled.

Deep breath, slowly out.

Chapter Twenty-Two

W arm light fused with shadows like a soft blanket wrapping around me. In that moment, I discovered magic. I carefully tiptoed between strips of peeled, whimsical wallpaper scattered across the dirt-smeared, chipped marble floor.

Wax dripped from fire-lit sconces shaped like birds on either side of the vacant hallway. I held my breath as I passed the first room, noting bits of clay and sand clumped at the door's threshold. Muffled voices hummed in the distance.

It was them. The rebellion. I'd actually found them. I clenched my fists, then opened them with each step. *Deep breath in, slowly out.* I steadied my steps, hoping my heart would follow. *Deep breath in, slowly out.*

The voices were indistinct. I couldn't pick a single word from the murmuring noise. I snuck past a sparsely lit room lined with cots. Blankets and clothes were strewn across them, left without care. The next room housed the former vault. Instead of money, worn boots littered the space, and a metal table stood in the center, a few weapons scattered on top. In the last room, a thin man hummed to himself while scrubbing a stove.

The hallway opened into what had once been the bank lobby. An orange glow enveloped the room. Fire-lit sconces lined every wall, and a roaring fire crackled from somewhere in the space.

The rebels appeared to be mostly twenty-somethings, some past thirty, and a few barley adults. At least fifteen stood in the lobby, although, I would have thought there would have been more. Each looked vastly different from the next, like individuals. None of them had a Suit approved haircut and a couple had unnatural colored hair. The men outnumber the women but only by a few.

The remnants of the old teller booths had been converted into a long table running along one wall. Rolled blueprints jutted out sporadically from the banker's drawers between seated figures. I peeked over the shoulder of someone poring over blueprints of an octagon-shaped building. The man mumbled something about the schematics.

The woman across him shook her head. "Nah, they'll see us coming."

"Not if we cut the power first," the man said, outlining one side of the building with his ink-stained finger.

This was it—the Rebel Underground.

She scratched her half-shaven head. She definitely didn't have a Suit approved haircut.

"That's a big 'if.' Do you even know where to cut their power source?"

"I work best on ifs," the man snickered.

She tucked two tiny braids behind her ear before replying. "We can't count on this working on an 'if.' We've got no real way in." She continued her protest.

I slipped behind the man she was arguing with, becoming engulfed in his shadow. Neither the redhead nor Phin were anywhere in sight.

If I could have found someone in charge, I wouldn't have been creeping around. There didn't seem to be anyone keeping watch. I wandered over to another table—an old door balanced on cement blocks. Highlighters in hand, a group flipped through documents bearing a Suit watermark. Could they actually read the words?

The room filled me with hope, courage, desire, and inspiration, penetrating through my skin. I took a deep breath, filling my lungs with the smell of melting wax, old paper, and burning wood. A hum of freedom stirred in their voices. We could all be free—not through mere words or protests, but with precise planning to reclaim our power.

I crept behind a man with black hair tied back in a messy bun. He scratched his thick eyebrow near a piercing, confusion furrowing his brow. The candlelight highlighted his smooth, light-tanned skin and the tattoo winding up his neck. He tucked a stray strand of hair behind his ear as he studied a document.

"Hey, I think—" He turned abruptly, stepping back onto my foot.

Yes, I was in the way, but how else was I supposed to see what he was reading? I yelped. The man jumped, bumping into the makeshift table. "Whoa, where'd ya come from?"

I stumbled backward into a firm body. Looking up, I met the dark, unyielding eyes of the rugged man I'd seen at the protest, gun strapped across his chest.

His angular jaw tightened; teeth gritted. "How did you get in here?"

Everything halted. *Run.* Every noise stopped. *Run.* Heads turned. *Run.* Blueprints were hastily rolled up and hidden under tarps. The group stepped closer, tightening around me.

Damn it. Will they believe I just accidentally stumbled in from Gohan?

I cleared my throat. "Hi, I'm here to join the rebellion." I extended my hand. The man crossed his arms. "Um, I came in through the tunnels. Sorry, the door wasn't locked." I shrugged, lowering my hand. "So, I just let myself in." I forced a weak smile.

The room rumbled with laughter. The man's Adam's apple bobbed as he swallowed, his sharp chin and cheekbones narrowing toward me like blades. He didn't laugh with the others, nor did his dark eyes blink as they bored into me. *Run.*

It felt like I was sinking into the floor. Each passing breath made me smaller. I dug my fingernails into my sweaty palms. His gaze flicked to the woman with the half-shaved head now standing behind me. She smelled of motor oil and sawdust. This wasn't going as planned. Where was the welcoming committee?

"You?" he snickered. "Isn't your daddy looking for you?"

Technically, yes, my father was still looking for me.

But how did he know who I was? My heart pounded in my throat, and I thought I might throw up. His eyes burned with spite.

"Fucking Suit!" someone in the crowd shouted, their laughter rolling.

Maybe, I should have asked before entering? Technically, I did knock the first time. I don't think the group would have liked me pointing out the technicalities.

I glanced down at my feet, sliding my trembling hands into my pockets. My cheeks burned, and my eyes stung from the smoke. Sweat dripped down my brow. *Run.* But my feet stayed rooted to the floor.

He chuckled, "So you wanna fight or something?" He shoved me, my cheeks flaming. The woman behind me pressed her hands firmly against my back, tripping me forward. I stumbled, barely catching myself before falling into his chest. Her snicker echoed in my ear. His laughter was deep, rattling my ears.

The crowd abruptly parted. "Now, now, now." The laughter stopped. "If someone wants to join the rebellion, it's not about physical strength. It's about mental strength." Phin's boyish, smiling face emerged as he gently pushed aside the sturdy man tormenting me. "Q, don't you have something else to handle? I've got this."

Q grabbed a glass of saps from the table, tipping it to his lips as he backed away, glaring at me the whole time." Right, I'm sure I do." He walked away without taking his glaring eyes off of me.

"You guys get back to work!" Phin waved his hand dismissively. "Now—" he wrapped his arm around my shoulders. "Why don't you come with me, and tell me why you're here?"

My shoulders stiffened automatically. The others returned to their stations, but their eyes followed me as Phin led me away. The blueprints stayed rolled, the documents hidden. Their distrust was palpable, their disdain muttered in barely audible whispers.

Phin guided me to a faded wingback chair near the fireplace. The mantel above the flames looked as if someone had smashed it with a sledgehammer, yet the chimney still carried the smoke out efficiently.

"Ginn," he called to a woman watching us intently at a nearby table. Her skintight black shorts hugged her butt just close enough not to reveal her cheeks. Under her golden hood, her bleach blond hair drooped over one side of her face to hide a cluster of acne layered beneath heavy makeup.

She scratched at her cheek, drawing attention to the streaks of gold paint dripping from her black outlined almond-shaped eyes. It looked as if she'd been crying golden tears. Everything about her screamed effort—not to blend in but to stand out. I had never seen someone dressed like her before.

"Get us another glass, please," Phin said, winking at her.

She nodded, rolling her eyes before walking off. Phin didn't look up until she returned, slamming a chipped glass on the table between us. She swayed her hips as she walked away, and Phin's unapologetic gaze followed every wiggle of her body.

Heat flushed my face as I adjusted my hoodie bunching around my stomach. Sweat trickled down my cheeks, sticking strands of hair to my skin. I tucked them behind my ears, silently hoping he couldn't smell the sour odor rising from me. Before he turned back, I sat straighter, pulling my shoulders back in an attempt to seem taller—maybe even more attractive.

Phin didn't notice.

He poured us each a glass of saps and handed one to me. Women weren't supposed to drink it, but I didn't care. I'd wondered about the taste for years. Tossing the rules aside, I took a bold swig—and instantly regretted it. The burn was unbearable. My throat felt as if it were on fire, and I doubled over coughing.

Why did people choose to drink this crap?

Phin snickered, his top teeth elapsing his bottom lip as he watched me. The flames reflected in his warm brown eyes. He had a comforting way about him. He was much past boyhood, yet he kept a youthfulness to his clean-shaven face. I placed the glass down containing the menacing contents and wiped my chapped lips.

"You'll get used to it." He nudged my shoulder, taking another sip of his.

I didn't know if I was supposed to speak. Everyone's eyes watched me. My arms seemed less like a part of my body than ever before. I fumbled with them, first putting them on the arms of the chair, then I crossed them over my chest, then flopped them on my lap. I wanted to know who he was; where he came from, I just wanted to learn more.

"I'm Phin," he said, leaning back casually. "Leader of this motley crew of judgmental fools." He grinned as if it were the easiest thing in the world.

"I'm Arabella. Arabella Freeman, I—"

He raised his hand, cutting me off. "I know who you are." My heart skipped a beat. "Everyone here does."

How could everyone in this room know me when no one outside these walls seemed to? "To be honest," he continued, "I thought you were dead." He shrugged, taking a slow sip of his drink.

"I'm not," I blurted, immediately regretting how stupid I sounded.

Phin chuckled, choking on his saps. He wiped his chin, his eyes twinkling with amusement. "Clearly."

I stared into the fire to avoid his gaze. The flames danced along splintered wood and bits of crumpled trash, their deep blue cores mingling with blistering orange edges. "How have the Suits not noticed the smoke from this building yet?" I asked.

"Most of the condo windows don't face this way, and even if they did, they wouldn't care. They probably think it's just homeless people trying to stay warm. And, technically, we are." He crossed one leg over the other, the picture of nonchalant confidence. "So, what brings you here? No offense, but you don't exactly scream rebellion."

Phin tapped his finger against his glass to a song he hummed under his breath. The same song Delilah would hum. He stared at the fire then off to Ginn who was fixing her hair.

I was rebellious; I ran away. How could he not see I was rebellious? "I—I just want to make my own choices. To be treated equally." My voice faltered. "I don't think who your parents are or what gender you are should determine your entire life. It's not fair." I stared at the indentions in my open palms. "I just—"

Phin's lips curved into a half-smile that didn't reach his eyes. "Right." He snickered, "Right." He took a long pause watching the fire. "Happiness for some is food and shelter. For others, it is truth and understanding. We all want something that we don't have. Some want more than others."

His words were a slap to the face. My chest tightened, and I bit down on my cheek to keep from crying. "I know," I whispered, my voice cracking. "I've been out there. They're lying to people, and the people believe it."

"I'll tell you this—I'm not a believer," he said, leaning in as though sharing a secret. "It's all bullshit, I just haven't figured out how to prove it to everyone yet." His gaze flicked to the group behind me, now back to arguing over the blueprints. "The Suits tell a good story, don't they? But you and I both know it's all lies. Every last one of them."

He leaned back, staring at his glass. "Anyone can tell a story. The hard part is, making people believe it." He grinned faintly. "So, what part of your story do you want to change?"

I had no story to tell. All I'd done was run. He studied my blank expression, his glass cradled in one hand. I looked away, focusing on the fire again. The blue in the flames reminded me of the vials I'd seen the well-fed man slip from his pocket.

"I want to be free of a predetermined life," I said firmly, meeting his gaze. His honey-and-caramel eyes were unreadable. A piece of wood snapped, sparking up embers. He licked his thin lips.

"That's a valid rewrite," he said after a moment. "But I'm still not sure you're the type of person who can handle this."

My heart sank. He didn't believe in me. Why had I thought I could just walk in and join? I was such a fool.

"I can't go back." I exclaimed.

"Back where? Your father's or the streets?"

"Neither." I shook my head.

"You're not a fighter. Some people don't have it in them." Why did he presume he knew everything about me? "There isn't anything wrong with you: you're just not." He shrugged.

I could be a fighter. Just because I never punched back doesn't mean I wasn't fighting the Suits. He needed to give me a chance. I had come this far; there was no turning back after this. He didn't know me. If this wasn't the place for me, where else could I go?

I leaned forward. The smell of saps lingered on his lips. "Then teach me."

I tried another sip of saps but didn't cringe from the burn this time. I set the glass on the table where it left behind a wet ring. He stared at me, his mouth ajar for a moment. I couldn't read what he was thinking on his face. My mouth ran dry. I wiped my palms on the chair's coarse fabric.

A smile gleamed across his face. "Alright. I'll do this for you. You can stay, if you become one of our fighters," He extended out his hand for a handshake and I obliged. "But it's not going to be easy. No one trusts you. You'll have to act differently around these guys."

"Differently how?" I asked, my stomach tightening. Was there a user-friendly guide to the rebellion?

He chuckled, clapping his hands together. "First, stop smiling so much."

I nodded, my earlier smile fading. "I can do that."

"Good," He snickered, clapping his hands together. "Then let's get started." He motioned to Ginn. "Another bottle and some snacks."

Ginn looked up from chipping her nails and sighed heavily, muttering under her breath as she fetched it. Across the room, the one he'd called Q watched me with a furrowed brow and an empty glass in his hand. His intense stare made me squirm in my seat, but I refused to look away.

Phin leaned back in his chair, filling our glasses once more. "Here, we believe in resetting society so everyone has a chance," he said, his voice serious." He spoke better than an average person off the street like he snuck in some formal education. "How does that happen? Well, it's a work in progress."

Ginn pounded a corked bottle of saps on the table then lazily placed a bowl of lukewarm rice balls between us. "Thanks," he said, watching her walk away.

His biceps flexed, opening the cork. *Deep breath, slowly out.* He caught sight of me watching him and winked at me. "These corks can be tricky."

He filled both glasses to the rim and placed the bottle by his feet. He took a sip before he continued, "There will be no upper class, no lower class. Everyone will be equal, no matter what you were born into—poor or rich." He paused, raising his glass slightly. "Male or female. We're all the same. Just human beings. We'd all love to live to the ripe old age of forty, after all."

I laughed but stopped abruptly, realizing he wasn't joking.

Phin kept the saps flowing, snapping his fingers at Ginn for another bottle when the first ran out. He drank most of it himself, but each glass I managed to gulp down seemed to lower my guard a little more.

With every laugh Phin gave, Ginn's irritation seemed to deepen. He appeared to enjoy provoking her, savoring her fake smiles more than her real one. He had a boyish tendency of wanting to irritate her. It was like they were playing a game I hadn't volunteered to participate in but had no choice.

He didn't ask me any more questions about myself. Instead, he spoke mostly, which I didn't mind. "I used to head downtown to try my luck with the Suits. I thought these dimples might score me some food." He grinned, pointing to the indentations in his cheeks. "They didn't."

I giggled despite myself.

"But most of the time, they were so annoyed they'd throw their food in the trash just to get rid of me," he said with a laugh. "And I'd snatch it before anyone else could. So, I guess it kinda worked."

Phin leaned in conspiratorially, his voice lowering. "One time, I snuck into one of their buildings and got lost. I was terrified they'd find me, so I crawled into the air ducts. Of course, I got even more lost."

I could see the story unfolding in his head as he spoke. "Then I stopped to peek into this meeting room. Everyone inside looked so serious. They were arguing, all puffed up and important." He clapped his hands together suddenly, making me jump. "And bam! I fell through the ceiling—landed smack on their boardroom table."

Saps spewed from his mouth as he laughed.

"Seriously?" I bent over laughing. I never laughed so hard in my life.

"Yeah, it was great. You should have seen the look on their faces." He imitated the Suits' faces. "Boy, get out of here." He wagged his finger in the air.

By the wee hours of the morning, we were completely drunk, and everyone else had gone to bed. The fire died out, leaving only a dim glow of embers. Phin slapped his knees and stood. "Well, I think it's time to call it a night. If you head down that hallway, you'll find a room with cots. Choose an empty one. It'll do for now."

I pushed myself up from the chair, my body weighed down by exhaustion and saps. Phin climbed the stairs with steady, confident steps, not a wobble in sight. I stumbled my way down the dark hallway and tripped into an empty cot, collapsing into the thin mattress. My head spun with saps, stories, and uncertainty.

Chapter Twenty-Three

M orning hit me with the thud of a weight vest dropped square-ly on my chest. My stomach churned, and I gagged. It hurt too much to be awake. Still, my eyes wedged open.

Q loomed over me. "Get up, fancy face. Time for training."

I rolled off the cot, landing in a heap on the floor. Why did it have to be him training me? Forcing myself upright, I cradled my pounding head and stumbled to my feet.

"Come on, I don't have time for this nonsense."

Nonsense? I was about to die. My stomach lurched as we entered the hallway. The rebellion was gathered in the lobby, their eyes fixed on me. Some stood silent, others whispered amongst themselves. Every stare carried the weight of disgust, cutting deep. I focused on the heels of Q's worn brown boots and kept my head down.

The wooden steps to the basement were clearly new, though poorly made. Crooked nails jutted from unvarnished boards and splinters caught on my fingers as I gripped the handrail. The staircase wobbled in places, and the uneven spacing almost sent me sprawling. It was clearly the work of a fine craftsman.

Dirt smeared the seven small windows in the basement, but light still managed to creep in. Three homemade punching bags dangled from the high ceiling, and six worn workout mats lined one of the brick walls. Beneath the stairs, barrels were stacked in neat rows. There were zero alternative exits.

It was cleaner than I'd expected. Someone had swept the cement floor thoroughly, and everything was arranged with care. Q stopped at a barrel in the center of the room, still not bothering to look at me.

He grabbed a roll of gauze and began wrapping his hands. "You ever punch someone before?"

"No," I replied, my voice small. Q felt like a coiled spring, ready to snap at any moment. "But I know what it feels like to be punched."

He stopped wrapping his hands. His broad shoulder rose, then lowered with a heavy exhale. "Sounds about right," he muttered under his breath.

Ripping the gauze with his teeth, he tossed it in my direction without lifting his gaze. It bounced off my hands and hit the ground. He sighed again, clearly unimpressed. "Well, you're gonna have to fight back today."

I scrambled to pick it up and began wrapping my hands, though I had no idea why. When it came time to tear the fabric, I tried using my teeth but only managed to shred it into long, useless strings. Did no one here believe in scissors? Frustrated, I placed the roll under my shoe and yanked until it finally snapped.

"You all set?" he asked, cracking his neck.

I tucked the loose fibers under my wraps, my cheeks burning with embarrassment. "Yeah, I'm ready." I placed the gauze back on the barrel gingerly. "So—"

He lunged at me. A startled yelp escaped my lips as his hand slammed into my shoulder. With the full force of his body, he shoved me, sending me skidding across the floor.

My head screamed.

"Get up," he grunted.

The heel of a polished black shoe tapped against the floor. Heel, toe. Heel, toe.

I exhaled shakily, forcing myself to my feet. The room felt like it was folding in on itself. Smack. Pain exploded across my face, and my knees wobbled. Sweat trickled down my trembling fingers.

"Fight back." Every muscle in my body froze. "Do something." He threw his hands in the air.

The cold voice of my father clamoring in my head, *"What's wrong with you?"*

I jumped back as the image of my father's hand came hurling towards me. The footsteps of the polished shoes drew closer. I squeezed my eyes shut, no one else was there. Sweat drenched my shirt.

It wasn't real. It was just Q and me. Only two people were in the room.

Heel, toe. Heel, toe. The sound grated against my nerves as Q circled me, lightly jabbing my sides and arms. "At least try to block me," he said, his tone dripping with exasperation.

Heel, toe. Heel, toe.

Run.

Why did I think I could do this?

My face flushed, my entire body trembled, and all I wanted to do was curl into a ball. I eyed the prime hiding location underneath the stairs, which was inconveniently blocked by a stack of barrels. I stood motionless, my breath heaving uncontrollably. I was going to suffocate from my own thoughts.

His chest puffed in and out. Every breath increased his irritation. He pushed me, tripping me back. "This is pathetic."

"You pathetic, useless bitch." Father's voice ricocheted from one ear to the other.

I was; he was entirely correct. In a flash, his fist crashed into my cheek, and my head smacked against the cold floor. I stopped breathing, or at least it felt like I did.

Q stood over me, "Get up." He shifted from one foot to the other.

Heel, toe. Heel, toe. *"Get out of my face, you, stupid girl."* Every part of me felt my father in the room. Heel, toe. Heel, toe. My heart raced. I couldn't breathe.

I gasped for air.

I tried to stand, but the weight vest pulled me down. Slowly, I pushed myself upright, as Q circled me like prey. The taste of blood lingered on my lips.

Deep breath in, slowly out.

"Sorr–" His fist sank into my face before I could finish. Pain streaked down my neck. Smack. Crack. My gut tightened. A sour taste washed over my tongue.

Smack.

"Get up," Q roared.

The ringing in my ears drowned out his voice. Blood dripped from my chin, soaking into the gauze wrapped around my hands. My vision blurred as I swayed on unsteady feet.

He patted my cheek. "Who took the fight out of you?"

Heel, toe. Heel, toe.

He spat on the floor. My arms hung limply at my sides, trembling fingers struggling to close into fists as blood ran to my fingertips.

Heel, toe. Heel, toe.

Smack. My teeth sank into my bottom lip, and blood splattered across the floor. Everything went dark.

Silence.

Knockout.

Chapter Twenty-Four

It was somewhere between night-time and dawn when I strained my eyes open to see him waiting at the end of the cot.

I jumped back, "How long have you been there?"

Q smacked his heart-shaped lips together, staring at his hands. "You gonna get up today?"

His stern jaw tightened as he waited for me to answer.

My head pounded, "Yes." I muttered.

I shut my eyes again, trying to find the balance to sit up.

I groaned, tasting the blood on my cracked lip. My eyes refocused on Q's disappointed face. "I don't have all day."

In truth, every part of me wanted to stay in bed. Everyone else's chests rose and fell slowly in deep slumber in the cots on either side of me. At least I'd avoid everyone staring at me. *Thud*. Q tossed the weight vest on top of me. "Put it on."

I grunted, sitting up. While I'd slept, someone had bandaged a cut on my cheek and washed the blood off my skin. Maybe Phin had scraped me off the basement floor after Q left me there to die.

Q stretched out his arms, yawning. My stomach growled. I realized I'd missed eating yesterday and now paid for it. I kept my mouth shut, though—stopping for breakfast didn't seem like an option.

A smaller crowd waited in the lobby, watching me shuffle out of the cot room. I struggled to round my shoulders and stand up straight. I needed to appear like one of them. They spoke just above a whisper. In the far back, the red-haired girl tossed her hair, laughing. I wanted to be her. I wanted to be on the other side. I wanted to be carelessly laughing. She gave me a side-eye glance while whispering into Ginn's ear.

"Don't worry about them. They aren't used to such regal women as yourself." Q snickered at his own joke as he ascended down the stairs.

Specks of my blood still dusted the basement floor. One large wet spot, previously splattered with blood, had been cleaned. Maybe the remaining drops were meant to intimidate me—they did.

Q wrapped his hands with gauze then tossed it to me. I caught it this time and smiled. He didn't notice. He was too preoccupied staring at the spots on the floor until I was done.

"Look, Phin let you join and told me to train you without asking me," He looked up from the blood stains. "If I had a choice, the answer would have been no—I don't trust you."

I gulped down the thick saliva forming in my mouth.

He scratched the coarse dark brown stubble shadowing his clenched jaw and exhaled, "You have to either learn how to fight or leave. Those are the rules he gave to you, whether either of us like it or not." He paused, "I am no Suit, I don't find joy in beating helpless women for fun. Are you gonna fight back today?"

I nodded.

His feet moved from side-to-side but before I realized he'd moved, a light jab hit my gut. I jumped back, crashing against a barrel. Smack.

"Put your hands up and block me." He said while lightly jabbing at my shoulders. "Do you wanna go back to your father?" I shook my head. "Then fight back."

I slapped his hand away then put up my arms to block him. His open palm belted across my face, splitting open the wound on my cheek. My knees crashed against the cement floor.

The light cut across his olive skin, defining his cut shoulder muscles. "Get up."

"Sorry," I mumbled.

"Don't say sorry." He tapped my shoulder, then the other. "Come on, hit me."

Father's shoes approached.

His next hit plummeted into my kidney. I yelped in pain.

"Fight back!" he screamed as his knuckles sank into my cheek. "Do you wanna quit?"

I clenched my jaw shaking my head no.

"Hit me."

Blood oozed from my cheek. Heel, toe. Heel, toe. I threw my arms up, shielding my face. Tears welled in my eyes but didn't fall. I braced myself as the room spun. Everything needed to stop. I tried to scream out, but before I could, a sharp pain split across my head. It felt as if the room had crumbled onto my chest, making it impossible to breathe.

***

The sun was long gone before I managed to squeeze my eyes open again. A cluster of candles on a small table in the corner reflected off the gray tin ceiling. Their light danced along the thin-lined flowers etched into each tile. Parts of the walls were punched out, exposing the brick beneath the sheetrock. The rebellion didn't believe much in interior decorating.

There was a familiar scent in the air—soup simmering on the stove. When I moved, agony radiated through my muscles. I gritted my teeth, sitting up, and a moan escaped my split lip.

Obviously, I won that fight.

Sweat soaked my shirt and hair. I wiped away the strands clinging to my face. Someone had re-bandaged my cheek and placed me on a cot. They'd even covered me with a light blanket. If only they'd injected me with a painkiller while I was out, I'd have been all set.

I stared at my shaking hands. *Deep breath, slowly out.* I shut my eyes but couldn't steady them. Out of the corner of my eye, a flash of a fist came at me. I jumped back, shielding my face. But as quickly as the image came, it disappeared.

It's all in your head, It's not real.

The room was silent. My heart pounded in my chest. Thankfully, I was alone. I rubbed my hands over my thighs and repeated, *Deep breath, slowly out.* I let out a trembling sigh as the air chilled the sweat on my face.

Sharp pains erupted in my stomach, but I pushed through to stand. Every wobbling step sent stabbing pain from my heel to my back. I braced against the wall to steady myself.

Their eyes watched me from the kitchen, yet no one moved to help. The cook glanced up, wide-eyed.

"Food." I swallowed the taste of blood. "Is there any food left?"

"Yeah. Yeah, of course, there is." He ladled some soup into a freshly cleaned, faded plastic bowl and gently steadied my arm. I flinched. "Hey—I'm not gonna hurt you." He positioned his hand under my hand to make sure I had ahold of the bowl. "You got that?"

I nodded, cupping my other hand under the warm bowl. "Thank you," I stammered.

"Oh, wait a minute," he called. I teetered in the doorway as he rummaged through a shelf. "You can have this too."

I snickered. "Bread?"

He shrugged, placing it in the bowl. "We nicked it earlier this week." He paused. "I thought it might be easier for you to chew." He pointed to my face.

Great. I looked as bad as I felt. A twinge of pain struck my cheek as I smiled. "It's great. Thanks."

He smiled back, running his fingers through his black curls. "I'll let you be."

I leaned against the wall, sliding to the floor with a grunt as pain arched from my back into my shoulders.

I clutched the bowl, inhaling the mixture of spices and comfort. The warmth against my chest eased my billowing anxiety. A pang of sadness struck me, and my lips quivered. I hadn't realized how much a kind gesture would mean to me. I sniffled, sucking back the tears.

The spices burned my split lip but washed away the metallic taste in my mouth. The soup instantly soothed my stomach. Relief filtered through me. I savored each bite of bread, soaking it into the broth. It was the best thing I'd tasted in months.

The cook walked over after I finished. "Do you want more? There's a little left." I shook my head. "Do you need help up?" He extended his arm, revealing a cluster of burn scars across his fair skin.

"No." I mustered the strength to pull myself up using the wall.

He stood close in case I slipped but didn't touch me. I steadied myself. "I'm fine," I said through gritted teeth.

***

This was where a smarter person would have said they'd had enough or ask for a break. Instead, the next day I repeated the same routine.

I woke up to Q waiting impatiently, then we walked through the crowd of haters. Q would tell me, "You can't cower in the corner, again."

I'd nodded, "deal."

Then I would proceed to crouch on the floor, trembling, leading to him to say, "I thought we just talked about this."

"Oh, right." I'd say, getting up.

Followed by—jab, uppercut, grunt, smack, jab, uppercut. Knock-out.

Q's frustration grew every day. His anger lessened the more he tired of my behavior. He uttered once, before he started the sparring, "I'd think you would be used to this by now."

I was used to it, used to trembling in fear. It was exhausting.

Every day I got up, and every day I felt like I could do it less and less. Every day the tapping of Father's shoes became louder.

What a great life I'd chosen for myself.

Chapter Twenty-Five

I opened my eyes to find no one standing over me. No sign of Q. The dull morning sun illuminated the room—the empty room. Was I still dreaming? I pinched myself. Nope, I was awake. Was this a trick?

After a week, I'd grown used to the soreness in my body and winced through the pain as I got up. *Where is Q?* I limped into an empty lobby, then tiptoed downstairs to the basement. Wrapping my calloused hands with gauze, I waited. Q came rushing down the stairs. I grinned, hoping to impress him by showing up before he did.

"It's about time. Where've you been?" he asked impatiently.

My jaw dropped. "I was here."

"No, you weren't. I've been waiting for you." His voice gruff and direct.

"Well, I just got here, but—" He'd changed the rules to this game we'd been playing. "You didn't come and wake me up."

"I'm not your daddy, little girl. You can wake up all on your own."

What a relief to hear he hadn't secretly been my father this entire time.

"Where is everyone?"

He threw two long, thick ropes into my arms. The weight nearly tripped me forward.

"That's none of your business." He paused, looking down at the bloodstained floor relaxing his voice. "They're on a mission."

I scanned the room, waiting for the sound of Father's polished shoes to enter.

"What are you always looking for?" He shook his head.

I jumped. "Oh, no one. Nothing." I paused, peering over my shoulder. "Do you ever hear footsteps in here?"

"Like from the floor above us?" He pointed to the ceiling.

"No, in the room with us."

He raised his thick eyebrows. "No."

"Oh. Okay." He thought I was insane. Maybe I was. "What are these for?" I asked, looking at the ropes.

He slipped his hands into his pockets. "Pull them," he commanded.

"What?"

I glanced at the ends of the ropes, tied to two large barrels. I'd gotten somewhat used to my routine of getting beaten every day. Why change it now?

"I said pull them." His voice was calm and steady, which somehow frightened me more.

I combined the ropes in my hands and yanked as hard as I could. The rough fibers burned my skin while nothing moved—not an inch. I let out a sigh.

Was there a lesson in this or just another sort of humiliation?

Q walked to the barrels and drew a chalk line on the cement floor in front of them. "When you move them past this line, come and find me."

"What?" I exhaled.

"I can't help you with this one."

"You're just gonna leave me down here?"

"Yeah, if you hear footsteps, it's me dancing above your head." He snickered, walking up the stairs. "Come and find me when you're done."

My shoulders grew overwhelmingly heavy. I slumped to the floor. There was no way he enjoyed dancing.

"Figure it out," Q yelled from upstairs.

What an ass. Was he doing this just to prove a point? The point being I wasn't good enough—strong enough.

I wrapped the ropes around my hands several times, set one foot back, and heaved on them. A scream ripped from my gut. The rope shredded my skin, and yet nothing moved. Blood soaked through the fibers, entwining with my damaged skin. I tried again every five minutes, yanking back unsuccessfully. Hours passed without even the slightest movement.

Was I good enough? Strong enough? Smart enough? They didn't think so. They looked at me differently: below the approval line once again.

I couldn't be one of them. The heaviness of defeat sank into me. Starin had said it all along—I didn't know tough. And they'd known it too, likely from the very first moment. What a fool I was to think I could be strong.

Sweat trickled down my bruised, swollen face. I unwrapped the shredded gauze, revealing torn skin. Tears rolled down my inflamed cheeks. I hung my head, biting my lip to stifle my sobs. *Deep breath, slowly out.*

The air burned my raw palms. I stared at them until the world blurred around me. Taking in one last deep breath, I gritted my teeth. A mixture of rage and disappointment surged through me.

I am worthless.

I raced over to the barrels, kicking them over and over. I let out a scream.

"I think that's considered cheating," Phin's voice came from the shadows.

My eyes widened, scanning the room. I wiped away any trace of tears.

"Don't worry, he left. He won't know. Your secrets are safe with me." He smiled.

"I can't move them anyway. I'm not strong enough." I leaned against one of the barrels and slumped to the floor.

"Oh, don't be such a downer." Phin strolled over, clapping his hands together. "Everyone is strong enough. You just need to find that strength within you." He crouched down. "You can't expect to carry the problems of the world on your shoulders without feeling the weight. You'll need a strong backbone—and maybe learn to deal with one problem at a time." He glanced up at the barrels. "There's no time limit for solving the world's problems. No reason to exhaust yourself." He studied my shaking hands. "Take your time. You'll figure it out. You're strong enough."

Oh, now he suddenly believed in me?

I shook my head. "This is impossible."

He tucked a strand of hair behind my ear. "You can do this." He winked. "I just gave you all the answers."

Then he left me alone with two unmovable barrels and my bloody, mangled hands. I tipped my head back, hitting the barrel. The shadows grew along the walls as the sun faded. Blood dripped from my throbbing hands, pooling on the floor.

"You gave me nothing," I whispered to myself. After an hour of moping, it came to me. I couldn't believe it had taken so long to figure out Phin's hints. "Deal with one problem at a time."

I wrapped my hands with so much gauze I could barely close my fingers. "You can do this." I untied one of the ropes and secured it to the opposing barrel. I had to show them I belonged here.

Deep breath, slowly out.

I wound the ropes around my shoulders, stood close to the barrel with my back to it, and lunged forward. Heat ripped through my shoulders. I gritted my teeth, releasing a loud grunt.

The barrel scraped across the floor. A jolt of excitement shot through me. I exhaled, smiling. I strained to take another meagre step forward. I could do this.

After twenty steps, I bent over, exhausted. I'd made it—a quarter of the way past the line. I caught my breath and picked up the ropes again. It took me until the middle of the night to pull both barrels past the line. My hands had gone numb, but my back felt like it had split in half. Moving the barrels across the line had taken everything I had.

I replaced the ropes to their original positions before going to find Q. Everyone stirred upstairs, engulfed in conversions while eating a bowl of some sweet concoction the cook whipped up. It smelled delightful. Q sat back drinking saps and laughing with Phin not paying much attention to the others around him. Ginn and the redhead giggled in their own world sharing a wing-backed chair near the fire.

The woman with the half-shaved head sat beside Q, filling his glass. Her jet-black braids draped over one side of her face. She glanced up at me like I didn't belong. The light caramel flecks in her mocha-brown eyes complemented her creamy dark skin perfectly. The soft candlelight illuminated two small scars along her cheekbone and a longer scar near her jaw that disappeared into her hairline.

"Hey, the Suit made it up here, guys."

"I—I'm finished."

Q glared at me. "It's about damn time. Let's go check it out."

The girl grabbed his glass and took a sip. "I guess this is all mine now, buddy."

"Save me a little," Q snickered, grabbing a lantern off of the table. "This won't take long."

She continued drinking from his glass. "Hmmm, I'm just not sure there's enough for you."

"There never is with you ladies," he laughed back.

The redhead whispered to Ginn while glaring at me. They burst into laughter, spilling their drinks on each other and screeching as more liquid splashed down their shirts.

Q rolled his eyes. "Phin, you coming?"

He gulped down the last sips in his glass. "Yeah, just one more sip before they drink it all."

Phin leapt down the stairs to catch up. I proudly placed my hands on my hips, presenting the barrels. Q crossed his arms over his chest, smirking. This time, I'd finally beaten him at his game.

Q crouched down, inspecting the line. "Well, you didn't move them that far past it."

Once again, utterly crushed.

Phin leaned against a pole. "Those aren't the rules, Q. You know it's not about how far they move them past the line."

"I guess you passed, kid. I'll see you early tomorrow morning." Q stomped back upstairs. Phin lingered a moment before heading up. "Oh, Arabella."

I smiled. Finally, there was a compliment coming.

"Mak said he saved some food for you. Make sure you grab it." He paused, "And clean yourself up, we got more water today."

Clearly, he didn't know how to compliment people.

"Who's Mak?"

"The cook. He gives you food every day. How do you not know his name?"

Really? That was the cook's name? "Oh, I thought he said his name was Tac. My bad." I gave an awkward smile.

Damn it, I needed to get better at learning people's names.

Chapter Twenty–Six

H e shook my shoulder profusely. *Shit, I'm in trouble.* I forced my eyes open. The light blonde highlights in Phin's hair glistened in the morning sunlight, obscuring his face.

He whispered, "Arabella." My eyes shut again. "Arabella." He continued shaking me.

I squeezed my eyes open to Phin's smiling face. The sun's rosiness made him look like a young boy. I pressed my fingers into my blood-soaked gauze covered palms releasing a sharp reminder of the night before.

"Come on, get up." He slapped my thigh.

"Shit, I have to get downstairs."

Everyone's cot was empty, their blankets and clothes left askew. The sun had crested past midmorning, slipping through the peeling newspaper at the tops of the windows. I was going to hear it from Q for being late.

Phin placed his hand on my shoulder, pushing me back down. "I told Q to let you sleep a bit. Here, I got this." His street accent crept in, as it sometimes did when he wasn't paying attention. "Thought of ya."

He tossed me a squeezy tube of numbing agent. The same brand my mother used with a bright red cap.

"Thanks," I winced, catching it.

"Yeah, no problem. Come with me." I awkwardly strained to loosen the cap while getting to my feet. "I wanna show you something." His voice rose to an almost giddy tone. "It's a beautiful day."

I gasped, unwrapping the gauze. The numbing agent felt cool yet burned slightly as I rubbed it into my palms.

Grabbing my hoodie, I sunk my burning hands into the pockets and found the lobby empty. Mak waved to me as we passed in the kitchen. He never seemed too busy for pleasantries.

I followed Phin up the stairs, eyeing the second floor. The green door, marked *Offices* across its dirt-smeared window, caught my attention. The leaders deemed worthy slept beyond the door. Did they have single rooms, or just one large sleeping area like us? Did they have real beds? I wasn't going to be invited in anytime soon. Q's room was probably as organized as he kept the basement.

From the flat rooftop, you could see the center of Iargulta and a small sliver of the vast beyond. The smog hadn't yet made its appearance, and I could see for miles across the city—from the rows of burned-down apartments to the polished skyscrapers of the elite, and further still to the factories beyond.

"You see that?" Phin pointed to the city center, where the Suits' headquarters towered like a bolt of lightning piercing the sky.

"The Suits' headquarters?"

"Yes, we call it their Glass House. It contains all the lies the Suits are keeping from us. It's kinda funny—the place where they hide their secrets is actually see-through, right?"

I nodded, staying quiet. The numbing agent was slowly easing the pain in my palms.

"One day, we're gonna take that place down and show the world all their secrets. Maybe not today, maybe not tomorrow, but one day." He paused. "We're going out today to do surveillance on the Hive. Nothing close to invading the Glass House, but every little bit counts."

My heart jumped. I rolled my shoulders and straightened out my back, finding the strength to stand tall once again. "I believe we'll get to the Glass House. I'm ready. When are we going to the Hive?"

"Oh, you're staying here." He snickered.

I released my shoulders, slouching again.

"Your face looks like shit. I can't let you leave. People will recognize you out there."

Why was it too dangerous? "But I lived on the street for months, and no one noticed me."

"Stay inside. I'm protecting you. I don't want you leaving the bank." His words felt irritatingly familiar. Clouds passed over the sun shadowing his face. "Okay?"

I nodded and complied, "Okay."

Phin reminded me, "Plus, you still need to train with Q."

"What? But I don't know how much more I can take." I pleaded.

"You have to learn to fight. What other use do I have for you then?"

"I can do more than fight to help you."

"I know you think that." He said sympathetically. "But that was not what we agreed on."

A deep, piercing pain started in my back. It spread throughout my body like a violation had occurred. "He's not even nice most of the time. Is he like this with everyone?"

"Arabella, don't be naïve." Naïve was my defining quality. "He's tough on everyone, but I told you—you need to prove yourself and he doesn't like you." He shrugged. "But I like you," his grin made me uneasy. "He's the only trainer I've got, so you'll have to deal with him until you beat him." Phin ambled to the roof's exit.

Beat him? He was going to beat me to death before I beat him. "What? But—"

"Arabella you have to act stronger than this to make it here. You can't act like yourself. You have to be one of us." He said it more like a demand than a suggestion.

My nerve endings froze realizing he wasn't there to protect me, after all.

"I'll be stronger. I want to keep training," I said, mourning the loss of who I had built him up to be.

"Okay." He nodded. "He has weak knees if that helps."

What? Weak knees? That didn't help at all. I'd have to reach his knees before he beat me to death.

"Arabella?"

"Yes?" I sighed.

"That name doesn't really fit you anymore. Do you mind if I call you Ari?"

I liked how it sounded when he said it. The name felt stronger than the former, like the person I wanted to be. It eased the unsteadiness developing in my heart. "Sure."

"Okay. Good luck, Ari." He smirked and shut the door.

Before I realized it, I was walking down the stairs, shoulders rolled back, face set stern. It wasn't me, but it was who Phin wanted me to be. So why the fuck should I disappoint him?

"Hey, hun." A peppy voice distracted me from my march.

I scanned the group of people coming up from the basement and gathering in the hallway leading to the tunnel system for the source of the voice. The woman with the half-shaved head waved while rummaging through the boots in the vault room.

"Hey," she glanced up and sighed. "I can't find the match to this boot anywhere." She smiled, melting away her hardened expression. "Do you see it?"

Was she talking to me like a real person? No one was behind me. I think she was talking to me. I shook my head, no.

She limped over, wearing one faded black boot. "Hey, I haven't introduced myself yet. I'm Naz." She extended her hand to me.

Was this a trick? "Arabella," I corrected myself. "Actually, you can call me Ari." I shook her hand, cringing at the sharp pain in my palm.

"Oh, Ari then. I guess I'll have to stop calling you Suit," She glanced down at my hands. "Ouch, those hands look nasty. That reminds me."

She limped back to a nearby table. "Q told me to bring these over to you, but you were talking to Phin." She handed me a pair of gloves. "They're supposed to help your hands heal or something like that. I wasn't really listening to him." She returned to searching the floor for the other boot. "They were supposed to go with the numbing stuff he gave Phin for you, but of course, Q forgot the gloves in his room. The man would forget his head if it wasn't attached, I swear."

"Wait, Q gave me the numbing agent?"

She kicked aside some mismatched boots. "Yeah, Q searched through the Suit stuff we stole for that yesterday." She jumped to the back of the room. "Yes, I found it!"

"Why would he give me something to help me?" I slipped the gloves on, marveling at their snug fit.

She pushed a thin braid away from her face. "Why wouldn't he? He bandages you up every night and gave you his blanket. He's just like that. But, of course, he can't give things directly to people. That would be too much—emotional attachments aren't his thing."

"Q's been taking care of me?"

She shrugged. "Yeah, he carries you up every night and tells us to go to hell if we laugh at you." She paused. "I only laughed the first time, by the way. I'm not a complete bitch."

"Q? The same grumpy guy who's beating the shit out of me every day?"

"Right." She fastened her boots, straightening out her walk. "Phin told him to make you a fighter and that's what he says he's doing. You know Phin." My eyes widened. "Oh, maybe you don't know." She paused, then added, "Anyway, Q told me you're doing good."

I chuckled. "No, he didn't."

What kind of conversations did they have about me?

"No, I'm serious." She looked me straight in the eye. "He said you don't give up. That's good in his book. Anyway, Phin gave you a name, so I think that makes you one of us now." She poked my side, giggling. "See you later. I have to lay out plans to save the world, after all."

"Yeah, see you later."

She rushed out of the vault room as the man with the bun, who blew my cover the first night, walked by. "Hey, Jun, wait up!"

He spun around, slipping his hands into the pocket of his baggy cargo pants while walking backwards. "Come on, we're late." He glanced at me. "Oh hey, sorry about stepping on your foot, by the way."

I shrugged, "I've had worse."

He snickered, bowing his head to me before they disappeared into the dark tunnel. Maybe I was still dreaming, and any moment now, a weighted vest would be dropped on me. The day was turning out very odd.

I watched them descend into the dark tunnel until they completely disappeared. When I entered the basement, Q sat quietly waiting for me on a barrel.

"I'm sorry I'm late."

He jumped off the barrel. "It's fine. Phin's a talker." He glanced at the gloves. "You all set?"

"Yeah. Phin gave me a numbing agent."

I watched for his reaction. His gaze fell to the floor. "Oh, did he? Good."

"Yeah. Thanks for finding it for him to give me."

He cleared his throat. "You're welcome." He paused, scratching his head. "Well, I can't have you whining about your hands all day, now can I?"

I snickered. "Right." Why was he like this? "Hey, are you the only trainer here?"

"No, Naz is a trainer. She's been training Jun for a while." Not everyone told the full truth, I guess. "Are you asking to trade or something?"

"No, no I was just wondering." Although Naz did seem way nicer than him. "I'm good."

"Are you sure?"

"Yes. Do you just train people— I mean is that like your only job?" I asked while awkwardly fumbling with my hands.

"No," he shook his head, "I'm usually the planner—like strategic services, infiltrations—um, along with Phin. Naz leads the supply runs and surveillance. We do this when someone is new."

"Oh, okay," I nodded.

"Um, so, we're gonna try something different for a while." He glanced at me and smirked. "I've actually gotten tired of beating the shit out of ya." Had he heard me complaining about him in my mind?

"So, let's start putting some muscle on you instead." He grabbed a few weights and brought them over to a mat.

"You will start every day eating breakfast." It already sounded like a great plan. "Then you'll come down here and work out with me. You'll need to keep up." He placed the weights neatly beside each other. "We'll break for lunch, then continue until dark. Does that sound okay to you?"

This was such a weird day. "Um, yeah." It sounded like the best thing in the world.

"After a while, we'll go back to learning to fight. Maybe I can actually get ya to hit me back." He clapped his hands together. "Okay, let's get started."

I nodded, smiling at him—then remembered I wasn't supposed to smile and quickly let it fall. I don't think he noticed either way.

By the way, I was wrong about working out being the best thing in the world.

Chapter Twenty–Seven

Sweat soaked through my t-shirt. I tied one end into a knot to stop it from flopping around. The pull-up bar wasn't my friend, and I had to focus on my form, not where my shirt was sticking.

After months and months of working out with Q, I had finally reached the point where it didn't hurt to sit and I no longer felt nervous around him. He changed the routine weekly, so my body didn't get entirely used to it but still, my muscles and joints now synced together better than ever before.

My arms strained to pull myself up for another pull-up. I learned to push through the pain, if not for only one more attempt.

I adjusted my ponytail. My hair had grown past the official Suit approved length. I relished in the idea, although I found it to be inconvenient while exercising. Still, I refused to cut it.

"Okay, let's take a break for today," Q said, popping up from his push up position.

It was still afternoon, with the translucent sun seeping through the dirt-smudged windows. The sweat on Q's bulging muscles glistened in the rays. His tank top clung to his skin, carving out his abdominal muscles.

He stretched out his arms, then rolled back his neck slowly. "You're gonna wanna stretch before this."

"Before what?" I widened my eyes putting my hands on my hips.

I spent so much time with Q that I forgot to pretend at times. I found myself censoring my gestures and expressions less every day.

"Before you learn how to throw a punch."

Every drop of sweat on me turned to ice. My arms fell to my side. "Can't we just continue with the work out for today?" I said as my hands caught my eye.

I hadn't noticed before that the skin ripped off of my palms healed over without the previous scars caused by my fingernails.

He shook his head although his eyes looked sincere. "You have to learn this eventually. Or Phin will have no use for you."

Why was I only worth something if I was a fighter? I could contribute many other things. I happened to be great at sulking.

"Can't we start this tomorrow?"

The sharp sound of polished shoes entered the room making the hair on the back of my neck stand up. I swallowed my thickening saliva.

"And tomorrow, you'll ask for the next day." He paused. "It'll help you to get out your anger."

I didn't want to deal with it this way. I didn't want Q to see what I was hiding inside. I bit down on my lip trying not to cry. Couldn't he close his eyes and look away like all the others before him?

I shrugged, "I'm fine. I don't have an anger problem."

He snickered. "Yes, you do." I shook my head. "Let it out. Just scream or something."

"I'm not going to scream. Someone will hear me." I crossed my arms over my chest.

He waved his hands in the air. "So, who cares? Just scream."

"No."

The polished shoes took a step forward.

Q leaned in, "Scream." I shook my head. "Scream." I dug my fingers into my palms. "Don't close your fists unless you're gonna hit me." He smacked my hands. "Stop hurting yourself. Scream."

I let out a faint burst of a scream. A feverish heat rose to my cheeks. My eyes stung. I didn't want to cry in front of him.

"That's it?" He threw up his hands.

"What do you want from me?" I gritted my teeth.

"Stop just standing there. Cry, scream, curse, fight—have an emotion." His arms sporadically moved up and down. "They basically dug a hole and buried you. Get pissed off."

I had no words. My arms hung by my side. Why was Q doing this to me? He really did hate me. There wasn't much I could say besides, "I'm fine."

"You're not fine. You are the least fine person I have ever met. You act like you're dead." He stepped forward.

I recoiled.

Heel, toe. Heel, toe.

They were coming for me.

Heel, toe. Heel, toe.

Q pushed my shoulder. "Come on, scream." His other hand tapped my side. "Scream."

"No," I whined.

Heel, toe.

"Scream." He shouted.

My bones rattled. "No."

Heel, toe.

"Then hit me." His hands came at me quickly—pushing and poking my body, over and over. "Scream." He roared. "Scream."

The polished shoes raced towards me from every corner. I wanted to scream so that he would stop, but I couldn't let it out. Their voices raked over me. My heart squeezed my lungs. I wanted to crawl inside myself and hide.

"Scream." Q's blaring voice splintered through them. "Scream. You're just gonna give up? Scream."

The Suits' screams pulsed around me. The room whirled. I lost control of my senses. I couldn't keep track of what was real and wasn't.

It wasn't okay.

I wasn't okay.

Heat raced through my body.

Pain struck across my face. "Let it out. Scream."

Sweat trickled from my brow. Their shouts ricocheted around me. I bowed my head staring at my palms.

Q gripped my jaw, digging his fingers into my skin. I glanced down at his bruised knuckles. "Look at me, you, useless bitch."

The words deafeningly echoed around me. *"You, useless bitch. You, useless bitch. You, useless bitch."* Their voices stabbed through my skin, burrowing deep within my bones.

My pulse raced. How dare Q speak to me like that. How dare he think of me like that. He was nothing but an impotent man who could not fathom the possibilities of a woman.

I am not giving in.

I am not useless.

I am not giving up.

I am not dead.

I am not giving up.

I will defy them.

A burst of rage filtered through my veins. It simmered then boiled until it overflowed. I clenched my fists.

A gut-wrenching scream escaped my lips. I would not allow their voices to tear me down anymore. I swung my fist. The voices shattered around me.

My fists flew up, wailing at him over and over. Every spark of anger I had ever buried within raced to the surface. The uncorked fury exploded onto him with every emerging scream. Hit by hit, I released the anger. They had created this anger.

My fist sank into his face, whipping his head back. He glared at me, stunned.

The mask of what happened fell. "S—sorry." I said, stepping back.

He wiped the blood from his lips. "That was a pretty good punch." He smiled, "Welcome back above ground."

Bits of pebbles bounced off the windows from people passing by outside. Our breaths heaved in and out. The polished shoes had vacated. The shadows lingering in the corners disintegrated, leaving only the sound of footsteps from above.

Q raised his hands to block his face. "Hit me again."

"What?"

"That was good. Hit me again."

"But I hurt you."

"Yeah, I want you to. Now, hit me again." He stretched his arms out, exposing his chest. "Scream if you want to." He pushed my shoulder back. "Come on, hit me."

I flung my fist forward, hitting him in the gut.

"Harder," he shouted.

Every punch he demanded to be harder. Each time, it sparked a flash of anger within me. I released a scream now and then, though he never acknowledged it. He just pushed me to fight harder and harder.

He grabbed my arm mid-punch, whipping me around toward him. His breath felt warm on my cheek. I shut my eyes, listening to his heart pound against my back. I never thought I would enjoy someone's touch. I didn't know it could be filled with safety and comfort. It steadied me.

He released his arm from around my chest. I let out a deep, slow breath. He looked at me without an ounce of anger—anger seemed to be the least of his emotions toward me. He gazed upon me with pride as a smile spread across his face. Happiness fluttered in my chest.

"Okay, we have to work on controlling that." Seriously? First, he wanted me to release it, now, he wanted me to control it.

"You have to think fast when you're fighting. You can't think if your mind is clouded by anger." He paused, taking a breath. "Let's work on your form first."

I nodded.

"C'mere. Stand beside me. When you're fighting, keep both hands up to protect your face." He demonstrated. "Keep your elbows in, like this. Bend your knees slightly and keep one foot back like this." He waited for me to adjust my feet to his position. "Okay, good. When you throw a punch, you have to extend your arm forward and rotate."

I curled my fingers into a fist and threw my arm forward, pulling my shoulder along. I could tell by the look on Q's face that I'd done it wrong. I sighed. "I'm bad at this."

"No, um—you just want to make sure you rotate when you punch and keep your arm up to protect your face."

I tried again, moving my body to repeat his movements.

"Uh—if you just—um, let me show you. Is that okay?" he asked gesturing if it was okay to touch me again.

"Okay," I nodded, swallowing a tickle of a thrill.

His fingers gingerly touched my shoulder, electrifying a delight throughout my body. He tapped his foot against mine. "Widen your stance a little."

His body radiated heat as he placed his hands on my shoulder and arm, guiding me through the movement. Sweat lingered down my neck, saturating my shirt. Lacing his fingers with mine, he smoothly led my fist into a punching motion.

"When you rotate your entire arm, shoulder, elbow, and fist at the same time it gives you more power."

An array of gold specks gleamed in his brown eyes before he looked away. "I'll show you better on the punching bag tomorrow." He cleared his throat. "We'll start working out in the morning, then, after lunch, we'll work on you learning how to defend yourself. Okay?"

"Okay." The word *defend* resonated with me more than *fight* or *punch* ever had.

He exhaled, smiling. "You did well. We're done for today. I'll see you later."

"But it's not night yet," I said, almost giddy.

He grabbed a towel, wiping his sweat drenched face. "Yeah, but I'm sure that was a lot for you. I'll clean up down here. You can go."

I smiled, lingering on his eyes too long. Diverting my eyes to the ground, I awkwardly slipped my hands into my pockets. "Um... thanks."

"Hey, Ari?"

"Yeah?" I paused on the stairs.

"Sorry for what I called you earlier. I was just trying—" He stared up at me, his brow furrowed.

"I know." I nodded.

Maybe he didn't hate me after all.

Somehow, it had been my best day and my worst day. Something happened that was indescribable: it was some type of relief. The heaviness wasn't gone but my body did feel lighter, the tension in my shoulders vanished, and my palms laid flat on the table without a nervous twitch.

***

After quasi bathing, I went up to the roof. The smog hung low with bits of sun seeping through creating spotlights. People on the street continued along with their day, either discovering new finds in the trash or caring for others. Sitting down, I hugged my knees. The day had felt so long. I drowned out the city noise staring at the horizon until the sun started to fade. My mind felt empty and quiet for the first time.

I arrived to dinner before my usual time. Naz sat down beside me with two glasses of saps. She slid one glass over without spilling a drop. "Looks like you could use this."

The atmosphere was lighter tonight. The rebels had split into smaller groups in the lobby and cot room, engaged in lively discussions. Bursts of laughter erupted and fell abruptly.

"Um, thanks, it was a rough day," I said, exhaling.

"Yeah, we all have those days. Most of mine feel like that, or like I haven't achieved anything at all. At least you can see you're achieving something. Your body's getting some muscle on it—looking good." She raised her sharp eyebrows, taking a sip.

Heat rose to my cheeks.

"Hey, hey, you watch yourself," Q said, pointing at Naz as he sat down.

She chuckled, tilting his chin to inspect his black eye. "What happened?"

"She happened." He nodded toward me.

Shit. Was I in trouble? I slipped my hands under the table, holding my breath.

"Damn, girl, you did that? You got him good." Naz laughed, holding her hand up for a high five.

I exhaled, giggling under my breath, and smacked her hand.

"Yeah, she got me good." Q ruffled the top of my head.

"What's up, guys?" Mak circled the table, passing a bowl to each of us. "Made something a little special today. Don't tell the others." He sat down, giving us spoons from his pocket. "Come on, dig in."

"It smells awesome, Mak." Q took a spoonful. "Oh man, that hits the spot."

"Damn, Mak, you're getting better every day," Naz said, piling a spoonful into her mouth.

I couldn't tell what the flaky white and pink dessert was, but it tasted divine. My eyes widened. Sweet and warm, it hit every note I craved.

"Thank you," I added.

"Yeah, cooking keeps my mind off things," Mak said, leaning in closer to Q. "Your face looks beat, Q."

I giggled, cupping my hand over my mouth.

"Still not as messed up as your crooked nose," Q smirked, before glancing at me.

"Ouch, that hurts." Mak clutched his chest dramatically. "You know I'm a lover, not a fighter."

They were all older than me, in their late twenties, although they had stopped treating me as a kid the prior month. They still acted with the ease of children at times. Joy encasing their faces as they laughed.

"Yeah, yeah. At least I did something today. What did you guys do?"

"I made dessert for you, man." Mak scoffed, grabbing Q's bowl away.

Q yanked the bowl back, scooping the dessert in his mouth before anyone else could take it.

"Hey, I did some surveillance on the Hive today. See? Told you—it always feels like I've achieved nothing in a day," Naz said, nudging me. "Plus, I'm working to get Mak's boyfriend out. Now that we've got a message from him saying he's there, we know for sure we've got the right place."

Q paused mid-bite. "I can't believe he got a message out. Who left the note?"

Naz shrugged. "I don't know. Maybe we've got a friend on the inside. That could be good."

"Can we trust them?" Q's eyes narrowed.

"I guess we'll see." Naz took a sip of her saps, her gaze fixed on the table.

Mak's eyes welled, "I can't stop thinking of him in there—what they might be doing to him."

Naz wrapped an arm around his shoulder "Hey, don't think like that. We know he's alive now. We'll get him out."

I scrunched up my nose, trying to follow the conversation.

Q snickered at my confused expression. "Let me explain. His boyfriend, Tantum—well, we called him T—was arrested during a protest. We'd organized a speech for Phin. It had been planned for a while, but it turned into chaos before he could even finish the damn speech. Half of us got caught and are being held as prisoners of the Suits. We're working on a plan to get them out, including T."

I swallowed, realizing I had been at the same protest. "I'm sorry your friend got caught, Mak."

"Thanks? You understand he's my boyfriend, right? We're not just buddies," Mak squinted his eyes, leaning over his bowl.

I frowned. "So, you weren't friends?"

Naz placed a hand on my arm. "Yes, but Tantum was Mak's boyfriend. They're in a relationship."

"Like a friendship relationship?" I could see in their eyes that they thought I was an idiot.

Mak took a deep breath licking some white flakes off his lips. "I love him, and he loves me. Just like you'd have a man as a boyfriend, I have a man as a boyfriend. As a man, I'm attracted to men."

Was that a thing? Oh no, they were mad at me. I totally didn't understand. A knot formed in the pit of my stomach. "I'm sorry, I'm not following."

"Guys, just let it be," Q said, placing his arm in front of me on the table. "She doesn't know. It's not something allowed or talked about in the Suit Society."

Naz raised a hand to silence Q and looked at me directly. "It's okay. We're not mad at you, hun." Her voice was calm and steady. "We're just not hiding who we are anymore in here, so we're gonna explain it to you. You can love whoever you want—man, woman, or whoever. You're free to do so here. You can be whatever gender here—man, woman, non-binary. Love is love. A person is a person. They exist, no matter what they identify as. We love and accept you for who you are."

I held my breath. There were other possibilities? This was something I'd entirely missed. I'd only ever seen a man and a woman together.

"I'm sorry. I didn't know," I murmured, rubbing my thumb against my index finger.

"It's okay," Mak said with a shrug. "You're not the first to ask questions, and you won't be the last."

"You can be who you are in here. Out there, you can't. If we love who we love outside these walls, they burn us alive in the square. But here, we're safe." Naz smiled warmly. "You're safe to ask questions. If you have any, ask me anytime."

"Naz and I just don't have to hide who we are anymore. We're safe within these walls, and it's refreshing. We weren't safe out there." Mak's hazel eyes held empathy, not anger. "We're open to questions and understanding."

Was I a terrible person for not knowing this?

Although I didn't feel comfortable asking more questions for fear of looking like a fool, I nodded, wide-eyed.

An explosion of laughter came from the other side of the lobby. Phin chased the redhead, tickling her waist as she playfully fought back. She yanked on his shirt, ripping it and exposing his firm abs. My heart pounded. I wanted to be her. She didn't care what anyone thought of her.

"Hey, we're trying to have a heart to heart conversation here." Mak huffed, "Could they be any more annoying?"

"Yes—just add Ginn," Q said, taking a sip and ignoring Phin, who was now getting drenched by a bottle of saps. A few onlookers roared with laughter.

"What a waste," Q groaned.

Phin laughed, tossing the remnants of his drink onto the redhead's chest. She shrieked and stormed off.

Naz chuckled. "She'll get him back."

The redhead frowned at the light brown stains on her now see-through white shirt as she marched upstairs.

"Who is she?" I didn't realize I'd said it out loud.

"Who? Dil? The hot redhead?" Naz asked, pointing to her.

I nodded.

"Oh, here we go," Q muttered, staring into his almost empty glass.

"What? She is hot," Naz said matter-of-factly.

"And fierce," Mak added.

Q shook his head. "Nope."

Naz threw her hands in the air, "Come on."

"She's fake and selfish. It makes her ugly."

"Okay, fine, she's not your type, Q, but that doesn't mean she's not hot," Naz said, turning her back to him. She continued, "Ari, look, I'll tell you like it is."

Q snickered.

"Don't mind him. Dil is hot and smart, and she knows it, which makes her highly annoying. But we also need her because of what she can do."

"The annoying part was at least true," Q added.

Phin rubbed his face as he walked over to us. He smacked Q on the back. "Never can please that girl, eh?"

"I wouldn't know. I've never tried," Q replied, taking another slow sip of saps.

Phin lightly tapped Q's growing bruise. "Looks like my girl clocked you pretty good there." He winked at me.

My stomach turned. Was Phin talking about me? I tried my best to not show the disgust in my face as my hands began to sweat. Had I missed a clause in the application declaring me as his girl?

Q clenched his jaw, pounding his glass on the table. "Yeah, and she'll do a whole lot worse if you mess with her."

"Come on, she doesn't mind me messing with her." Phin winked again, stepping towards me. "She likes me."

Q blocked him from moving forward with his arm.

Phin crouched down and made a pouty face to Q. "What's your problem?"

My heart raced. I pressed my feet into the floor, standing completely still. I wished, I could have just walked away as Dil had done to him.

Q's neck muscles balled up as he released a heavy breath. He placed his arm on Phin's chest then pushed him back. Q's rope was fraying, ready to snap.

"Back, the fuck up," Q growled, staring at the wall past Mak, barely acknowledging Phin. "You're drunk, loud, and wasting supplies. Those are my current problems. The Suits are going to hear us in here with the way you're acting. Clean your act up."

Phin giggled, pressing his finger to his lips. "Okay, shhh. I'll be very quiet," he whispered dramatically, then backed away. "No fun at all, this guy." He stumbled, catching himself on a chair. "Oh, Naz, can you grab the truck battery tomorrow? Dil needs more batteries for her computer lab, and I need bonus points."

"Sure," Naz said with a polite smile, though Phin had already wandered off before she answered.

Q exhaled sharply, his muscles tense. "Irresponsible dipshit."

Naz pounded her glass on the table. "He's really leaning into being a full-fledged asshole, that one." She chuckled darkly. "Man, we'd better find more saps in the truck tomorrow, or he might die of thirst—and then what would we do?"

"And I present to you our fearless leader," Mak added pretending to bow to Phin. "If you need him, he'll be passed out on the floor later tonight. Don't bother picking him up."

The tension in Q's eyes lifted for a moment, and he smiled. "Hey, control your food, man," he said, nodding at Mak's dessert, which was teetering dangerously on the edge of the table.

Naz nudged me. "Hey, you guys should come tomorrow. We could use you."

"Yeah, I mean, if Ari wants to," Q added, his glare still following Phin as he bounded down the hallway like a child, arms flailing in the air.

"I can't. I can't go outside," I blurted.

"Why not?" Naz turned her questioning gaze to Q.

Q raised his hands defensively. "Don't look at me."

Mak shrugged. "It's okay if you don't wanna go outside. I don't."

"I think your reasons are different, hun," Naz said softly. "Why *can't* you go outside, Ari?"

"Because." An alarm went off in my head at the thought of crossing Phin. "Because Phin told me I can't go outside."

"What?" Naz exclaimed.

Q pounded his fist on the table. "Damn it, Phin."

Naz's jaw dropped. "Ari, you mean to tell me you haven't been outside since you arrived because that guy—who's currently pretending to be a robot—told you no?"

I nodded hesitantly. "I've gone up to the roof a few times."

Mak threw his arms up. "Oh, hell no."

Q let out a frustrated breath, placing his hand over mine on the table. The warmth of his hand travelled up my arm, grounding me. "You are not a prisoner here," he said firmly. "You can leave whenever you want. None of us can tell you otherwise—not even that fool." He inhaled a deep breath. "If you are not in control, you are under control. Don't let him control you. Do you wanna go outside?"

Phin slid back into the room, skidding across the floor before tip-toeing out again, clearly trying to avoid notice.

"I don't want to make him mad at me," I admitted, my voice cracking.

Q shrugged. "Then blame me if he gets mad. Tell him it was a training exercise."

Jun plopped down at the table, banging his knee against the edge. He winced but quickly forgot the pain when he spotted the dessert. His brown eyes widened as he snatched the bowl from Q and began shoveling the last bits into his mouth. "Where did you get this?"

Q sighed letting him keep the treat then snapped his focus back to me. "You wanna go?"

I took a deep breath, then nodded.

Q smiled, his expression softening as he turned to Naz. "Count us in. I think it's time for a little fresh air."

Jun looked up from the bowl, crumbs dusting his mouth. "Did I miss something?"

Naz shook her head, laughing. "Stop being late, and you won't miss stuff. They're coming with us tomorrow."

A roguish smirk spread across Q's face.

Chapter Twenty-Eight

The paper-covered windows diffused the somber moonlight as dawn approached. I hadn't been able to sleep all night, knowing I was going outside today. Jun wasn't awake yet. His body was curled up on his cot, clutching a blanket so tightly that no one could have stolen it during the night. I tiptoed to the door, brushing off the layer of dust that had settled on me during the night.

Naz's voice carried softly from the hallway. "It'll fit. I was sizing her up all night." She paused. "Oh, come on—it was for this."

I crept closer without her noticing. Her small braids were woven into one thick braid that hung over her muscular shoulder.

"Do you want to wake her?" Her eyes were wider than anyone's should be before dawn.

Q glanced over at me standing behind Naz. He looked down at the folded clothes in his arms. "Hey." He paused, clearing his throat. "We found these. We thought they might fit you." He handed me the clothes awkwardly. "Well, she did most of the work."

I scratched my head, yawning. "Okay, thanks."

Naz smiled. "Just try them on. If they don't fit, we'll look through more stuff."

"Sure." I nodded, inspecting the faded, used clothes.

"I'm pretty sure I've got your size down. Come find me in the vault after you're dressed to get some boots that fit. It's a pain to find a matching pair." She started walking away. "We have to wake up Mak to make us some grub before we leave."

Q grinned, leaning toward me. "He's gonna hate us."

I snickered.

"If he wants us to get him food to cook with, he won't whine," Naz said, wagging her finger in the air as she ascended the stairs. "I don't know why no one likes mornings around here." Her voice trailed off.

I frowned at the musty smell radiating from the clothes. Who had they belonged to? I examined the holes and stains in the pants. It smelled like someone had died in them.

"You, okay?" Q asked, his concern evident.

"Yeah, I'm good."

I wasn't. My heart rattled against my ribcage, and I couldn't swallow the lump in my throat. It had seemed like a great idea last night, but I hadn't been outside since finding the rebellion. *Deep breath, slowly out.* It couldn't be as bad as I currently felt.

Mind over matter, right?

His voice softened to a whisper. "Are you lying to me?"

Was I that bad of a liar? "Probably." I shrugged.

"You'll be safe with us."

"I know. I'll be fine once I'm out there," I lied again. "It's just the anticipation," I added, more to convince myself.

He nodded. "You can tell me if you're not okay with something, you know."

"Yeah, I know." Even though I did know, I wasn't comfortable saying so. "I'm gonna go change."

"Okay. I get to wake up Jun," he said menacingly.

I knew I wouldn't be going out alone. Q and Naz would be there. Still, I couldn't shake the anxiety brewing inside. What did raiding a supply truck entail? Why did I need different clothes? Was it too late to ask questions?

A thud followed by a quick yelp startled me. Jun sprang up from the floor, rubbing his head. I was glad I'd woken up myself.

"What the—?"

"Time to wake up, sunshine."

Q needed to work on his bedside demeanor.

I slipped into an empty closet and stood a flashlight upright to shine on the ceiling. I struggled into the tan pants, wobbling on one foot at a time. The frayed spots at the knees tore open as soon as I squatted to pick up the brown shirt.

"Damn it," I muttered, examining the holes in the pants. "Whose pants did I break?" I sighed.

The thin shirt was comfortably loose but nearly see-through. I slipped on the green cargo jacket and rolled up the sleeves to expose my hands. I took a deep breath, shaking the nerves from my fingers.

"You can do this," I told myself.

By the time I was done, pots were clanging in the kitchen, accompanied by groans from being woken up. Naz sat on the table in the vault room, swinging her legs until she noticed me.

"Hey, how do they fit?"

I tugged at the pants. "A little tight."

"Oh, those will stretch out. You look great." She hopped off the table. "Okay, so you look like you have smaller feet than me. I put the smaller boots in this pile."

She gestured toward a small collection of mismatched boots. Some had heels worn to angles, while others had scuffed sides.

"Okay," I said, sitting on the floor and tossing aside the obviously too-small pairs. "Um...so, what happens during a raid?"

Naz grabbed a pair of once-black calf-high boots, now coated with layers of white and brown dirt. "Well, we usually take out the guards first."

Oh no, I had to fight a guard?

"Then, we tie them up," she casually continued.

I hadn't been trained in tying knots yet.

"Then we take what we want and leave."

Come to think of it, I didn't really need anything.

"It's pretty simple."

None of it seems simple.

"Oh, okay. Yeah, that sounds simple," I said, nodding.

It sounds absolutely terrifying.

Naz stomped her foot into one of the boots, wedging it in place. She didn't seem fazed, calm as if it were just another day for her. I slipped on a pair of calf high, brown leather boots over the pants. They fit well enough for me to give up searching further.

"I'm not sure how much help I'll be. I'll probably just get in the way."

"Nah, just hang back with Q and watch. You won't have to do much. Plus, there are way more helpless people here than you." She wrapped an oversized knit scarf around her neck and adjusted the asymmetrical clasp on her dark gray knit overcoat. "You'll be fine. Come on, let's get some food." She patted me on the back, guiding me out of the room.

Mak's eyes were barely open as he meandered into the kitchen empty handed. He had lit two candles by the stove keeping the room dim. Q hovered over one of the four bowls set out on the teller's table. Steam rolled off the porridge into the faint dawn light.

I folded my arms across my chest. The room was cold and empty with so few people. I had forgotten it was once occupied by Suits.

Q stopped eating and tossed me a yellow bottle labeled *Sunblock*. "Here, so you don't get burnt."

I barely caught it in time but he didn't notice. He went back to eating, hardly chewing.

"Thanks," I replied, rubbing the white lotion onto my face.

Naz grabbed a stool by the table. "Oh, not worried about my skin, huh?"

"You're outside every day. She hasn't been out for months," Q said, scooping up a spoonful of porridge.

"Likely story." Naz scoffed, snatching a bowl.

I dragged the stool beside Q out, revealing a scarf and goggles draped over it. I stared at them for a second then immediately pushed the stool back in. "Sorry, I didn't know someone was sitting there." Heat rose to my face.

Q pulled the stool back out and pushed it toward me. "No, those are for you. We're going into the mountains. You'll need these to cover your face."

"Look at that," Naz added with a wink. "He's got you covered."

"It's windier the higher you go up," Q explained, pointing out the window.

"Okay." I nodded, talking between spoonfuls. "Thanks."

Jun meandered into the room, rubbing his head. He adjusted the shoulders of his long dark brown coat, which hung loosely off his lean, tall frame.

"Hey, Jun," Naz said, swallowing her porridge. "Nice of you to finally join us."

"Yeah, yeah, yeah. I'm here," he mumbled, yawning and running a hand through his ruffled hair.

Q slid a bowl toward him. "Rise and shine."

Jun glared at Q, then inspected the bowl. "Morning," he muttered, rolling up his sleeves to reveal his tattooed covered forearms. "Why can't the trucks run later in the day?"

Naz smirked. "Take it up with the Suits. Maybe they'll reschedule just for you."

Jun mimicked her words silently, rolling his eyes.

I spooned the porridge into my mouth, trying not to laugh. It wasn't Mak's best creation—bland and barely scented—but it was hearty enough to fill my stomach. No one else at the table complained, scraping their bowls clean.

Mak waved to us as he slumped back up the stairs.

"Thanks," we mumbled in unison.

He didn't respond.

Q exhaled. "So, is this it?"

"Nope, there's me!" Ginn announced, appearing out of nowhere. "I'm finally ready."

"You're not ready," Q groaned, eyeing her outfit. "You're not going out with us like that."

"Why not?" Ginn sauntered over to the table, her hips swaying. "I'm on a mission for Phin." She twirled one of her pigtail braids, smirking.

Her outfit—if you could call it that—was absurd. A white scarf draped over her head and looped around each side of her breasts barely covering her. Short shorts revealed more of her tan skin than they concealed. A leather utility belt hung low on her hips to complete the look. "Are we ready to go?"

"Go change. You'll burn your ass off dressed like that," Q said, pointing upstairs.

"Yeah, but I'll look cute doing it," she countered.

Naz shrugged. "She's not wrong."

Jun nodded, not taking his eyes off his bowl.

Q threw his hands in the air. "No. Go change."

Ginn snickered. "I'm sure Phin would disagree. Let me go wake him up. Oh, Phinney." She yanked on her white shorts. "Phinney." The shorts snapped back, smacking against her butt. "You know, Dil hates being woken up early."

Jun's eyes widened. "Oh, no."

"Don't wake him up, Ginn," Q snapped.

"We've gotta leave soon, Q," Naz interjected, stacking the empty bowls. "We don't have time for this."

"Like I'm going to let some man tell me what I can and can't wear. Aren't we working on not doing that?" Ginn smirked.

Naz snickered. "True."

"Aha," Jun added, slipping a black beanie over his thick eyebrows. "True."

Q rolled his eyes. "Fine. Burn your ass. Let's just go."

Ginn, although only a few years older than me, had a power over Q that I hadn't seen before. Her control didn't lie in dominance but in her pull with Phin. It made me curious about the games she played with men. She gave them a little and got triple in return. Men may have found her to be simple, but she knew exactly what she was doing. She even had a way of looking at me that made me feel inadequate.

I followed the group to the wall leading into the tunnels. Q stepped aside, letting everyone descend before him. I stopped, taking a breath before stepping down. He held out a flashlight for me.

"After you," he said.

Deep breath, slowly out.

I lowered myself into the dark tunnel, one step at a time. The sound of their footsteps echoed, bouncing off the walls and ricocheting back to me.

Bang.

I jumped as Q shut the door behind him. I braced myself against the wall, my pulse quickening. His footsteps descended quickly.

I clicked on the flashlight, its beam timidly illuminating my path. The others swung their lights confidently as they stomped forward. Q patiently stayed behind me while I shuffled ahead as if I might fall off the edge of a cliff at any moment.

Deep breath, slowly out.

At the center of the tunnels, we veered away from the city. The others moved without hesitation, clearly knowing the way. Ginn hummed to herself, skipping ahead.

The tunnel stretched toward the city's edge. At the end, sunlight poured through a giant metal grate. Piles of wagons, tangled in a ripped red flag, cluttered one side. Sand drifted between the wheels, gathering in the corners.

I attempted to shake the nerves out of my fingertips. Hardly able to fill my lungs, I reminded myself to breathe. There was just sand behind the grate. Nothing could hurt me.

The sunlight traced the edge of Naz's high cheekbones. "Here we are," she said with a smile, glancing at me. "Jun, help me over here."

"Coming," he called, rushing to her side. Together, they worked to remove the grate.

"You good?" Q asked me.

I wiped my sweaty palms on the tight pants. "Yeah." I nodded, pulling the scarf tighter over my mouth. "I've got it." I lowered the tinted goggles over my eyes.

Deep breath, slowly out.

There was no other option but to be okay. I couldn't just sit in the tunnels waiting for them to return.

Jun slid his copper-rimmed goggles over his eyes. "Why's the sun so bright in the morning?"

"Come on, whiner," Naz teased, nudging him as she headed toward a large, covered object.

She and Jun pulled off a brown tarp, revealing a beat-up truck parked just outside the tunnel. The sudden gust of sand sprayed us. Ginn squealed, ducking.

"I'll let you drive," Naz said, tossing the keys to Q. "Since you're a little rusty on the rest of it."

"How kind of you." He smirked, opening the door. "Get in." He gestured for me to climb up.

Naz and Jun hopped into the truck bed and began dumping out buckets of sand. The passenger door creaked open as Ginn plopped into the seat. I climbed in beside her, making myself as small as possible. She twirled the end of a white ribbon braided into her pigtails, entirely ignoring me. I kept my hands under my legs, trying not to touch her.

"You guys need to clean this truck once in a while," Q muttered.

Naz yelled out, "I did clean it. You clean next time, you'll love it then."

Q slammed the door shut. "Let's get going."

He turned the ignition. The engine sputtered but didn't start.

"Damn it," he muttered.

Naz knocked on the back window. "You gotta give it some love sometimes." she yelled.

"I'm not giving it some love," Q grumbled. He turned the key again, and the engine sputtered. Letting out an exaggerated sigh, he tried one more time. The truck roared to life. "Yes." He smiled.

I was already sweating through my shirt by the time we rumbled out of the sand. Maybe Ginn had the right idea with her outfit? She delicately slipped on a pair of bedazzled goggles, careful not to mess up her perfectly bronzed face.

Her makeup included cheap, tarnished fake jewels glued along her cheekbones and brow line in an intricate pattern. Sitting between her and Q, my body felt like it was baking. Sweat trickled down my back, soaking into my waistband. The truck cab was too small and only seemed to get smaller with every minute.

The dust rolled over us in a burnt umber haze, the sand flickering faintly in the light. The truck followed an unmarked street along the edge of a crumbling dune that encased the outskirts of the city until it opened to the endless desert.

The shadow of a giant mountain emerged on the horizon. Father's dark house loomed beside it in the distance. A flash of anger rolled over me. I gritted my teeth, gulping down the spite brewing within me.

Daddy dearest, are you watching?

The dunes looked like ocean waves—enchanting but deadly. They curved and swelled, never breaking. Between them, jagged boulders jutted out like islands.

I had never seen a sea nor a tree before in real life, only rumors of them in the past. It's not because of my so-called sheltered life but because they vanished long before I was born.

The once-lush world had been consumed by the creeping desert, leaving only bones and dry sand. My parents' generation had likely seen the last trees die, though even they could never fully enjoy them.

Their predecessors had drained the land, and now everything was gone.

They never respected the land. The Suits siphoned out the resources, mining every ounce of profit they could. All that remained was a constant reminder of humanity's greed—and the knowledge that one day, we'd all follow.

Q parked the truck behind a boulder crumbling into a dune. He adjusted his scarf and goggles, covering everything but his nose.

"Let's split up. You two bury the explosives under the sand and wait for them on the other side of the dune," he instructed Naz and Jun. Then he turned to us. "Ginn, Ari, you're with me."

Ginn scoffed. "Of course, he thinks he's in charge."

"Ginn, I can hear you," Q said, deadpan. "I'm standing right here."

"I don't care."

"I did let him drive the truck," Naz added with a shrug.

Jun brushed a strand of black hair from his face. "Whoever drives the truck is in charge. It's a fact."

Naz nodded. "Facts."

Ginn crossed her arms. "You're not in charge."

"I am, actually. I outrank you. Now get up there." Q pointed at the dune.

Ranks? When had that been a thing? I really needed to ask more questions.

Ginn let out an exaggerated sigh and stomped toward the sand dune. With every step, her feet sank, and the sand cascaded down around her. She eventually dropped to her knees and began crawling, her face twitching as the hot sand pressed into her bare skin.

I stepped forward, digging my boot in the sand for balance. The dune seemed to collapse beneath me with every step. I followed her, getting down on my hands and knees when I couldn't maintain my footing. The coarse, scalding sand dug into my palms.

The wind howled against us, and I braced myself, struggling to maintain balance. Ginn kicked up a flurry of sand that landed on me, but she didn't seem to notice—or care.

By the time I reached the top, Q was already squatting there, scanning the horizon. "This looks like a good spot," he said, setting his goggles on his forehead. "Now we wait."

Ginn plopped down with a dramatic sigh and clapped her hands together to shake off the sand. "Oh, my favorite part—finally."

Q pulled out a pair of binoculars from his jacket. "You didn't have to come."

She snickered, lying back on the sand with her arms behind her head. "And let you get first dibs on all the stuff? Please. Plus, I need to work on my tan."

"What did Phin tell you to get that he couldn't ask me for?" Q asked, the binoculars glued to his eyes.

"You'll see when I find it," Ginn said, humming to herself.

"I wouldn't have asked if I was okay with waiting to see."

"It's some kind of meds," she muttered, her tone dismissive.

"Meds, my ass," Q mumbled under his breath.

The wind whipped around us, sending sand flying in sheets. Down below, Naz and Jun were digging shallow holes in the dirt road where faint tire tracks crisscrossed. They placed explosives into the holes, glancing over their shoulders before quickly covering them with sand.

Q handed the binoculars to me. "They'll be coming down that ridge soon," he said, pointing toward a jagged cliff. Jun and Naz darted behind a small rock formation. "Just watch for the dust cloud from their vehicle."

I scanned the ridge through the binoculars, shifting my gaze back and forth. "It's so smoggy out there. How will we see anything?"

"Yeah, they're really cranking out smoke at the factories today," He tapped the binoculars in the direction of the factories.

The chimneys loomed above what looked like faint cliff dwellings carved into the mountain.

"Do you know what they make in the factories?" I asked, handing the binoculars back to him.

"Not really sure. Maybe we'll find out someday."

I pointed to the dwellings. "Who lives in those mountains?"

Ginn perked up, a mischievous grin spreading across her face. "Oh, the cliff dwellers? Let me tell you."

Q groaned, shaking his head. "No, it's not true."

"They're totally real," she shot back.

"What's real?" I asked, intrigued despite myself.

"The cliff dwellers," Ginn began, her eyes lighting up. Well, that part made perfect sense. "They look like us, but they crawled out of the pit behind the mountain."

"That's not true," Q said flatly.

Ginn ignored him, launching into her story. "The pit was created by the evil from the old towns. It spread into the land and changed people."

"Evil?" I echoed, growing skeptical.

Q shouted, "The pit is not made from evil."

"Yes, evil!" she exclaimed. "The smoke and chemicals from the factories make people crazy. Deformed. Savage. The cliff dwellers." Ginn's eyes grew wide.

"Crazy people?" Okay it was starting to sound like nonsense.

"She's the only crazy one."

"Yes, crazy people. Anyone who passes that mountain is never seen again." Ginn pointed to the caves. "I heard they eat them while they're still alive."

I squinted at her. "But if no one's ever come back, how do you know they exist?"

Q let out a loud, "Ha."

"That's not the point!" Ginn snapped, slapping her hand into the sand. "You're not listening."

"And why don't the factory workers turn crazy too?" I asked, trying to poke a hole in her theory. I'd never met someone who worked in the factories before, but I'm sure I would have heard if they started eating each other.

"Right makes no sense," Q continued laughing. "You're the crazy one."

"What about the pit then? How do you explain that?"

I looked at her questionably, "The hole is from a mining failure. A mountain collapsed into the land from the Suit Corp. mining the mountain too much. It happened a long time ago."

Ginn glared at both of us. "Whatever. The cliff dwellers are real."

"No, they're not," Q said firmly.

"This is ridiculous," Ginn muttered, crossing her arms. "No one ever takes me seriously."

Q smirked. "Maybe it's the outfit."

Ginn huffed back, pouting as the wind toyed with her braids. "I put a lot of work into being me."

I studied her from the corner of my eye. Ginn had an intimidating presence. She stood out in every way, from her clothes to her attitude, and she seemed to revel in it. That kind of confidence was foreign to me, though I couldn't help but admire it.

Would Q judge me differently, if I chose the wrong clothes one day?

Sand particles delicately picked up by the breeze settled back onto another dune. The tension between Q and Ginn grew into an uncomfortable silence.

"So, how did Phin recruit you?" I asked Q to break the silence.

"Ha." Ginn jumped up laughing. "Oh, I can't wait to tell Phin this one."

Q groaned. "He didn't, we started this together. He's my best friend," he said, scowling at Ginn. "Now sit down before someone sees you."

"You guys are best friends?" I asked, surprised. That was honestly more surprising than the cliff dwellers. They didn't even seem to like each other most of the time.

"Yeah. We grew up together. His parents took care of me," he shrugged. "I mean, we don't always see eye to eye, but we balance each other out. He's good at talking and getting attention, and I...get shit done." Q paused glancing to the left. "You know that story he told you about falling through the ceiling during a Suit meeting?"

I nodded, my mouth ajar.

"What he didn't tell you was I was with him and also fell through the ceiling and that we got caught," Q raised the binoculars to his eyes smiling. "They threw us into a prison for three days," He snickered at the memory. "The only reason they let us out was because they were tired of hearing us cry."

"He doesn't tell that part of the story because it's boring." Ginn interjected.

Q rolled his eyes. "One day, we're going to storm the Glass House together and tear that son of a bitch apart."

"Oh, you mean her daddy," Ginn giggled.

"Zip it, Ginn." He glanced at me. "No offence."

"None taken," I said with a small smile. "I'd like to tear him apart too."

A cloud of dirt and dust rumbled toward us. My heart thumped wildly. Q placed a whistle between his lips, the binoculars glued to his face.

The high-pitched sound sliced through the wind.

Ginn squatted, a mischievous grin spreading across her face as she readied herself to pounce.

Chapter Twenty-Nine

Bam. Boom. Cap. The sand exploded upward.

My heart skipped.

"Let's go." Ginn rushed down the dune, nearly tumbling.

Q placed his palm on my back, pushing me forward. "It's time."

I raced down, trying my best to keep up with Q. I wasn't sure if I was breathing or how my legs were moving.

Sand and rocks rained down, pelting the truck. Shadows emerged from the smoke. A Suit tripped out of the truck, coughing. I thought my heart was going to pound out of my chest. Three whistles bit across the wind one after another. A dart zipped across from the rock formation.

The Suit fell as another one stumbled to his feet. Another whistle came from Q's lips, then a dart whizzed by us, hitting the guard in the throat. He clutched his throat, collapsing to his knees. I stopped, watching his eyes staring at me until they faded away. The dart's little red tassel lay between his still fingers.

"Good shots, Naz," Q said, standing over the bodies.

"Whoa," Jun shouted, springing up from behind the boulder, finally awake. His beanie sprinkled off bits of sand as he bobbled his head.

Naz jumped out, swinging the dart gun. "Thanks."

"What were those?" My breath heaved in and out. The scarf engulfed my face with heat. I yanked it down to breathe. "Did you kill them?"

"No, of course not." Q pulled the dart out of the Suit's throat. "Don't worry. They're just gonna sleep for a while."

Naz tapped the other Suit with her foot. "Yep, completely out. Jun, go get the truck."

Q tossed Jun the keys.

"Got it," he gleamed, rushing past the mangled supply truck.

"Should we tie them up?" I asked, worried they would wake before we were done.

Naz squatted down, "Nah, they look out of it to me."

Q grunted. "Let's get in there before she takes everything."

"I'll get the battery out first," Naz yelled out walking to the front of the vehicle.

Ginn rushed to the back of the truck without waiting for us. She bit down on her lip, straining to cut the lock off the back. Q stood behind her with his arms folded over his chest. She grunted, squeezing the cutter tighter. She let out a breath when the lock fell to the ground.

"Yes," she mumbled, tossing the cutter back and swinging the doors open.

Ginn climbed in, wedging herself between the large boxes, pushing aside smaller ones. Q pulled out a box and handed it to me. He jumped up and tossed two lighter boxes out.

He extended his arm to me. "Get up here."

I bit down on my lip.

"Let's go." He yanked me into the tightly packed truck.

I found it quite uneasy to be standing in the same place where a Suit once stood. I wondered what he'd touched. I imagined them loading up the truck in a stark white warehouse. They would have worked like robots in an assembly line to get the boxes stacked in a precise order, their faces vacant of a single expression.

Now, the boxes were barely held in place, ready to topple out altogether. The weird gaps from the explosions put the boxes at slight angles and upside down. Ginn stood on her tiptoes, attempting to read the label on each box

"This one has some food in it," Naz said, inspecting some of the freeze-dried packages. "I think at least." She dumped the box out. "There is some kind of grain, I think."

"Nice." Q grabbed an oversized box and jumped out. "Ari, grab the boxes and toss them down to me."

Most of the boxes weren't too heavy for me, the ones that were, I pushed to the side. Ginn continued rifling through the boxes and leaving the half-opened ones for me to grab.

Jun came around, parking behind the truck. "I took a loop around. Doesn't look like anyone saw the explosion."

"Awesome. Load this in the truck." Naz pointed at the items she deemed worthy for us to take.

"Yep." Jun put his hands on his slender waist letting out a heavy breath while surveying the boxes.

"Tell me if you need help," Naz called out.

He nodded. "I'm good."

Naz mumbled under her breath, "The kid would rather die than ask for help."

Jun was closer to my age than the other rebels. Even though he was no longer a teenager the spark of his youth remained. He had a slight dance to his movement, loading the truck with boxes, ignoring anyone that might take notice.

"I can't find anything in here." Ginn tossed a box, spilling out red bungee cords all over the back of the truck.

"Stop making a mess. You can search through the stuff once we get it out of here," Q yelled at her.

She whined, climbing deeper into the truck. "Damn, you're so bossy."

I grabbed another box and squatted down to hand it off to Q. Two boxes toppled over toward me. I ducked as a box of soaps emptied out over my head.

"Ah, vanilla," I mumbled, taking in the overwhelming scent.

"You're picking those up," Q jumped up yelling at Ginn. "We could use those. Let's get this shit out of the truck first." Q tossed the bungee cords back into the box.

"This is why I hate it when you come out with us. You're no fun. You're such a nag." Ginn said, tossing back a box.

"Nag? You're reckless." He huffed back.

I squatted down to lift up a wooden crate with the letters *D.A.B.S. 387* stenciled on the side with a half oblong circle underneath the letters. I gritted my teeth, straining to move it. "What is this?" I grunted, placing it back down. "I can't move this."

"Let's see. Let me help you." Q tugged the crate out of the corner. "Jun, get me a tire iron." He dusted off the writing. "What do these letters say?"

"Dabs? It's not a real word." I said scanning the box for any other wording. "I don't know."

"It better not be what I'm looking for," Ginn yelled out from behind a box covered path.

"Shut up, Ginn." He shouted back.

Q wedged the tire iron under the lid, pulling up the nails. The box cracked open. My heart sank. Q removed a vial of iridescent blue liquid from the crate. "What is this?"

Ginn tossed aside a box. "Oh, those are mine."

"No, they're not." Q peered over my shoulder.

"I mean, they're Phin's." She snatched the vial out of his hand.

"What does Phin need with those, Ginn?" His voice grew sharp. "Tell me, or you're not getting them. You didn't even find them." He grabbed the vial back. "You know the rules."

She sighed, putting her hands on her hips. "That's unfair."

"Ginn, wh—"

"It's supposed to make you stronger," I blurted out. "And take away your pain?"

Q's eyes darted at me. "Have you tried this?"

I shook my head. "No." Shit, I should have kept my mouth shut. I started rambling, "I just heard about them. They were giving them out on the street, saying they stole them from the Suits. But I have never seen the Suits use anything like that."

Q tossed the vial back in the crate. "So, Phin wants these to have a shortcut to being stronger?"

"Well, yeah" Ginn nodded wide-eyed. "Who wouldn't?"

"Hey, hey stop fighting," Naz yelled, putting her hands in the air. "Ari, you found this shit. Do you want it?"

I shook my head no.

"Okay, then it's up for grabs. Ginn you can have it."

"What the fuck, Naz? You're on her side?" Q lashed out.

"I'm not on anyone's side. Those are the rules and everyone follows them."

"Okay, fine. He can take the easy way out instead of putting the work in." Q kicked the box. "You're picking it up and putting it in the truck, though. I'm not having any part of this shit."

"Pffsh, I can do that." Ginn glared at him.

"Good." Q gritted his teeth. "Let's get all of these boxes, the battery, and the rest of the useless crap so we can leave."

Ginn scoffed, "So much for best friends."

Q raised his voice as if Phin could hear him from the middle of nowhere. "That shit isn't good for him. There isn't some magical thing you can take that will make you stronger. Strength is gained by the effort you put in. This is bullshit."

Ginn rolled her eyes, "Oh, here we go."

"I'm just stating hard work and discipline give you results, not that bullshit."

"Oh, everything is bullshit now when you disagree."

"Yes," he shouted back at Ginn.

I tiptoed, jumped off the truck and lingered near Naz to avoid them. She dumped over a box frowning over the scraps of fabric. "Is there anything good in this load?"

My scarf was suffocating. I unwrapped it, letting the fresh air dry the sweat dripping down my neck. The scraps of fabric scattered, drifting in the wind. I picked one up, spreading it out over the sand. It was a decent size of smooth gray leather.

Naz tossed the fabric back in. "Just another box full of crap."

I traced the line of old stitching marks in the fabric. "Can I have it?"

"That piece?" She said, shoving the fabric in the box.

"No, the entire box. I could make myself a coat or something."

The Suits didn't save useless items. They wouldn't have put useless crap in the truck unless it was worth something. It was quite hard to find fine leather anymore.

She shrugged. "Sure. I don't want it." She tossed the box to Jun. "Load it in the back."

Q, finally done arguing, stomped to the back of the truck, placing in the box of soaps. I jumped into the cargo bed, folding the leather piece into the box, and moved the box back into place.

Ginn's face was turning red from carrying the box to the back of the truck. Her skin became covered with scrapes and splinters. She placed it down with a loud thud.

They wrapped the tarp over the boxes, then tied it down with a rope and some of the new red bungee cords. Ginn sat in the front, pouting with her arms folded across her chest.

"It's time to head back," Q said, jumping off the cargo bed.

Suddenly, I felt a hand slithering around my ankle. I glanced down to see the Suit's eyes fluttering up to the sky, before focusing on my face. "Hey! Help! Aren't you—"

My heart stopped. He knew my face. I snatched the scarf, wrapping it around my face.

A swift kick smacked against his head. "We have to go – now." Q tugged my arm. "Get in the front."

Q watched the Suit lying on the ground in the side mirror as we drove away. Q didn't let out a breath until the Suit was barely a speck behind us.

When we arrived back at the bank, the others met us at the stairs to assist in bringing the items up. Their faces lit up at the sight of us returning. I couldn't help but smile too. Someone passed me a glass of saps in celebration. There wasn't a familiar face until Mak peered out from the kitchen, giving a nod of approval.

Phin stomped his feet on the floor, shouting. Followed by Ginn shouting back, she skipped over, hugging him tightly. She looked around, whispering something in his ear as a smile grew larger across his face.

I unraveled my scarf and drank down the saps in one unsatisfying gulp. Their voices muted into a void surrounding the room. Phin's eyes watched, lingering on me longer than I wanted, as his hand rested on the small of Ginn's lower back.

Deep breath, slowly out.

A bottle smacked me in the gut then fell to the floor. "Hey, are you okay?" Q picked the bottle of water up and tried to hand it to me again.

I stared down at the water for a moment before I grabbed it. "Yeah, fine."

"Guys, guys, if we could all get a glass now to cheer these guys on." Phin took a step closer to me. "These guys went out today and risked their butts for you rotten fools." A low chuckle rumbled through the crowd.

Something in my gut felt wrong. Phin took another step toward me with his arm still gripping Ginn's waist. "If you could all hold up your glasses for my buddy Q and his team." They put their glasses in the air. "And don't forget my new girl—Ari."

His hand slithered along my hip, slowly grazing my butt then wrapping around my waist. His touch felt different from Q's, instead of warmth, an icy chill crawled up my spine.

My muscles stiffened. I gritted my teeth. The deafening sound of my heart took over every other sound.

The smell of saps on his breath lingered down the nape of my neck. The odor engulfed my senses, suffocating me. I wanted to slap his hand away, but I couldn't move.

Q wedged himself between Phin and me, flicking Phin's hand away. "Hey, why are you taking away from my glory, man." He gave Phin a heavy whack against his back. "You're crossing the line. I thought we were buds here."

An unsteady expression spread across Phin's face. Q wrapped his arm around my shoulder, lightly melting the bitter knots forming in my neck, and I let myself exhale. The crowd cheered, not noticing the awkwardness between Q and Phin.

Q smacked Phin's back again. "We need to talk about what was on that truck," he said without moving his mouth. "And she isn't yours."

Chapter Thirty

C old sweat soaked my shirt. The cot room was silent, except for the constant breathing of deep sleep. My heart hammered against my eardrum.

It had been just a dream.

Deep breath, slowly out.

I couldn't stop thinking about the nightmare of them finding me. Going back to sleep was impossible.

I walked softly out of the room to avoid waking anyone. The glow of a single candle danced in the dark, consuming the lobby. Pages ruffled, followed by a sigh. I tiptoed along the side of the wall.

The thin candlelight scarcely outlined Jun's androgynous features. His shoulders slumped with a heavy breath as he let the papers fall onto the teller table. Defeat and exhaustion hovered over him. Rubbing his face, he brushed his hair back.

I grabbed a candle from the kitchen and went into the vault room, not wanting to bother him. The floor had been recently swept, with the dirt and pebbles piled into a corner. I gathered the pebbles and placed them on the empty metal table. The stool made a slight noise when I moved it. I held my breath, hoping it didn't wake anyone.

I needed to find a way to soothe my racing heart. Pushing my sweat-soaked hair back into a ponytail gave me some relief from the radiating heat. I let out a breath, blowing the sand onto the floor.

First, I placed a pebble in the middle, then repeated. Delicately placing them in a spiral pattern, the rhythmic motion eased my breathing.

"Excuse me," Jun stood in the doorway, a candle and papers in his hands. "Sorry, am I interrupting you?"

I peered down at the precisely placed pebbles on the table. "No, I'm really not doing anything."

"I was wondering if you could help me because you're smart and I'm kinda stuck."

I snickered, placing another pebble in place. "I'm not really smart."

He took a small step into the room. "Well, you're smarter than me. You can read the Suit way, right?"

"Yeah, I can do that."

A smile grew across his face as he let out a heavy breath. "I have these documents, and they told me to look for this one word, and—" He stopped, looking down at the pattern of pebbles. "What are you doing?"

"Oh, um, just being weird." Heat rose to my face. "What word are you looking for?"

"This word." He handed me a torn piece of paper with the word HIVE written on it.

"Hive?"

"That says hive?" He shook his head. "That's crazy." He wrote down *Jyb* next to it.

"That is the way you spell hive? That's not even close. Where is the v sound?"

His eyes widened. "What? It's right there."

"There is nothing there that makes that sound." I giggled.

He shook his head. "The way you spell things is so confusing. I think they made it make no sense. I would have never guessed that says hive."

"Did you just need help with what the word was?"

"No, I went through all the pages and highlighted all the ones with that word and divided them up. Now, I have to figure out what they say but I can't read in the Suit way." He took a breath. "I have been up every night for weeks and haven't gotten anywhere. I really don't want to get another one of Dil's looks of how stupid I am when I tell them I have nothing tomorrow."

"Does Dil know how to read the Suit way?"

"No." He shook his head.

"Then why is she giving you a look?"

"I think that just might be the way her face looks." He let out a small laugh that made me smile. "I don't know why they wouldn't just ask you what it says."

"I think they don't trust me."

He scrunched his face. "Why?"

"Because I am an outsider, maybe?" I shrugged.

He passed me a document with with both his hands. "That's stupid."

A watermark covered the center of the page not obscuring the words. They were transcriptions from Suit headquarters. Each page was either a recorded phone conversation or new protocol.

"How did you get these?"

"Off of the supply trucks. Sometimes we find boxes of these and keep them, just in case."

"Well, this one is just changing the lunchtime for the guards. They went from twenty-minute to thirty-minute breaks." He give me another page. "This one is saying the repairs on the plumbing system were scheduled, and from the date, it looks like it was completed last month." I scanned several more pages. "None of these seem important. Is this helpful information for what you're looking for?"

"No, not really yet. What about this one? It came out of the truck that time you went with us."

I snickered. "They are talking about the guards accidentally falling asleep on the overnight shifts."

"Falling asleep? Really?" Jun peered over my shoulder, inspecting the document.

I pointed to where the conversation was. "Yeah, it looks like in the morning when the new guards come in, they have found some asleep. They are staggering the guards' shifts and are cutting shift lengths during the hours from three a.m. to eight a.m. They are working with smaller teams."

Jun turned over one of the documents and started writing down everything I said. "What does s-staggering mean?"

"It means they are not all starting at the same time. So, like a group may start at eight, then another group at nine."

"Then the eight o'clock group will leave an hour earlier than the nine o'clock group?"

"Right."

He shook his head writing more down. "Thanks."

"Does this help?"

"I think so. Thank you." He stacked up the papers in a pile on the corner of the table. "Why are you awake at this time?"

"Oh, um, bad dream."

"You wanna talk about it?"

I wiped my sweaty palms off on my stained pants. "I'm not really good at talking."

He shrugged. "Okay."

He walked over to the dirt pile and picked up some pebbles then placed them on the table. Not saying a word, he started with one pebble in the center, then placed another next to it.

I peered over his arm reaching for the center pebble. "What are you doing?"

He quickly placed his hand over the pebbles.

"Hey, hey, this is mine. You work on yours. It's a competition."

I snickered. "It's a competition?"

"Yeah, mine is gonna be better than yours." He looked down at my spiral, flicking off one of the pebbles. "You better get started. I am beating you."

"Hey."

His face scrunched up into a childish laugh as he blocked my arm from swiping at his pebble pattern.

"What does the winner get?"

"Um." Jun stared out into the dark hallway, then at me. "If I win, you will teach me how to read the Suit way and if you win, I will teach you the street way?"

"Deal."

Chapter Thirty-One

The paper in my diary had become crisp. Turning the page, I feared it would tear. Over time, each page evolved into a mess of inked words and doodles. Some were of people I'd met, and others were just squiggled lines in the corners of the pages. The diary was my quiet place, although some of the words weren't always peaceful. At least every word was my own thought—something they couldn't take away.

The sweet smell of breakfast lingered in the room. Like an alarm clock, it roused—the few late sleepers, who stretched out on their cots and staggered to their feet. Q would already be in line for food with Naz by now. Phin always woke up too late for breakfast but just in time for lunch. I wrapped the fraying twine around the diary and slipped it between the folded leather scraps evenly placed under my cot.

By the time I waited in line and got my quinoa breakfast bowl, Naz was already sitting with Jun at the teller table. I didn't understand Jun's ability to never sleep. I was exhausted. My mind raced with ideas of how to teach him to read. Maybe, I could steal a Suit's children's book somehow.

Mak had judged our pebble designs just before sunrise, and I'd finally gone to sleep. I think Mak was biased in choosing a winner, though, mostly because I lost. Okay, fine—Jun's was better than mine.

I drizzled some toasted nuts and chocolate sauce from the mixing station while searching for Q.

"Where's Q?" I asked, sitting beside Naz.

"He already ate," she said, mixing up her quinoa. "He's waiting downstairs for you."

"Hey, do you wanna play a game of gonggi?" Jun looked up at me wide-eyed.

"Huh?" I coughed, almost choking on the nuts.

"Jun, no one wants to play that game with you." Naz rolled her eyes.

"It's fun if you would just try," he sighed.

"Shit, I'm late." I snatched the bowl off the table.

"He can wait. He's not doing anything important." Jun said, slightly annoyed while chewing.

Naz nodded. "Yeah, he's probably just aggressively cleaning a spot."

"Thanks," I said, rushing towards the stairs.

"Anyone ever tell you to relax?" Naz shouted after me.

"Always, actually," I mumbled under my breath.

I hadn't missed eating with him in months. Was I that late? Q swept around a new machine covered by a tarp in the corner, possibly a new torture device. This wasn't going to be a good day.

"Sorry, I'm late," I said, shoveling some quinoa into my mouth.

"It's fine. I got up early." He grinned, staring at a spot on the floor, then to the tarp. "Naz and I went out and picked this up for you." He yanked the tarp off, exposing a machine.

A hard knot started forming in the pit of my stomach. "What is it?"

The excitement fell from his face. He raised his arms in the air as if I'd immediately understand what the metal machine was for.

"Naz said you wanted that fabric to make a coat."

"Yep, I did say that." I said, still unaware what machine was standing in front of me.

"It's a sewing machine."

My eyes widened. "Oh."

I hadn't ever seen a sewing machine before. Technically, I had no clue how to sew. It just seemed like a good idea at the time to make a coat. I had watched the housekeeper hand sew many items before but never with a sewing machine.

"So, we found one for you," Q said, more chipper and awkward than usual.

"Oh, thanks." I blushed.

A smile spread across my face. A gift. I'd received many gifts before but none from someone who listened to what I wanted. I took a step closer to inspect the machine.

I bit my lower lip, unable to hold back my joy. He had cared enough to clean it, some spots even looking polished. There was no needle or thread but I wouldn't have a problem finding that in a dumpster if I looked.

"Naz remembered we'd seen it at one of our other bases. So, we went out early to grab it," he paused watching for my reaction. "I think it is still in good condition."

"Yeah, I think so too. Thank you." I said placing my hand over my heart.

He exhaled a heavy breath. "Glad you like it."

"Wait—you guys have other places?" I exclaimed.

"Yeah, just in case we get discovered here or need to get out of the city. You'll learn where they all are at some point." He folded the tarp into a small square. "There isn't much to them right now. That was under a bunch of trash at one of them."

I wasn't sure if he didn't trust me enough to tell me the locations, or if they were a secret to everyone but a select few.

"Oh, cool," I shoved another giant bite into my mouth in the most unladylike fashion.

"You can take your time eating that." He laughed rubbing his thick, dark brown hair.

I swallowed the last bite, wishing I had grabbed something to drink too. "I'm good." I placed the bowl on top of a barrel. "Let's get going."

It was the same old workout routine until we took a break for lunch. Q grabbed two sticks leaning in the corner along with the broom.

"Have you ever seen one of these?"

I studied what I presumed was a weapon. It looked like what was leftover if you removed the brush part of a broom. "Have I ever seen a stick before?"

He snickered. "No, it's not a stick. Here." He tossed one to me. "It's a bo staff."

The stick wobbled from one of my hands to the other. "How do you—" There was a dull blow to my side before I could finish my sentence. "Ouch!"

"You gotta be on your toes." Q spun the stick in his hand like a professional show-off. The bo staff tapped one of my hips then swung around to my other hip. He flicked the stick to strike me across my face. I blocked it with my forearm and grabbed his stick at the same time.

"Hey, give me some time to figure it out."

He laughed. "You got it." He tapped my shoulder, then swept the bo staff back. "Think about where I'm gonna hit you before I do, then pounce."

Why did he find this so funny? I tightened my grip around the bo staff, blocking him before he could hit my thigh. I swept the staff around, chopping at the back of his knees. His knees buckled, tripping him forward. His bo staff clattered on the floor. I rushed over, snatching up his stick.

"I guess you weren't thinking hard enough, huh?" I laughed. "He was right—you do have weak knees."

He gawked at me, shocked. "Who said I have weak knees?"

"Phin."

"What? I don't have weak knees." he brushed his hands off on his pants. "I can't believe he told you that."

I shrugged, "It came in handy."

"Okay, ha-ha. Hand the bo staff over." He extended his hand to me.

I slipped both of them behind my back. "No." I shook my head.

His body towered over me, shadowing the sun. A slight jittery feeling bubbled up in my chest.

A smile cracked on his face. "Come on, give it to me."

He wrapped his arms around me, grabbing for the staff.

I giggled. "No." My skin danced like fire.

"Come on." He laughed.

"I see you guys are working hard." Phin's voice cracked through the laughter.

My heart sank. How long had Phin been standing there watching? A chill ran over my body. Q snatched his bo staff from behind my back.

He cleared his throat. "We're learning something new today." He casually rested his arm on the staff. "Hey, did you tell her I have weak knees?"

Phin leaned against the doorway. "You do have weak knees."

"I do not." Q shrieked. "Stop telling people I have weaknesses."

Phin snickered. "You have weak knees, bro. Just accept it." He folded his arms across his chest. "And stop fooling around." He licked his lips. "We have all the information for the Hive we need now. It's happening next week."

"Awesome. We can go over the plans tonight."

"You should start training now." Phin snickered "She's coming with us. Get her ready."

"The Hive?" I mumbled.

My heart shook against my ribs.

"Bullshit—she isn't going. She isn't ready." Q shook his head.

Phin spat back. "She said she was ready the second week. She's going."

I'd like to remove that statement from the records, please. It was obviously an arrogant mistake of mine.

Q gritted his teeth. "I am her trainer, and no, she isn't."

"She is. Too bad. We voted," Phin said nonchalantly.

"Who?" Q lashed out, yelling. "Why wasn't I at this meeting?"

Phin shrugged. "She's your trainee, remember? Get her trained, then."

Hello? Did I get a choice in this?

"You're going to get her killed." Q rushed to the stairs, his chest heaving up and down. "She's not ready."

No, of course, I didn't get a choice in it, men were talking. Listen up, little girl, these are your *keepers* speaking here—*you* have no choices in life.

"Stop fooling around, then," Phin snapped at him.

"Stop being reckless, Phin." Q's steps shook the staircase. "She'll be a target out there."

"You went out two weeks ago, and she was fine." Phin puffed out his chest.

"That's different, and you know it." Q lowered his voice. "They'll tear her apart if they get ahold of her."

Phin took a step back. "Well, she's your responsibility, so you better get her ready. She's going with us." He backed out the door.

"Phin." Q disappeared through the door. "Phin."

He stomped back in and tossed his head back. "Fuck," Q screamed.

There was more fear in his eyes than anger. His arms hung by his sides, utterly defeated. "What an ass," he said, staring at the ground. "He's doing this to get at me."

Why wasn't Phin including Q in important meetings? For best friends, they seemed to feud a lot, mostly at the expense of all of us.

"Maybe, you should scream; it'll help you get your anger out." The words slipped out before I realized what I was saying.

In a flash he glanced up at me. "Oh, you got jokes now?" The tension in his shoulders eased, and a smirk cracked across his face. "Do you think you're ready to break into a prison with us?"

My eyes widened. "The Hive's a prison?"

"Yeah. What did you think it was this whole time?"

"I don't know. I didn't really think it out."

No, I wasn't ready. Okay, yes, Q was right about me not being ready, although I would have liked to say it myself. I couldn't prepare myself mentally to walk outside the Suit Headquarters, let alone break into a Suit prison. A small tremor started in my fingers and crawled into my heart. I couldn't even look him in his eyes. "Why? I mean—what? No, I'm not ready."

"Why are we breaking in?" He confirmed what I was mumbling about. "It's to release the protesters the Suits are keeping there. You'll find out as soon as they tell the rest of us, I guess." He paused. "Since I apparently haven't been included in the planning of this bullshit."

His words sucked the air out of the room. I just stared at him with my mouth hanging open.

He sighed. "Come on, let's get out of here."

"What? No. But. Shouldn't we be practicing nonstop now?" I started rambling. "I still don't know how to use the stick thing. I'm not capable of anything."

"First of all, remember to breathe." *Right. Deep breath, slowly out.* "Second, we both need to get out of here right now." He took a deep breath. "Let's just clear our heads."

"I don't want to get in trouble for leaving again."

"You know, Ari, you should really start thinking about how you can make trouble rather than worrying about what might happen." He smirked. "No one has ever succeeded without making trouble. Plus, we're rebels. We don't follow orders. And screw him." He paused. "Also, if we stay, I'm gonna punch him in the face."

I would have enjoyed seeing that, actually.

Chapter Thirty-Two

"Shit," I muttered under my breath, squeezing the door handle. The truck bounced and rumbled as it climbed the side of a mountain.

"Don't worry, I drive up here all the time," Q shouted over the wind.

Worry? Who said I was worrying—besides the entire expression on my face? "Nah, it's fun," I lied, digging my nails into the handlebar.

A cloud of dust billowed behind us, catching the sun's rays and turning them golden against the vast, barren landscape. The scent of sunbaked earth filled the arid atmosphere. Evidence of the city's existence had long disappeared. We had arrived at the thin line between freedom and uncomfortable isolation—a place that could absolve you of your emotions, if you let it.

The warm breeze blew my hair back. "Where are you taking me?" I asked, gulping down my thick saliva.

"We're almost there." Q rested his elbow on the door. "It's just a place I like to go to clear my mind."

I guess I needed to clear my head. It felt as though I'd been crying all day, even though I hadn't shed a tear. Yet—somehow, I was at peace. We drove past dunes sweeping into graceful waves of soft brown with hints of red. Mesmerizing ripples cascaded down, leading to nowhere.

The wind slipped along the dune's side, blowing the sand into endless peaks. I took a deep breath, completely filling my lungs. I wanted to hold onto the moment forever. Particles of sand floated free in the sunlight, dancing before settling delicately on the desert floor once the disruption was over.

Q turned off the engine. "We're here."

The blankets of sand embraced us, absorbing the sounds of chaos we'd left behind. My boots crunched against the sand, splitting through the silence. Sand dunes stood on either side of us, shadowing us from the unforgiving sun and cooling my skin. A shiver ran up my spine as sweat slithered down my back. I wiped my forehead, scratching sand into my parched skin.

We had driven to the end of the world. "Where is here?"

Q exhaled. "We're where everything ends. All the drama, all the chaos. You can just let yourself breathe. Come on, follow me."

"Do you come here often?" I followed him around to where the wave in the dune turned inward.

He shrugged. "Just whenever I feel like getting out."

The tension in his jaw, which made his face appear more angular, vanished. His arms swung by his side. We had entered his comfort zone. I realized the tension within me had been left back in the truck, also.

Q sat down where the ripples in the sand flattened out. "Okay, this is a good spot."

"Spot for what?" There was nothing here but sand.

He lay back. "Take a seat and relax."

"Relax for what?" The muscles in my shoulders retightened.

"Just lay down, close your eyes, and think about whatever you want. You'll feel better."

"You want me to lay down with you?"

"No." He laughed. "Go lie down wherever you want. Just close your eyes and stop talking. Let whatever you want out. Think about whatever you want."

"This is weird." I sat down on the warm sand.

"It's not weird. Close your eyes and stop talking." He exhaled.

I slipped my hood over my head and laid back. The sand hugged every curve of my body as if it knew me. Beside me, Q relaxed, spreading his arms out.

I sighed. Closing my eyes felt ridiculous. How was this supposed to make anything better? It was only a few days before I would probably die, and here we were lying in the middle of the desert. Why not just take the truck and keep driving until the gas ran out? Running away from a situation wasn't exactly new for me. What if I was captured and held in a small box for the rest of my life, staring at four dark walls?

A familiar feeling resonated within me then expanded—four black walls. I was suddenly back, enclosed by fear. I couldn't tell if there were walls there without pounding my fist against them. My chest heaved up and down.

Why had I been put in there? What had I done? His polished shoes echoed on the floor outside. Warm tears poured down my cheeks. Heel, toe. Heel, toe. The sound of his shoes was deafening. The steps stopped just before the door. I didn't want him to open it.

Hide.

I crawled back deeper into the closet. The stale scent of the house slithered up my nose. I let out a trembling breath, spreading my arms to push back the suffocating sand.

The door clicked open. Light spilled in. *Run.* I recoiled further into the closet. His hand gripped my tiny ankle. I flung my arms out, reaching for anything. *Run, run, run, run, run.* His fingers dug in deeper, dragging my body out. My heart was in my throat, hammering. I thought I might choke.

Starin's eyes widened at the sight of me. I grabbed the doorframe, pulling and yanking, frantically trying to get away. His youthful cheeks flushed.

"Man up, boy. Get in your room," Father spat at him.

My fingertips clung to the doorframe as Starin's eyes welled with tears.

Father yanked my legs. "You're a fucking pathetic disappointment. Boy, kick her fingers."

Starin looked stunned.

"What kind of man are you?"

Starin crouched down, avoiding my eyes while he pried my fingers loose.

"No, no, no," I whimpered.

I held my breath as my small body flung into the room. Father's shadow expanded, looming over me. The clock ticked with every step he took forward. Pain split across my back. Cold sweat drenched my hair. I trembled as his fist smacked across my face.

"Learn your place, girl." Father's hand beat down again.

I let out a cry. "Stop, Daddy." Agony radiated through my body.

"Keep your mouth shut." His shoe struck my head.

My stomach churned as stabbing pain cut through my gut. His fists pounded over and over.

I let out a breath. Heel, toe. Tick, tock. Heel, toe. Tick, tock. He paced back and forth. I staggered up. My fragile young body swayed.

Drops of blood splattered across the floor. I stared at them as they puddled into shapes.

"Stupid girl." His belt snapped.

I flinched, squeezing the sand in my hands. Tears rolled down my cheeks. The breeze gently swept sand over my body, evaporating my sweat. Strands of my hair stuck to my tears. I unclenched my fists, letting the sand slip through my fingers.

I could feel Q without him touching me. The energy flowed out of his fingertips, seeping into me. It was a warmth that settled in my chest, easing my heavy heart. I opened my eyes, letting the tears pour down my cheeks.

Sand swirled tranquilly above my head. The particles rearranged with one another, then settled upon me. The tiny pieces were so fragile, yet together they built the strong unforgiving desert floor.

Entering the prison could be my final attempt at defying them. It could also be the downfall of everything. The Suits could tear me apart, cut off my feet. I had to be ready for either outcome. I swallowed down the knot in my throat.

"You okay?" Q glanced over at me.

I wiped the tears from my cheek. "I'm f—" I paused. "No, I'm not okay." I sat up. "What if they take me?"

He stretched out, sitting up. "That's not gonna happen."

My eyes stung. "How do you know?"

"Because you're not gonna let that happen." He mustered a smile. "You hit back now."

I exhaled. "They're bigger than me."

"So am I, and you hit me. You can do this." He paused, waiting for me to answer. "Did this at least make you feel a little better?"

"Yeah, maybe. I don't know." I drew a line through the sand. "Can I ask you, what do you think about when you come out here?"

"Um, yeah." He paused. "I think about my mother. I try to remember the way she looked at me."

My heart ached. "Is your mother no longer here?"

He shut his eyes, then stared down at the sand. "Um." He took a deep breath. "My mother died when I was very little. The way I like to remember her, she was stunning." The breeze swept the sand between our bodies. His face twisted in sorrow. "She was so beautiful it attracted the wrong type of attention from the Suits. The Suit guards would grab her in the street and pull her into an abandoned building. She would tell me to go play. She'd say, 'I'm fine, and I'll find you later.' She always came back disheveled and red in the face." He cleared his throat.

"I was curious about why she told me to run and play. So, one day, when the guards pulled her away, I didn't listen. I followed them into the building, hiding in the corner under the stairs." His eyes welled with tears. "I was too little to help. I don't even remember being able to move." He paused, trying to swallow. "My mother fought back. She did. Although she knew it caused her more pain, and she didn't know how to fight, she fought back." He reassured himself with a small nod. "They beat her, then raped her, then beat her until she was dead that day." Tears rolled down his cheek. "The assholes even left her there, exposed for everyone to see." He wiped away his tears. "I try to remember what she looked like before that moment." He paused. "Most days, I can't."

"I'm sorry." I wanted to hug him, console him, but I didn't know how. Instead, I hugged my knees against my chest, wishing I could offer more comfort but feeling utterly inadequate.

"Don't apologize. You're not at fault. Don't let them make you believe their actions are your fault in any way. I know what the Suits do to women. They beat you down until they kill you. If they can't physically kill you, they'll kill your spirit until there's nothing left." His voice grew firm as his tear-streaked face turned toward me. He stared into my eyes. "You have the power not to let them take that from you. Don't allow them to take it from you. No matter what happens out there, remember you have strength within you. You were born with it." He paused, his expression softening. "My mother knew it. Even though they killed her—she didn't let them take her power away."

I nodded, though the words felt like a challenge rather than reassurance. It was a whole lot easier imagining being powerful than being that person in the moment. Yes, I wanted to be a strong person, but yes, I quivered at the thought of entering that building. The idea of standing up to them, fighting back—it felt far away, like a dream I couldn't quite reach. I swallowed hard, my throat dry as the desert air.

Q gazed at me for a moment longer before speaking again. "You're stronger than you think, Ari. You just need to trust yourself."

I wasn't sure if I believed him, but for a fleeting second, I wanted to.

Chapter Thirty-Three

P hin's arm rested on the crumbled mantel as he tapped his foot to an unheard beat. Bits of trash scattered onto the floor, barely missing his faded blue sneakers. He stared at the saps swirling in his glass, seemingly oblivious to the rest of us standing before him.

I shifted from one foot to the other, the minutes stretching unbearably long as I stared at him wide-eyed. The others remained silent but restless. Dil leaned over the teller table, propping her elbows on its surface, her cleavage visible as she studied the blueprints spread before her. Her heavily outlined sapphire eyes scanned the plans, the faintest smirk on her cherry red lips.

Ginn plopped down beside her, whispering something in her ear. Dil giggled, then glanced at me before rolling her eyes. Did she know everyone's secrets? Ginn threw her head back, laughing. Clearly, I'd missed the joke.

Q's jaw tightened at the sound of their giggles. "Can we get this started already?" he huffed, folding his arms across his chest.

Phin stopped tapping his foot and looked around the room, his gaze settling on each of us in turn. When his eyes locked on mine, heat rushed through my body. The moment felt awkward, too long, like he was searching for something in me that wasn't there.

"Okay, it seems like most of us are here," he said, finally placing his glass beside the blueprints. He paused, allowing the weight of the moment to settle, "Let's get started on Mission Freedom."

I dug my nails into my palms, forcing myself to remember to breathe.

"This mission," his voice dropped lower, "is not just about rescue. It's about making a statement—to become a threat to those who oppose us. Are you with me?"

Ginn howled, tossing her head back dramatically. The others pounded their fists on tables and walls. I wanted to throw up.

"We will use the protest tomorrow as our cover. That's when we'll break our guys out," Phin continued, a smile creeping across his face. "The objective is to infiltrate the Hive."

My mouth went dry. Was I really ready for the Hive? Absolutely not. Even after a week of training, my stomach churned with unease. Naz caught my eye and smiled reassuringly. My eyes must've been as wide as saucers. If she could see my anxiety, could everyone else?

Phin resumed pacing among the group, "My girl, Dil will hack into their computer system. The security room is below the prison." He clapped her on the back before moving on. "So, as usual, cover Dil. She, is the key to this working. Q, Ari, Ginn—you'll be going down with Dil and me to the security room."

Why me? I should have volunteered to be a lookout three towns away.

"The rest of you will divide into two other groups. One will keep the crowd outside active and engaged. We must blend in with the protesters. If anyone stands out, the Suits will know something's up."

Yet another reason why I should stay back at the bank. "The second group will enter the prison directly. Naz will lead that team."

Naz shot to her feet. "Yep. Everyone with me, keep your eyes open and your mouths shut until we get the signal from inside the security room. We want everyone to come home, including everyone here tonight. So, until they signal us, we don't make a sound. After that, take down each fucking guard with darts as quickly as possible. Meet me after the meeting to go over our entry and exit plans." She pointed nonchalantly to the basement.

It all sounded simple enough, minus the fact there were a few dozen armed Suits, locked doors, and the only way for it to work was to rely on a smug redhead and a cocky blond. Fuck, what was I getting myself into?

Phin gestured to the kitchen. "Mak's gonna get breakfast ready before dawn. If you miss it, too bad—you'll go hungry until we regroup later. Mak will also be ready for any injuries when we return. Everyone here has a job to do tomorrow."

What? That wasn't a plan. I needed a full report plus illustrations to understand the mission and all I got was a lame speech?

"Stay focused. We're rescuing our friends from imprisonment—from torture. Who knows what they've endured in there? This isn't about standing out or being a hero. We are a team, and that includes those in the Hive." The room erupted in cheers and pounding fists. "If you mess with one of us, you mess with all of us. Let's start this damn rebellion!"

The cheering escalated. Was I the only one who noticed how vague this plan was? Maybe I could fake a sprained ankle.

Q jabbed me in the shoulder. "Get some sleep. See you in the morning." He walked off, stopping to chat with Mak before heading upstairs.

"Wow, that was a long wait for a short speech. I should've been late this time," Jun joked. "Hey, do you wanna play gonggi?"

"What?" I frowned. "I have no clue what that is."

"It's a game that you play with stones," he explained, his eyes lighting up. "You have to grab the stones before you can catch the ones you toss in the air."

"Huh?"

"Okay, I'm explaining it badly. I'll teach you."

"You want to play a game right now?"

"No, tomorrow, after we get back," Jun smiled, exposing his dimples.

"You're thinking about playing a game instead of the fact that we're breaking into a prison, everyone's probably going to be hungover, and I have no idea what I'm doing?"

"Right." He nodded earnestly. "If you think about gonggi, you won't worry about the prison stuff."

"How are you not scared?"

"Well, I'll probably be scared of something in the moment, but I won't make myself scared until it actually happens."

I let out a heavy sigh. "That's—actually kind of smart."

"See? And then, when I do get scared, I have playing gonggi with my friends to look forward to."

"Seriously?" I couldn't imagine being in such control of my emotions to be able to change my focus.

"Not this game again," Naz groaned, slapping Jun on the shoulder. "We'll get your friends out tomorrow, and then they can play the game with you."

"Yeah, but Ari's my friend. She can play too, if she wants."

It's official people, I have a friend.

Naz smirked. "Ari, don't let him sucker you into it. You don't have to play."

"I think I will just concentrate on the prison part first, then see."

Jun shrugged, "Okay."

Naz smiled, "Good plan. As we should be doing." Naz swung her hands into a clap. "Everyone on my team, let's head downstairs to have a chat."

Her team perked up and marched to the basement. Jun spun around and gave me a reassuring square smile as he descended into the basement. I guess it was just time for me to try to sleep.

As I turned to leave, a hand grabbed my arm. "I need to speak with you," Phin said.

"Sure." My stomach churned.

He drained the last of his saps and wiped his chapped lips. "I wanted you to know you're doing great. I know Q can be a grumpy ass."

Why was he suddenly my cheerleader? It had been months since he said an encouraging word. I didn't need him telling me who Q was. I didn't need him to approve of anything, least of all me.

I took a step back. "A grumpy ass? He really isn't. Q is–"

"Good, good." He cut me off. "How do you feel about tomorrow?"

His bloodshot eyes narrowed, already half-drunk but still calculating. "I'm fine," I lied. He was the one forcing me to do this, and suddenly he cared about my feelings. "Q's got my back, and I don't have a choice even if I wasn't okay, right?"

Phin grinned and slung his arm around my shoulders. My muscles tensed into a tight knot. I've got your back too, don't worry. I believe in you." His thumb rubbed against my shoulder gently. "I'll protect you; there is no need to be nervous. You're important to me." Stomach acid crawled up my throat. "You know that, right?"

He was some weird enigma, I couldn't figure out.

I gulped down my fear. "Yeah, I know." What I knew was that he was a liar.

A smile spread across his face. Why was he smiling? "Okay, go get some sleep." I stepped away, so his hand fell from my shoulder. "And check in with Ginn and Dil in the morning. They are gonna make you up to be one of us." That's funny, I thought I was one of them, already. "They'll make sure you're ready. You'll look like a warrior."

I'd rather be a warrior than just look like one.

With a sigh, I walked away. Great. My morning would start with Ginn and Dil giving me a make-over. At least if my once upon a time husband was there, I would make an excellent first impression. Father told me he was in Intelligence. What did that actually mean? Did Intelligence detain prisoners for information? Maybe tomorrow will be the end of it all.

Tick, tock.

One day left.

Tick, tock.

Chapter Thirty-Four

Dil huffed in my face. She looked disappointed at the arch of my eyebrows. I couldn't exactly tell what they were doing, but I knew I'd be disappointed.

"Um, this isn't coming out right," Ginn whined, tugging my hair back.

"You've gotta pull it back tighter." My head pulled as she yanked on my hair. Any tighter, my hair would have fallen out.

"Are you sure that's red?"

"I'm telling you it's red. It's just bad lighting in here." Dil was getting increasingly irritated by Ginn's questions. "I can't work like this; her skin is so dry." She frowned.

"You know, I can hear you, right?" I glanced up, wrinkling my forehead.

"I told you to stop moving. You're ruining this." Really, I was the one ruining this precious moment? "You need to stay still." Dil spread out my skin using a red lip liner to draw across my forehead.

The weight of the make-up felt as though my skin could have slipped off my face at any moment. It was a form of torture that I hadn't experienced before. I let out a heavy breath onto the powder container creating a cloud of dust.

I didn't think warriors cared about their looks so much. Naz never wore much make-up, and she pulled off a beautiful warrior regardless.

I tugged at the tight pants they told me to wear. The fabric barely held together with a series of tears, zippers, and scraps of fabric. The belt was more like a strip of knotted fabric, with chains hanging down on the side. It made me feel off-center when I walked.

I adjusted the breastplate from digging into my stomach. Fragments of a fabric dangled from the breastplate to my belly button with two belts strapped to keep them together. An armor covered in spikes protected my shoulders, which I feared would poke me in the face. I wiggled my toes in a pair of platform leather boots that were slightly too big and were way too heavy to walk in.

I was beyond uncomfortable. Dil's and Ginn's presence only made it worse. Did they know how people on the street dressed? It mostly was whatever you could put together from a dumpster and their sacred twine, not a crafted look.

Dil pinched my chin, pushing my head back. "How am I supposed to make her look like one of us? Do you see what I have to work with?"

Ginn tugged on my hair. "I don't know; he wanted her to look this way."

"He cares more about this than getting our people out." Dil furiously stroked a brush across my cheek.

"Looks are important." Ginn sighed. "I try to look good every day. Some people just don't get it."

Heavy footsteps stomped in. Q's hefty brown leather coat hung in layers over his broad frame. He inspected my face then raised my chin gingerly without smearing the make-up. I was waiting for an objection to the frivolous activity. I wanted him to say *stop, she doesn't look like herself*, but those weren't his words.

"She still looks too sweet." What was wrong with that? "Put more on make-up, completely cover her if you have to."

What?!

He left without actually looking at me. Since when was complete detachment his thing again? Was there anyone who viewed me as an alive person? Maybe I should have taken a poll.

I slouched. Q didn't like how I looked naturally. My eyes welled up. *Deep breath, slowly out.*

Ginn yanked my head to one side. "Hand me the red spray paint."

My eyes widened. Did she just say spray paint?

Dil passed a can of spray paint to Ginn. "What are you doing?" she asked with a mischievous smile.

"I'm gonna put red streaks in her hair." Ginn shook the can by my ear. "It's gonna look so cute."

"Awesome." Dil grinned.

"Um, excuse me." I pushed Dil's hand out of my face. "Stop; what are you doing to me?"

Dil grabbed my shoulders, pushing me back down. "Chill out; it's gonna look awesome."

"Are you spray painting me," I exclaimed.

Ginn smiled, "Just your hair."

"Is it gonna come out?"

They shrugged, staring at me. "I don't know." They really had no regard for my opinion.

"But you're gonna look badass." Ginn jumped in front of me. "It goes with the whole outfit. Don't worry I've got you covered, girlfriend."

Great, that's what I was worried about.

"It will wash out eventually." Dil looked up to the side, thinking. "Or it will just grow out."

I was never getting it out of my hair. "Fine." My eyes fell to the floor as the spray paint can hissed behind me.

Dil relined my eyes with black then drew spikes down my forehead.

Once they were satisfied, the sun was nearly up. Dil sat back and tossed the red pencil in her pink make-up box. "There, that's all I can do."

Ginn piped in, "I'm done too. This hair isn't gonna move for days."

Just what I was looking for in a hairstyle. "Thanks?" I heard immovable was all the rage this season.

Dil scoffed and rolled her eyes.

"Ya look great." Ginn picked up the make-up box and skipped out of the room.

I stepped forward to view myself in the tarnished mirror. My hair was pulled back tight into a ponytail that Ginn tweezed to expand into almost a mohawk with thick streaks of red. She sprayed my roots red with the color fading into my forehead, where Dil colored in three red spikes. A thick strip of red outlined in a thin black-streak across my eyes. A desaturated blush narrowed my face, pronouncing my cheekbones. I wasn't sure if the look made me better or worse looking. She used highlighters and contours to manipulate my face to appear slender and gaunt. My plump lips were covered in a dark purple and underlined, making them look thinner.

I couldn't find any part of me left. A hollow feeling grew in my stomach. They wanted me to be someone I couldn't be. Just like my parents, they wanted me to be something different than me.

My eyes stung. I swallowed down the urge to cry, creating an ache in my throat. I wanted to throw up. How was I supposed to blend in looking like that? I just wanted to be me finally.

"Hey, looking good." Naz peeked in. She was wearing black from head to toe. She adjusted her corset tightened with several belts that led to a utility belt weighed down by a dart gun beside a densely filled pouch. "Ready?"

I sighed, "What am I doing? This isn't me."

"Yeah, of course, it's not. You're in hiding. You can't look like yourself."

Okay, that made sense, but still, it didn't sit right in my stomach. I wanted it to be different. Couldn't they have made me look different and less exposed? The scars on my stomach and back were visible for everyone to see and judge.

I yanked at the frayed fabric hanging from the top, ripping it slightly. "It feels like I'm taking a step back."

She stood beside me, staring in the mirror. "When you're ready, you can wear your own face." She paused. "But this does make you look like a badass." She snickered.

Wait, did I not look like a badass regularly? I adjusted the breastplate. "Looking like a badass is quite uncomfortable. Shouldn't a badass care less about how they look?"

She slapped my back. "Very true." She slipped on her black hood and pulled out her braids. "But we look damn good, though."

I sighed, "No matter how much make-up you put on me, I'm not a badass. All I can think about is running. What does that say about me?"

"That you're a real person with real emotions. Girl, if you weren't scared, I might think you're crazy." She chuckled. "This stuff we're doing isn't easy for all of us. It's just death for us if we continue letting them control us."

"I know how that feels." I nodded.

"See, you're here with us, and we are all here behind you too." She patted me on the back. "Plus, I've run before. I've run from many things: from fear, from truth, and even lies. I ran from it all for a while."

"What fear did you run from?"

In Naz, I only could see strength. I couldn't imagine her being anything less than the strongest person in the room, in both body and mind.

"The Suits, they treat us like poverty is a disease, and the darker you are, the more contagious you are. They killed my older brother for sitting on their steps. Like he had infected their house, and the only way to get a cure was to rid themselves of him."

"What? That's awful. Why?"

"They don't need a reason, and if they did, they would just make up one. He was sitting on their steps, and they kicked dirt and screamed at him. When he got up, the Suit shot him in the head. I remember his head snapping back and hitting the ground. I still see it in my dreams. After they killed him, they looked over to me and I ran. I ran as fast as I could out of there. And for a while, I ran every time I saw one of them until I realized I wasn't the problem; they were. Everyone runs sometimes but eventually you stop, and that's when everything starts for you and ends for them." She paused. "Today, I hope that moment starts for you."

Chapter Thirty-Five

They came in waves, marching and chanting. The stomps shook the ground above the tunnels. My heart quickened, pounding in my throat as we ascended the stairs.

The old city hall building's ground floor was empty. The vibrations from the protesters rattled the thin walls. In the corner, mangled chairs teetered, on the verge of collapse from the faint breeze seeping through the slits in the windows. The wearisome morning sun climbed over the horizon, illuminating the elaborate gold carvings in the decorative ceiling. My family's insignia stood proudly in the center; sand gathered in the deep curves of the lettering.

The faint scent of rot filled my nostrils as sweat trickled down my arm. I let out a trembling breath, closing my eyes and taking in the shuffling sound of feet against the pavement. I licked my chapped lips, tasting the chemical flavor of the lipstick. I'd tasted worse.

Phin peeked through the wooden planks over the windows. "Okay, they're coming back around," he whispered. "You know where you're supposed to be."

Did I really know? A reminder wouldn't hurt.

Q glanced down at me. "Stay close to me."

That was the best plan I'd heard all day.

Deep breath, slowly out.

I tried to shake the nerves from my hands.

Phin glanced back. "Okay, let's divide up." He pointed to Naz. "Be safe. See you later."

"See you guys on the other side." Naz raised her fist to Q.

"Be safe. Get them out," Q replied, bumping fists with her.

"I will. Watch your back."

Phin propped the door open as Naz and her team slipped out of the building in slow spurts, blending in with the protesters. Q, Dil, Ginn, and I remained behind with Phin.

Boom. Boom. Boom. Every pound of the drums shook me. My heart could have rattled out of my chest.

Phin's lips curved up into a grin. "Let's go kick ass, guys." He stepped out, merging with the march.

Once we exited the building, my heart stopped. My breathing halted. I stepped forward, but I wasn't sure how I was still alive. How had I gone from sulking in my room to invading a prison?

Ahead, Jun and Naz dropped burlap bags into barrels, one after another. Fire roared from the barrels, producing a dense yellow smoke and engulfing the protesters. Their figures disappeared into the thickening haze.

Q gripped my hand, yanking me forward. "Stay beside me."

This was it—what I'd been waiting for since I left. I didn't run. I didn't scream. I didn't chant. But I stayed solid, and that was all I could offer at that moment. I was there. I was in the streets with them.

Sweat soaked through my frayed fingerless gloves. A quiver started in my fingers, radiating up my arms. My saliva felt too thick to swallow. Every second, I became smaller with Q's shadow towering over me.

But I stayed solid. I wouldn't crumble.

Ginn and Phin threw their fists in the air, chanting with the crowd, "We will rise! We will rise!"

Q's body tensed as his eyes darted around, scanning faces through the smoke. His unease made me nervous. Above the smoke, the morning sun lit the copper dome of the Hive, casting an aura of mockery against our grim determination. The sun bathed the city in golden, serene eerie beauty like life was in slow motion. The crowd's chants lifted into the air, while the stone building remained cold and earthbound.

Familiar faces popped in and out of focus in the crowd. They raised signs high toward the dome, keeping the protesters' attention concentrated on the building. The group formed a continuous orbit around the Hive, creating a blanket of cover for us.

The Suit guards stood motionless by the doors, watching people pass by and scream. They all looked the same—hair slicked back, clothes pressed, and guns strapped across their chests. None of them strayed from their positions.

The number five above a door caught Phin's eye. "Here we go."

He quietly approached one of the guards, who was distracted by the crowd.

"We will rise! We will rise!" The crowd chanted. "We will rise!"

Phin smirked and reached into his pocket. In one swift move, he jabbed a taser into the guard's abdomen. The guard twitched uncontrollably before collapsing to the ground.

My chest heaved as panic set in. I wasn't ready—not for this. I took a step back as the ringing in my ears muted the crowd's chants. I forgot to breathe. The faces around me blurred.

Run.

Phin's mouth moved, but I couldn't hear him. "Come on. Let's go." He mouthed to us.

Run.

Q crouched, zip-tying the guard's hands while Phin gagged him. Maybe I could slip back into the crowd unnoticed. I took another shaky step back, struggling to catch my breath. The layers of makeup on my face felt suffocating. My knees wobbled, and I stumbled back.

Who was the enemy here? Right now, we looked like the bad guys.

Phin hovered over the door, punching in a code from a crumpled piece of paper. The light turned green, and the keypad clicked open. Q grabbed the guard's arms, helping Phin drag him through the door.

"Get in, quick," Q's voice cut through the ringing in my ears.

Run.

Someone bumped my shoulder, jolting me back into focus. I let out a heavy breath. The chaotic sounds came flooding back.

Phin grabbed the guard's gun. "Let's show them who we are."

I stepped inside, although every part of me said *run-a-way*. The door slammed shut, hushing the chants outside. Phin turned over the crumpled-up piece of paper to a poorly drawn map.

"I guess the inside guy came through." Q whispered.

Phin shrugged using a hand signal for us to follow him down the dull lit hallway. Ginn smiled back at me, almost giddy. Every step she took pulled the stitching on the side of her tan pants tighter. It looked like someone had sewn two pairs of pants together unsuccessfully. The stitching tore apart at the top of her thighs revealed her bronze skin.

A door sprung open. I jumped back. A guard exited, staring at us.

"Hey, who are you?" A guard yelled, reaching for his walkie.

Run.

Q leaped forward, grabbing the guard's head and smashing it against the wall. His head ricocheted off the wall as a surprised expression fell from his face. My heart jumped. The guard's body collapsed on the floor beside Ginn. She recoiled and tiptoed around him.

"The crowd around the building is expanding. All guards to their posts." The walkie called out.

"Let's get down there." Q grabbed the walkie, dropping it into his pocket.

I sprinted, following them blindly to a stairwell. My eyes darted back and forth, hoping they knew where they were going. The stairs ended at the basement level. Phin's hand flew in the air halting us.

Thick and sticky, my salvia stuck to my tongue making it hard to swallow. Make-up melted down my face accumulating at the base of my neck. I carefully itched around my nose with the tip of my finger. A gob of make-up smeared off on my finger. I wanted to remove everything from my body: from the clothes down to the make-up.

I crept forward. Our shadows expanded on the shiny white walls as though we were giants. Q pulled the walkie out of his pocket, placing it by his ear. A static voice splinted over the heaving breaths. "The west door has been compromised. All security personnel to their stations."

"Shit," Q mumbled. "Book it."

My heart plummeted.

Phin poked his head out of a doorway then waved his hand for us to go through. I yanked on the breastplate digging into my side. Gulping down my fear, I almost choked on my salvia. We entered a wide hallway where water damage spots ran along the cement walls as we gradually descended deeper below the ground.

The dull buzz from the overhead lighting elapsed our steps. Q's calculated breaths inflated the tension in his shoulders. The deeper we descended below ground the tenser his shoulder became. Phin wandered in front of the pack out of sight as the hallway circled to the left. I hid behind Q, peeking over every few steps to see what was ahead.

A short grunt blistered through the silence. I made a low screech that I don't think anyone heard as I jumped back. Q leaped forward, rushing to Phin out of sight. *Run.* I didn't know which direction to turn away from the fight or towards it. I looked back, trying to remember which way we had come. Dozens of needles danced across my skin. I couldn't fathom what could happen beyond that moment. I held my breath.

Phin panted, wiping his forehead. "He came out of nowhere." He exclaimed to Q.

Q walked past Phin, ignoring him. "Let's get moving. It's clear up ahead, now. We have to stay together." Q grit his teeth. "Phin, stop going ahead." He wagged his finger in his face.

Phin rested his hands on his hips. "We are almost there." He motioned for us to continue down the hallway.

I stared down at Q's feet. I was too scared to look at what might be coming. He stopped just before the hallway circled again at two locked metal doors with an authorization screen on the side. Q placed his finger against his lips and mouthed *Stay here*.

A bead of sweat trickled down my arm to my fingertip then dropped onto the floor. I shut my eyes. *Deep breath, slowly out.*

Dil swiftly swiped a device on the authorization screen. The screen blinked red twice. My mouth ran dry.

"Your guy didn't give us the right sequence." Q impatiently whispered, staring down the hallway then back to her. His rapid breath made my breathing uneasy. I wanted to tell him, *deep breath, slowly out.*

"Yes, he did. He has been good for us so far." Phin whispered back.

"Both of you, shut up." Dil breathed out slowly, swiping over it again biting her red lips.

Not a shred of doubt ran through her body. She was the calmest among us. Somehow, she wasn't even sweating while I was melting into a puddle of a person.

We waited in silence, watching the little light blinking. The light flashed green. I let out my breath and sprung towards the wall. Phin pushed her aside as the doors slid open.

I dug my nails into my palms as two guards sprung up from a circular security desk, reaching for their guns. I shrieked, crouching down. Phin snapped the taser off his belt and released it into a guard's neck. His body twitched, smacking into the control panel. Q rushed in.

I pressed my body against the cold cement wall and covered my head. My eyes grew wide, clinging to the wall. I couldn't move. The sounds alone were too much for me to handle. Grunts and groans met smacks and slams shattering through my muffled ears. They rose and fell as quick as my chest. I couldn't follow who was attacking who, so instead, I stared at the small wet spot on the floor where my sweat gathered and focused on my breath.

A guard slammed on a button. "Lockdown, intruders." The zap of a taser released, contorting his scream.

The doors shut down the hallway like dominos. A strobe light flashed, flooding the room with red, followed by a shrieking siren. I covered my ears.

"Shit," Q screamed.

Flashing lights bounced off the walls. "Get in here. They know where we are," Phin shouted as he pistol-whipped a guard across the face.

Someone yanked my body up. Ginn's voice came into focus, "Come on. It's the fun part."

What kind of person finds any of this fun?

Q shouted, dragging an unconscious guard to a corner, "Dil, turn the damn alarm off."

"I'm on it." Dil raced in the room, jumping on the computer station.

The lights and siren rattled from one ear to the other. Ginn let go of my hand and skipped over to Dil, who was furiously typing. As quickly as it started, the alarm silenced. A collective sigh of relief radiated through the room.

I meandered around the room, rubbing my fingers over my thumb. Dil examined every inch of the control panel. Ginn, meanwhile, plopped down in an office chair and spun herself around. "Ah, silence."

"It's temporary," Dil said, zeroing in on the screen ignoring Ginn's frown. "That's the best I can do for now."

"Fine; just get the cell doors open." Phin pointed to the panel.

Ginn rested her elbows on the desk, "What can I help with?"

Dil swung her backpack off and removed an electronic device. She inserted one end of the device into the panel while typing in code after code. Phin paced back and forth around the room, glancing from side to side.

I shut my eyes for a moment to slow my breath. One, two, three, four, five. I opened them, pooling my focus to Dil.

"We're in." Dil shrieked.

"Yes, that was quick." Phin smiled.

"The code was made by simple, unimaginative men. What do you expect?" Dil snickered, not losing concentration. "Ginn, find the alarm setting on that computer."

Phin shrugged and walked away.

A buzzing sprang up from a short hallway connected to the security room. I jumped, moving quickly behind Ginn, who was staring wide eyed at the other side of the room.

"I'll check it out." Q rushed out of the room.

Slam. A door shut then another: rattling the room. My eyes darted around the room.

"What was that?" Phin demanded pounding on the desk.

"Someone's just put in a manual override to lock down the interrogation rooms." Dil typed away. "They blocked me out. There isn't anything I can do. The override locks the system out for an hour."

"Who's in them?" Phin beat his fist against the desk again.

"I don't know." She didn't look-up. "Chill the fuck out. This isn't helping."

I was shocked how sharply Dil spoke to Phin. Ginn smirked with her eyes darting between the two.

"Fine, you do your thing." Phin backed off.

A body slammed against the wall down the hallway. I couldn't help but tremble. A faint blue light outlined their obscure shadows bouncing off the dark walls as they fought.

Phin sprung back. "Great, trouble."

"I found the alarm settings." Ginn piped in.

A grunt ripped down the hall. I dug my nails into the sweat-drenched gloves.

Dil kept her eyes laser focused on the screen. "Ginn we can't completely disable them for good. Is everything in red on the page?"

"Yes," Ginn said confidently.

"Okay once that switches back over to green that means they were able to get the alarm back online. Once that happens, we will have a few minutes before the alarm starts screaming again." She paused, not losing her focus. "That doesn't mean they are not searching for us now, still."

I gulped down the knot in my throat. It felt like a ball of tar tearing apart my insides as it fell to the pit of my stomach. Ginn sat up alert, watching between the door and the screen. I stayed in the corner of the room with my arms hugging my chest tightly. My breath heaved in and out staring down the dark hallway. Sweat dripped from my furrowed brow.

A yelp of pain echoed from the other room, then a heavy slam as a shadow collapsed to the ground. I shuddered. Footsteps approached in the distance. My mouth ran dry while an ache grew in the pit of my stomach.

Q wiped his bloody knife off on his pants. I exhaled, staring at the blood on his pants. Did he kill someone? My heart squeezed my lungs.

"We're good, but the guy locked down some doors back there. I can't get them back open." Q said, out of breath.

"Yeah, we know." Phin rolled his eyes.

Dil shrugged. "The holding cells are what we came for. I'm not wasting time on a few interrogation rooms." She didn't bother looking up.

She was brilliant. I never saw someone type so fast with such concentration before. Her eyes darted across the screen like a machine. Where had she learned how to use a computer? It wasn't like she had one growing up. No matter how annoying she was, they couldn't claim she was useless. They couldn't do this without her.

Phin rapidly tapped his foot, peeking out of the entrance doors. "Let's get moving, Dil."

"I'm going as fast as I can. You can come over and do it yourself if you think you can do it better." She snapped back.

Phin put up his hands, withering away. "I'm good."

Dil pressed her lips together into a smirk brushing a loose strand of hair aside. She ignored Q pacing behind her with the fresh blood on his pants. I found it nauseating. The stagnant air was going to suffocate me. I fanned my face. The heat radiating off Q made the room hotter with every second we stayed in there.

I stepped back towards the dim lit hallway where a delicate hint of cool air seeped out. A chill shivered up my spine. I breathed in the cool air letting the darkness draw me in.

A faint whine breathed out from the next room. Q hadn't killed him. What had Q done for the man to sound like that? I tiptoed with the dull ache in my stomach crawling back up my throat. My heart choked me. One polished black shoe laid upon the floor. Drops of his blood trailed into the room. How badly did he hurt him?

"Hey." I jumped as Q yanked me back. "What are you doing?"

"I think he's still awake," I mumbled.

"He's not gonna do anything; he's tied up. Get back over there." He tugged my arm.

Ginn chuckled, still staring at the alarm system. "How much longer?"

Dil sighed, "Not much."

Ginn sprung up with her eyes wide. "The alarm went off. I mean, the alarms are gonna go off again."

Phin leaped over. "What do you mean? I don't hear anything."

She pointed to the green lit screen. "Look."

Run.

Dil rolled her eyes. "I told you we had a limited amount of time."

"Shit. We need to get out of here." Phin squeezed her shoulders.

Run.

Dil's arms fell to her side. "I'm done. It's done." She tossed the device in her bag. "The cells are open. Give them the signal." She grabbed her bag walking out of the door, "Let's get the hell out of here."

Phin smirked and pulled a pager from his pocket. "Naz's got the signal. Let's give them a distraction." He cracked his neck, his grin widening. "Get ready to make some noise."

Chapter Thirty-Six

Every nerve ending fired off as I rushed out the door after Ginn and Q. My breathing eclipsed the blaring sirens. I whipped my head back and forth, nothing looked familiar. Were we going the wrong way? Footsteps marched toward us in the opposite direction. Red lights flashed across my vision.

My body flung forward, smacking against the floor. Pain radiated across my back, but before I could catch my breath, his fist hurled toward me. I let out a screech. The Suit appeared out of nowhere. I threw my arms up, blocking him. The sirens screeched.

Adrenaline surged through my veins as I strained to stop his next blow. The force of his weight struck my face, whipping my head back. The pain stunned me. I staggered to my feet, forgetting to breathe. In a blur, his body hit the ground before I could stabilize myself.

Run.

Q stood over the fallen Suit. "Run."

Finally, someone agreed with me.

Suits swarmed in from every direction. Gunshots rang out. I ducked, covering my head as shards of glass rained down. Phin ripped a gun from a guard's body and fired into the chaos behind us. Every nerve froze. I couldn't tell which way was right or wrong. Who was the enemy?

I surged forward, barley dodging shadowed figures. In a flash, my body slammed against the wall. I curled up, bracing myself as sharp pain blistered down my spine. A fist beat against my head, followed by another pounding against my ear. My lungs exhausted, wheezing to take another breath, I gasped for air.

I needed him to pause, just for a moment, so I could get a shot in. Instead, his fist pummeled into my gut. I yelped in pain as the Suit's body abruptly was yanked off of me, and in one quick flash, his body smashed to the ground.

It became clear—I was the enemy.

Q crouched down. "You okay?"

I exhaled shakily. "What? No." My eyes widened. "Do I look okay?"

"Can you get up?" he shouted, extending his bloody hand to me.

I gritted my teeth, fighting through the pain.

"We have to go!" Phin yelled over the gunfire.

"Go!" Q screamed, dragging me forward. I tripped over a Suit's lifeless body.

Phin raced ahead, holding down the trigger and firing rounds into the center of the Hive. My legs trembled as Suits flooded the area, surrounding the central staircase. I needed to keep moving. My lungs burned as I raced up the steps.

We were a viable threat now. No longer just voices screaming outside, we were deep inside, prepared to dismantle everything. The rebels knew their enemy, but the Suits hadn't known theirs well enough. We were there to shatter the system, piece by piece. We were there to fuck the norm.

Phin snickered. "Ready, bro?"

"Let's go," Q replied, tossing something from his pocket at the Suits below.

Boom. An explosion ripped through the air. Smoke engulfed us, choking my lungs. Phin threw another grenade. Boom.

"Come on!" Phin screamed.

Q tossed his last grenade and shoved me up the stairs. "Go."

The explosion threw me forward. My teeth sank into my lip as my knees crashed against the steps. Blood filled my mouth. My head spun, the room blurring around me. Coughing, wobbling as I tried to rise, I collapsed onto the hard stairs.

Chaos erupted around me. Ringing eclipsed their voices.

My body trembled. I clung to myself, digging my nails into my skin, trying to ground myself. Pain bit through the drumming in my head. I couldn't stay here.

Smeared bloody handprints streaked the cold, white marble stairs littered with blackened blast marks. Muted footsteps scrambled past my head. I reached for the next step.

A stream of blood trickled from his polished black shoes dangling over the top of the landing. Blood seeped from his ankle, the creases in his trousers still sharp. I knew who he was. He—was my enemy.

Wiping my tears, I grappled to stand. My thighs ached, and my ankles wobbled, but I pushed through. I stood up. I would remain solid.

Q gripped my shoulder, moving me forward. The flashing red alarm cut through the dense smoke. I gasped for air as a shadow darted in front of me.

My fist connected with him. He grunted, stumbling back as I stepped over him. The smoke burned my eyes, tears cutting streaks through the makeup caking my face. My lungs ached with every breath. My pulse raced.

In the distance, light spilled from an open door at the end of the hallway. I pushed forward. Smoke followed, billowing through the doorway. Q's hand tightened on my shoulder. I tried to fill my lungs with fresh air but doubled over, coughing up the smoke instead.

Q glanced over his shoulder, grabbed my hand, and pulled me into the crowd.

"Keep your head down," he mumbled.

My vision refocused as the Suits swarmed out of the building, infecting the crowd. They began yanking down hoods and tossing people aside as they searched for us among the protestors. The sour stench of their desperation clung to the air.

I tightened my grip on Q's hand. I stopped myself just before digging my nails into his skin. My heart pounded, threatening to explode. Though our pace was calm, marching in line with the protesters, every step felt like agony. Sweat drenched my face, and my legs quivered, ready to give out at any moment. I focused on the person in front of me, forcing my breaths to steady.

Deep breath, slowly out.

Their footsteps quickened behind us. The walkie in Q's pocket crackled. He snatched it out, dropping it under his feet to be stomped on by the next person.

"They're going to find us," I whispered.

Q's eyes darted around without his head moving. "No, they aren't."

The Suits' voices shattered behind us. "Find them."

"They're here somewhere."

"Get them!"

The Suits had never had to defend themselves before. Their panicked faces searched the crowd, the cracks in their invincibility starting to show. Everything they stood for was starting to crumble: their dogmatism, their ignorance, their misogyny, their brutality, their manipulation, their hypocrisy, and their tyranny. This was a little crack in their invincible glass tower they'd built, so high above us all. Proving that their tower, like any, could fall.

Q tugged my arm. "This way." He cautiously veered into an alley.

His steps were heavy, his free hand balled into a fist.

"Hey!" a voice called.

I froze.

"Don't stop," Q said, loosening his grip.

"Hey, no name." Her scratchy voice rattled behind me.

I knew that voice.

"Delilah?"

Chapter Thirty-Seven

Delilah staggered out from behind the dilapidated boxes, dragging her foot awkwardly behind her. Her body twitched in odd places as if her muscles didn't know how to react to her movements. She scratched her matted hair, shaking her head erratically.

My heart ached. "Delilah?"

What had happened to her?

She grinned, splitting her blistered lips. "Hey, got some?" A mixture of pus and blood seeped from the cracks in her mouth.

"Got what?" I took a hesitant step toward her.

Her face snapped toward Q. "I know ya got some of it."

"Who in the fuck is this?" Q grabbed my arm, yanking me away from her.

I yanked back. "I don't have anything." My stomach sank. "Delilah, I don't know what you're talking about."

She lurched forward. "Don't lie ta me." Her bloodshot eyes bulged wildly. "Give it." A faint blue glow lined her veins, old puncture wounds oozing with infection. "Give me it," she snarled.

Something was lost within her. The happiness I once knew was gone, replaced by something unrecognizable—something inhuman. I bit down on my split lip to keep from crying, the metallic taste of blood pooling in my mouth.

"I have nothing," I said, opening my palms to her.

Q gripped my arm. "I think we should go."

"Go? No, no." She cradled her face, rocking on her heels.

"I need to help her." I turned to Q.

"We have to leave." Q glanced behind us. "We don't have what you're looking for, lady."

She leapt toward me, grabbing my face with clammy fingers that dug into my skin. "Where are they? Where are they?" she screamed hysterically. "Where are they?"

My eyes widened as I met her gaze. There was nothing left of her but an insatiable hunger for something I couldn't give. Tears streamed down my inflamed cheeks.

I tried to pry her hands off me. Her breath was rancid, the smell of rot seeping from her.

"Where are they?"

"Stop!" I cried. "Stop!"

Delilah was gone.

Q yanked her off me, sinking his fist into her face. "Shut up."

Her frail body slammed to the ground, lying motionless. I clutched my stinging face, my lips quivering.

"She wasn't like this before. Look at her arms. What did they do to her?"

"I don't know, but we'll figure it out later. We've got to go." Q wiped his hands on his pants, grimacing in disgust.

"We should check if she's okay." I crouched down beside her frail body.

Q grabbed my arm. "We have to go.

I pushed him away. "No."

He scaled the boulder, extending his hand to me. "We have to go, Ari," he said, his voice calm but firm.

Her chest rose and fell faintly. At least I knew some part of her was still alive.

"Hold on to yourself, Delilah," I whispered.

I reached out gripping Q's wrist, and he pulled me up into the old Record Holdings building.

Light streamed in through the open roof, suspended in the dust-filled air like time had paused. Fresh footprints marked the dusty floor, leading nowhere. I let out a trembling breath. Outside, the noise roared, escalating into a riot.

"Are you sure she's, okay?" I asked, my voice wavering.

A familiar scent lingered in the room, a mix of starch and musk. I breathed it in, letting it fill my lungs before realization struck. "Do you smell that?"

"There's no ti—" Q's head snapped back.

I gasped. A taser clamped onto his neck, and his eyes widened, staring at me as his body convulsed and collapsed to the floor.

Heel, toe. Heel, toe. Sharp footsteps echoed in the silence. A shiver ran up my spine.

Run.

"Tsk, tsk, tsk, tsk. Looks like Daddy's girl is in trouble again," the voice hissed. "Do you know how much trouble you got me in?" The beady-eyed guard from Father's house stepped closer. "You're going to get me my job back, little girl."

Run.

I stumbled back, bumping into an old desk.

The guard's voice was a sinister melody, rising and falling in volume. "He can't help you. Stop looking at him." My hands trembled. "Now, you're all mine."

He unbuckled his belt. "All, all mine, little girl." He licked his lips. "Hmm, not so tough now, are you?"

"Others are coming," I choked out.

He cupped a hand to his ear mockingly. "Hmm, I don't hear anyone." His head snapped back as Q moaned weakly. "Stay down," he grunted, pressing the taser's trigger again.

Q's body convulsed violently. The muscles in his neck tightened with every volt.

"Stop it!" I screamed, tears stinging my eyes.

"Make me." His tongue flicked out, licking his lips before he smacked them together.

Run.

RUN.

I cringed, my heart breaking as Q's muscles spasmed.

"I can't wait to watch them cut off your feet."

My teeth chattered

"You know, I caught her for him. I watched him cut off her feet—the housekeeper, the one who helped you escape. She wasn't a good runner." He snickered. "Starin sawed them off slowly—one by one. Then we watched her bleed out all over the floor." He stepped closer, lowering his voice. "They reassigned me because I couldn't find you."

Sharp pinpricks spread across my skin. What had I done? Tears streamed down my cheeks as I wiped them away, smearing red makeup on the back of my hand. I stared at the streaked red, paralyzed.

"For such a worthless little thing, you've caused so much trouble." His dark eyes glared into mine.

The word *worthless* carved itself into my temples.

He stepped forward pinning his body against me. I held back the vomit as my stomach churned. His breath lingered down my body, paralyzing me. He sniffed up along the curve of my breast then stopped hovering along my neck. "Hmm, just the right scent of fear."

His hands clamped down on my wrists, pinning me to the desk.

Run.

"Let go of me," I whimpered.

"Who's going to stop me?" His eyes devoured every inch of me, rubbing himself against me. "Hmm, I always imagined how good you'd feel." He bit his lip.

Run.

"Get off." A heaviness sunk my feet into the floor.

"No, stop," Q groaned, struggling to move.

"Shut up," the guard barked.

The zap of the taser shattered my nerves, and I gagged on the sour taste creeping up my throat. My fingernails dug deeper into the desk. There was nowhere to run to. There was nowhere to hide. I was alone. Pleasure grew in his eyes with the fear that rose in me. I could feel the more I trembled, the harder it made him.

Q groaned, straining to move.

Run.

"You killed her," he hissed, his slimy tongue licking the side of my face.

My skin crawled.

"You worthless bitch."

I met his cold, lifeless eyes. I stared into his eyes until there was only one word screaming in my head.

Fight.

I threw my head forward, headbutting him. He staggered back, shaking his head in surprise. Blood surged back into my veins.

"I said *no!*" I screamed.

He never stopped to think he was part of the problem, not me. Her death was not my shame. The shame was all his.

"I didn't kill her. You did," I lashed out, cracking my fist into his face. The impact made me feel like I was taking a piece of myself back. I swung again, collecting another piece as blood spewed from his nose, staining his pristine white shirt. My fist sank into his gut, and his body crumbled to the floor.

"You killed her!" I screamed.

An explosion of tears seeped out of me. He was all of them—every person—who had tried to bury me. A scream rippled out of me. Every shame, every cruel word, I pounded back into him.

"You did it." I released a wailing scream. "You killed her." My fists released every ounce of anger within me. "You did it."

Over and over, I beat him. I couldn't stop myself.

Arms wrapped around me from behind, prying me off him. But I wasn't going back. I flung my arms, punching behind me. I let out a cry.

"It's me. It's me," Q's voice stuttered in my ear. "Shh, he's gone. It's okay."

The guard's bloodied body lay motionless. I'd beaten the last breath out of him. There was nothing left. I let out a trembling sigh. The pleasure was gone from his beady eyes staring upward in fear. My eyes fell to Q's trembling arms, embracing me.

I exhaled and wept, melting into his warm body. He rocked me as I curled up in his arms. I couldn't stop my body from trembling, but neither could he. Tears poured down my cheeks.

"Shhhh." He whispered into my ear. "We're okay."

I wish I could say I felt whole again. I didn't. But at least I had taken back the pieces of myself they'd stolen. Maybe I could rebuild now that I had found those pieces again.

Light filtered through the boarded-up windows as sand settled around us. His faint whispers filled the space. For a moment, I let my defenses fall, shedding every mask I clung to. His embrace seemed as much for him as it was for me.

Chapter Thirty-Eight

It was well past evening by the time we made it back into the tunnels. Every muscle in my body ached. Red and black streaks ran down my neck, remnants of the make-up I couldn't wait to wash off. It wasn't mine—it never had been. Everything I wore today didn't belong to me. Maybe, earning the look came with an attitude more than an achievement. Either way, it wasn't me. The longer it stayed on, the more disgusted I became.

The walk back to the bank felt longer than usual. I worried about who had returned and what they knew. Maybe they had already realized how useless I'd been at the Hive. Instead of helping, I'd only gotten in the way.

Laughter exploded from the lobby as I slid open the pocket door. I exhaled a wary breath. People packed the bank's lobby drinking and embracing each other. Some I knew, and some were new—gaunt faces with hollow eye sockets.

Jun danced gleefully with two young men I didn't recognize. His smile lit up his face with contagious joy. At least now he had someone who would play a game with him. Somehow, I was jealous of them.

How horrible was I?

"Bro, I thought they got ya," Phin exclaimed, spilling some saps on himself.

"Nah, just had to wait it out a bit." Q scanned the crowd of unfamiliar faces. "I see you were so worried you decided to start celebrating without us."

"Come on, grab a glass." Phin grabbed an almost-empty bottle off the table.

Q snatched it from him. "Slow down, man. At least let me catch up." He slapped Phin on the back.

"There's no slowing down this train." Phin let out a full belly laugh. "Come find me when you wanna party." Phin raced off, shouting.

Naz clapped Q on the back. "Glad to have you back. I was worried there for a minute."

"How did it go?" Q looked around the room. "I don't see everyone."

"Not everyone's back." Naz looked over to Mak, frantically searching the crowd. "It's gonna kill me to tell him." Mak smiled, waving over to us.

My heart sank.

Q waved back, "It's gonna kill him more."

My stomach churned.

Naz sighed. "I know. We emptied every cell, but we came up six short. T was one of them."

Q rubbed her back. "I'll go with you to tell him. You got something to get this blood off my hands, first?"

"Yeah." Naz snatched a dishrag from the kitchen.

They didn't need me for this. I couldn't even console myself most days, I'd only make things—worse. I meandered back down the hallway.

Q wiped his hands, "You coming?"

"I'm going to wash my face." Guilt stabbed at me for backing away. "I'll be right back."

His benevolent eyes questioned my answer from under his furrowed brows. He knew I was lying. "Okay, I'll see you later."

I nodded and retreated, stepping back. Hanging out with a ragtag team of happy people felt like the most uncomfortable place I could have been. The candles flickered near the door to the washroom. My reflection in the cracked mirror was horrifying. Black eyeliner bled under my eyes, making them look sunken. Red streaks—some make-up, some blood—ran down my face. Sand, spray paint and blood crusted my hair and streaked down my aching neck.

The muffled cheers rose and fell from the lobby. I ripped off the breastplate and let the heavy shoulder pads drop to the floor. Bruises shadowed every muscle on my stomach. I rolled my shoulders back, releasing a heavy breath. Part of me felt empty. If not for the pain, I might have believed I was dead.

I dragged a bucket along the tub of water, distorting my reflection. Scooping water into my hands, I splashed it onto my face. The murky liquid stung my sore cheeks, and I winced, clenching my jaw. Streaks of red and black dripped off my chin, swirling in the bucket until the water was both all and absent of the colors at once.

"Who am I?" I whispered.

I grabbed a dirty cloth from the floor and scrubbed at the crusty blood on my arms—again and again—until my skin burned. The familiar harshness of trying to erase someone else's touch returned to my skin. I clutched my cheek where the feeling of his tongue lingered and held my breath.

The ache boiled up from my marrow, shredding me from inside. I gritted my teeth, trying to contain it, but it hurt too much.

Why did the pain never leave?

Exhaling sharply, I let the tears fall. My knees buckled, collapsing me to the floor. Drenched in tears, I curled up and let myself mourn as long as I needed. I was mourning the person I was once.

Time didn't pass; it remained still until I finally pulled myself up.

I shuffled out of the washroom quietly. In the lobby, Phin was laughing with Ginn, Dil, and a woman with long, thick black hair.

"Sky, baby, I've missed you" Phin stretched his arms wide, wrapping them around the woman. "I'm not letting you out of my sight again." Their laughter sprinkled faintly over the room's chatter. "Let's dance."

Everyone knew each other.

No one noticed me standing there, almost naked, watching them. I slipped into the vacant cot room, where there weren't enough cots for the new arrivals. Whoever's bed I had taken would be wanting it back now.

I pulled on my hoodie and pants and laid down. I didn't think I could move again. Moving forward wasn't my thing, anyway. I stared at the tin ceiling, trying to make out its floral design in the dim light.

The day had been a disaster. I was a disaster. Maybe, I could hide away in the cot room forever.

No one would bother to find me.

I'd been so sure this was who I wanted to be. I'd been so sure I could do this. I'd been so sure this was where I belonged. I'd been so wrong.

I had been such a naive fool, thinking I could have pulled off being one of them. This life was too difficult. I wasn't made for a life like this. Who I wanted to be, wasn't anywhere close to who I was today. A person like me was made for a life a whole lot less challenging than this one.

I dug through my bag for my diary. My stomach turned sour as I opened it. I clenched the pen, although my knuckles stung. I flipped to a blank page and started to write: *Today, I attempted to be braver than I am. I failed. I was surrounded by many people stronger, braver than me, and I could not rise to the occasion. This was a mistake. Everyone knows I don't belong here. I know I don't belong here. I haven't figured out where I belong yet. Maybe I will figure it out one day. But I doubt that I ever will. I need to move on, so I don't cause any more damage here.*

Phin's laughter penetrated through the walls. I tossed the diary in my backpack.

No one would notice I was gone.

I rolled back my shoulders and cracked my neck. The pain in my ribs took my breath away. I held my chest dropping my bag next to the door to watch them one last time. I would miss them. Phin spun around bowing to the crowd. Well, I would miss most of them.

None of the new faces glanced my way. No one bothered introducing me to any of them. I didn't bother introducing myself, either. Everyone was back exactly where they belonged—everyone but me.

Mak stumbled out of the kitchen, pressed his back to the wall, and slithered down. He cradled his head in his hands. His shoulders shook as he spoke, "No, he had to be in there. If he's not, he's dead."

"That's not true." Naz knelt beside him. Q meandered into the kitchen, retrieving him a bottle of water.

My heart ached. I couldn't help but stare. If this was the ache that defined love, maybe, a part of me loved myself today.

"You know it's true. If T's not dead now, he will be after this." Mak sobbed.

"Tantum is strong. He'll fight." Q placed the water beside him.

"We'll find him, Mak," Naz calmly spoke while stroking his dark curly hair. "Hey, look at me." She tipped his chin up. "We won't stop searching. He's out there."

Music drowned out his tears. Phin broke out dancing between the laughter. He wasn't a great dancer by any means, but there was pure joy on his face. Dil and Ginn yanked the new faces' arms, trying to make them dance in the center of the room. Ginn kissed every guy and girl on the cheek, leaving behind smeared red lipstick marks.

"I'm gonna get us a drink." Q said, walking off.

I slipped behind the doorway until he was out of sight. It was horrible to watch, but I didn't know how to make Mak feel any better. Naz embraced him, letting him weep on her shoulder.

Phin jumped on the teller's table, wobbling until he found his balance. "Alright, alright," he shouted, brushing back his sweat-soaked hair. "I want to thank everyone involved with this today. It's good to see some familiar faces back."

Mak sunk his face deeper into Naz's shoulder.

"Let's all raise our glasses and take a swig." Phin raised a half-empty bottle of saps above his head. "To everyone who kicked ass today to get our friends out." A loud cheer rushed through the room. "And to all of our friends that kept going under imprisonment, we drink to you, to your strength and your willpower. You are back where you belong. And finally, to all of us that showed the fucking Suits, we're not to be messed with—cheers!" Phin tilted his head back, gulping down the rest of the bottle without taking a breath.

The glasses smacked against the tables in unison, then the singing carried on. I slipped on my backpack and nudged my way through the crowd. No one noticed I was there, not even when I shoved past them. The rhythmic clapping grew louder, followed by bursts of laughter and dancing. The further I ascended toward the roof, the fainter their joy became, while my despair echoed louder.

The roof was silent. It was just me and the twinkling stars, barely visible through the light-polluted sky. The towering condo's light sparsely lit the rooftop as I breathed in the crisp air, filling my lungs. Who knew when I'd get another view of the city like this? I rubbed my arms, holding myself tight against the cool breeze.

In the distance, the Suit headquarters stood illuminated like a crystal sword, slicing the night sky in two. Its sharp lines and cold brilliance loomed over everything, casting long shadows across the desolate streets below.

The protesters were gone, leaving the streets eerily quiet. Every so often, an armored truck rolled by, its floodlights scanning alleys. Red emergency lights flashed sporadically between the shacks and burnt-down apartments. Father's voice droned over the speakers, ominously.

I peered around the corner, catching glimpses of life inside the Suits' luxury apartments. Their brightly lit windows displayed pristine domestic scenes—families seated at dinner tables, eating mounds of food, talking about their day. Every scene was the perfect Suit family: spotless, clean hands, perfectly displayed hair, polished, flawless clothes, and the women's faces set to please.

Goosebumps covered my body. Every window was the same—the same family, the same dinner, the same misery beneath the surface. A knot tightened in my stomach. A similar agonizing miserable feeling settled into my gut. That world felt so far away. I didn't belong there either.

"Running away?" Q's voice startled me. He stood behind me, a half-full bottle of saps in his hand. "Planning to go back?"

I shrugged. "No. I don't think I belong there either."

He took a sip watching the Suits in the window. "Whatta you mean, either?"

"You both want me to be someone I'm not." I exhaled, staring at the boots I didn't bother to return. "Even you."

His face twisted in confusion. "I never asked you to be anyone but yourself. When you asked to join—"

I cut him off. "You made them make me look like someone else today. I looked 'too sweet,' remember?"

He sighed. "I wasn't trying to change you. Just hide your face." He glanced over to me, gulping down some saps.

"It felt like you were." My heart sank.

"I was trying to protect you. Out there, you have a target on your back." He took a step closer, lowering his voice. "Especially breaking into a place like the Hive."

I shrugged, taking a step back. "I'm just a liability, right?"

"It's not like that." He stepped closer, softening his shoulders, "I see it in your face when your anxiety takes over. You let it get the best of you. Hiding behind that mask, you could hide who you are at least, it gave you a chance to get through it."

"You never asked what I wanted." I spat back. My voice trembled with suppressed emotions, "If I wanted to hide myself."

His shoulders slumped. "I'm sorry," he let out a heavy breath, "I didn't mean it that way."

"I'm just gonna leave. I don't belong here." I paused trying to catch my breath before my voice cracked, "No one's gonna care if I'm gone."

He stepped closer, again. "I care. I don't want you to leave. You do belong here. You belong here when you're yourself. Not the person everyone pushes you to be or who you think everyone wants you to be. The person you are when you're comfortable being yourself. That person belongs here."

I swallowed down a knot of emotion tightening in my throat. "Me?" I paused. "I'm dangerous when I'm me. Look what happened." My voice cracked, "I—I killed a man."

"I know." His tone softened. "But you also saved a man today. You protected yourself." He took another step towards me. "You also helped a bunch of people escape today."

"Helped them? I fell apart." I stared at the bits of dry blood in the cracks of my sore knuckles trying my best to hold back tears.

"I didn't see you fall apart." He leaned closer, his voice steady. "I saw you get back up and fight."

I shook my head, tears welling up. "Q, don't you see? I'm not a fighter. I'm a runner," my voice sharpened, "that's who I am. All I wanted to do was run away as soon as I entered that building today."

Exhausted, I slumped my aching shoulders. I barely could keep myself up with the shooting pain in my back.

"That's not true. You asked to learn to fight. You've been fighting since you got here, even if it didn't look like it to you." He paused. "You're only a runner until you stop running."

The weight of his words hung in the air.

Q was all brood, no bite. He showed emotions just like me. I found it alarming to figure out a man could wear sadness as I had before. It quickly consumed all his features. "Just don't run." His voice fell to a whispered, "please."

"I'm not strong enough not to run." My eyes welled up.

"Yes, you are." His words terrified me.

I shook my head as my eyes started to sting from holding back my tears, "No, I'm not. I endangered you and the mission today because I'm not."

"We'll work on teaching you how to fight and work on your anxiety. You have it in you. You've had it since you arrived. And if you don't want to fight, you can help Mak with cooking or something. I'll make Phin let you stay." He brushed his wavy hair out of his eyes. "Please, stay, and we can work on anything you want. You can make yourself whoever you want to be" he stared deep into my eyes, "but I would like if you wanted to be you."

I turned away. The empathy in his eyes made me uncomfortable. It hurt my heart to take a step away from him. Tears rolled down my cheeks. Instead of wiping them away quickly, this time I let them remain seen.

"I can't do this," I said in a whimper of a breath.

"Look at where you've come from—not where you haven't reached yet. You're standing here, arguing with me. You could hardly look me in the eyes when you arrived. You're fighting me right now. Look at your hands—they don't shake anymore. You look people in the eye now. You dare to ask questions. You can show emotions for damn sake." He took a deep breath, looking in the apartments then back at me. "I don't want you to leave, but I'm not gonna make you stay. It's your choice."

He handed me the bottle. "Here. You might need this more than me."

A choice. Somehow having the choice given to me made me uncomfortable. His body teetered on the side of exhaustion with the reflection of my emotions in his eyes. The air stood still between us.

On the flip side of the moment were two very different lives. I just needed to wait for the moment to pass. The voice in my head went silent. Not screaming *run*, not whispering *hide*.

I stared at the bruises and cuts on my steady hand holding the bottle. My shoulders ached but hung relaxed. I breathed without needing to remind myself. I found it terrifying that possibly he spoke more truth than me.

"I'll hold you back," I said softly, taking a sip of the saps.

"Then I'll just have to be a better trainer." He snapped back.

I took another sip then held out the bottle for him to take. The burn rushed down my throat warming my stomach. A woman in one of the window scenes stared at her plate while the man spoke, wagging his finger towards her.

A tinge of anxiety prickled in me. I wanted to save her. I wanted to tear down the door and free her from him. No part of me wanted the Suits to win. There wasn't any piece of me that told me to run away from the enemy. Every piece of me wanted to run towards them and fight.

"Okay," I said. "I'll stay."

A grin spread across his face, lighting up his eyes.

I took a step towards him. "But I'm not depending on you to protect me. You're gonna teach me how to hold my own in a fight."

"Deal." He grabbed the bottle from me then nudged my arm. "Glad to meet this version of you, who stands up for herself." A smile cracked on his face. "Tough looks good on you."

Heat rushed to my cheeks. "Thanks."

He chuckled. "We'll start training tomorrow, then?"

The pain in my back flared, shooting down my leg. "If we could wait like a week or so that would be great. Honestly, once I sit down, I don't think I'll be able to get back up."

He snickered, "Yeah, I'm sore too, let's wait a week and then start."

I raised an eyebrow. "Sure, you are," he laughed trying to act a little sore, "Sounds like a deal."

He exhaled, tilting his head back to gaze at the sky. "It's peaceful up here. We should come up here more often."

Two stars shot across the sky, lining up perfectly as if they were meant to meet. They streaked through the night like they knew each other, like they respected each other's paths.

"Yeah," I murmured, shutting my eyes and wishing for more than I'd ever dared to dream.

"Oh, I almost forgot." He reached into his pocket and pulled out a small tube with a red cap. "I thought your knuckles could use this."

I laughed softly. "My knuckles? I think my entire body could use that."

He smirked. "I don't think we've got enough for that. Here, let me help you." He unscrewed the cap and carefully applied the numbing agent to my bruised, raw knuckles. His touch was gentle, deliberate.

"You wanna go back down or stay up here a little longer?"

Surrounding myself with a herd of drunk, dancing people didn't sound appealing. My chest still ached with everything I'd been through. "I'll stay up here a bit longer."

"Okay." He sat down, leaning against the sidewall. "I'll keep you company, if that's okay."

"They'll miss you at the party."

"Nah, they're drunk; they won't notice I'm gone."

I would have noticed. I slowly made my way down to sit beside Q, holding my knees against my chest for warmth.

He tipped the bottle to his lips. "We're gonna tear this place apart one day, and you'll be there standing right beside me. You'll see."

So, there we sat on the cusp of either greatness or disaster. The unknown didn't make me cringe this time; instead, it excited me for once. For the first time, I was not alone in the world. I was part of something bigger—something that believed in a better world. In a world, I could stand side by side with a man. I finally felt like me—whoever that was, I would find out eventually. I actually kinda liked me.

I'd been sold, beaten, and lost. But in the end, I'd freed myself. I was free to do whatever I wanted with my life.

I now have a voice of my own — the voice of a fighter.